This is a work of fiction. Names, characters, places, and incidents either are the product of the author's imagination or are used fictitiously. Any resemblance to actual persons, living or dead, events, or locales is entirely coincidental.

Copyright © 2020 Gareth Ellis

All rights reserved. No part of this book may be reproduced in any form on by an electronic or mechanical means, including information storage and retrieval systems, without permission in writing from the publisher, except by a reviewer who may quote brief passages in a review.

Web: GarethEllis.co.uk
Twitter: @GaxTZ

For Alex. Thank you for believing in me.

"Computers will overtake humans with AI within the next 100 years. When that happens, we need to make sure the computers have goals aligned with ours."

-Stephen Hawking

by
Gareth Ellis

Chapter 1

19:42 26th October 2138

The coppery stench of blood rushed into his nose as he reached the threshold of the room. It was everywhere; smeared and splattered up the walls and pooled on the floor. It didn't help that the local cops and EMTs who'd got to the scene before him had walked through most of it—either accidentally or on purpose—traipsing bloody footprints around the room, spiraling towards the body like some macabre yellow brick road.

He hated the mess that was left in the wake of an AI killing. They didn't just kill someone cleanly; there was always a show to be seen.

All that remained of the unfortunate victim in the middle of the floor was an already congealing puddle of blood, feces, and torn flesh.

Despite the chaos, the authorities would know who the victim was by the intact severed hand that would be pinned to one of the nearby walls with a six-inch spike—just another of their calling cards.

Lifting the crime scene tape, he walked through the doorway into the horror show beyond. He reached into his coat pocket and pulled out a small tin. Opening it, he rubbed some menthol talc under his nose. It wouldn't shield him from the stench entirely, but it would help.

No matter how many years he'd done this job, he still couldn't get used to the smell. He remembered going to his first AI cleansing. The mess wasn't half as bad as this—they hadn't perfected their art yet—but the sight of the blood and the maelstrom of odors that hit him made him vomit as soon as he'd entered the house.

He'd gotten used to the sights now; they didn't faze him at all. But the smell, the smell always got to him. Thank God for the talc.

He stepped through the room, treading carefully. He didn't want to further spread the gore, least of all get it on his shoes and take it away with him.

Taking a quick look around the dank space, he noted that the local cops were still picking up pieces of the victim and taking blood samples from various spatters. Maybe they'd get lucky and find some synthetic AI blood. It was a long shot; but you never know your luck.

The apartment was sparsely furnished, but the furnishings that were present were old and damaged. A portion of the damage could be attributed to the apparent struggle that had occurred here recently, but some just looked like it hadn't been cared for.

The walls of the home were painted what quite possibly used to be white. Mold stains highlighted each corner of the room, and water could be seen seeping through the drywall in numerous patches. This wasn't the home of a wealthy person and not one to someone who took pride in their life.

As the countless other emergency professionals busied about their work, he stopped in the center of the room next to the biggest of the blood puddles; the victim's remains.

No one paid him any attention; at least this was better than some reactions he'd had.

He looked around at the chaos that surrounded him and pressed a finger to his temple. His vision swam with text:

```
Loading...
Sierra Security Software... Version 10.3.56
Loading...
Welcome Lieutenant William Kell
Loading...
Please select an option:
```

    1. Scan Fingerprints
    2. Scan Suspect
    3. Scan Room
    4. Connect the Dots
    5. Upload to Central Server
    6. Call
    7. Connect
    8. Erase

Three, he said to himself.

The text disappeared as the room was covered by intersecting lines forming a grid.

He looked around the room and saw that several objects were now highlighted within the network of lines.

His optical processor enhancement behaved as though he were the only one in the room with the other people milling around him faded as if they were ghosts.

Completing his three-hundred-sixty-degree rotation, he was back facing where he began.

He focused on the items the scanner had picked out:

There was the pool of victim; a smear of blood trailing from the door to the remains; the front door itself; two glasses of wine on the nearby countertop; pans on the stove; a picture frame that was lying face down on the floor; and a phone next to the sofa, where more blood was pooled. On the wall opposite the door, a hand was impaled by a six-inch spike.

Four, a figure appeared in the room, this one more solid than the faded people but much less real; it was light green in color. The figure stood at the stove.

Kell heard a hollow knock on the door. A scene played out where the green figure walked across the room, looked through the peephole, and opened the door. Another shape entered the virtual playback, this one red.

Green turned and started back towards the stove, red reached out and grabbed the green figure's arm, and in a single fluid movement, a green hand was now on the floor.

Green slumped down to its knees, holding the stump of its arm as if screaming in agony; Kell could imagine the cries.

Red stood behind green and kicked out at its back; the figure went down face-first into the floorboards.

Red then bent and grasped hold of greens ankle and started to drag the injured figure across the floor over the highlighted blood smear.

At this point, green managed to break free of Red's grasp, crawled to the sofa, reached up to the side table, and knocked the frame and phone down to their current locations.

Red pounced on top of green and, with balled fists, began beating down upon the other figure.

Green managed to struggle free once again and dragged itself over to where the large pool of blood lay; within less than a second, red caught up and savagely beat and dismembered the flailing green form. Blood and flesh were thrown across the room.

When Red had finished and Green no longer appeared in Kell's view, it went across to the previously severed hand, picked it up, walked to the opposite wall, produced a spike, and with a single thrust, pushed the spike through the flesh and into the wall.

The red avatar then strode calmly towards the door through which it had entered and left the apartment.

```
Simulation Complete
```

Kell pressed a finger to his temple again, and the text disappeared with the room coming back into full focus.

Walking across the room where the knocked off frame now lay, he pulled a blue latex glove from his pocket and stretched it over his hand, releasing the wrist with a snap.

Crouching, he picked up the frame, flipping it as he did. Other than a smear of blood, the frame was undamaged from its fall.

Inside was a photo of a man and woman; the man was very average looking, reasonably tall, short brown hair, glasses—just seemed like your average Jo-schmo. Though, the woman was a beauty by anybody's standards, way out of this guy's league. She was a head taller than the male with long, straight black hair and dazzling green eyes. She would undoubtedly stand out in a crowd more so than the man.

Kell placed the frame back on the side table and stood.

He made his way to the small kitchenette where his implant had highlighted the pans on the stove along with two glasses.

Three pots sat on the top of the cooker hobs, all with food inside, potatoes, beans, and something that he couldn't quite figure out; it looked like someone had eaten it already. The two pans with the veg had boiled dry and started to burn, and the other stuff looked like it had set as solid as week-old concrete.

He turned on his heels and looked at the glasses, both still full of white wine. *This guy was expecting someone. Maybe the woman from the photo? He wasn't expecting what happened, though.*

Leaving the kitchen area, he walked back across the room to the hand pinned to the wall.

He shook his head, always the same; a hand pinned to the wall with a six-inch metal spike.

They wanted us to identify this mess; they always wanted us to find out who they'd killed.

To them, it was right; they were doing the world a service.

He examined the base of the hand where it had been removed at the wrist. Whatever it was they used, it was red hot. It cauterized the cut, stopping the blood flow immediately after the amputation. Why they did this was a mystery, the victims were always torn apart. Maybe they didn't want them to bleed to death; perhaps that wasn't justice to the AI.

He pressed his finger to his temple again; after the loading screen had flashed up, he gave the command, *one.*

A blue flash filled his eyes as the implant scanned the hand. At this, several techs turned to see what the light was, but upon seeing that it was just him, they turned back and busied themselves with what they were doing.

```
Searching...
Searching...
Searching...
Searching...
Match found
```

An image popped up, surrounded by text. The picture was a photo of a man, the same man who was in the photograph he'd picked up off the floor. The text read;

```
Name: Martin Howard
Date of Birth: 01/17/2116
Date of Death: 10/26/2138
Age: 22
Sex: Male
Ethnicity: Caucasian
Height: 5" 7'
Weight: 170lbs
Hair Color: Brown
Eye Color: Brown
Employment: Janitor - PTech Analytics

Previous Arrests:
Narcotics Possession - 2133- 3 Months
Robbery - 2134 - 6 months
Assault - 2136 - 1 year
```

He pressed his temple again to dismiss the display.

So this Howard had previous, makes sense that they'd go after him, he was undoubtedly a repeat offender, and his crimes were definitely escalating, from possession to assault in a couple of years, the logical next step was—

His thoughts were interrupted by a soft ringing behind his eyes, *answer.*

A voice rang out inside his head, "Kell!" it was his superior, Captain Crane. A good man, but his voice was terse. Lately, he'd been getting a lot of pressure from above to solve these murders.

Sir

"What's going on over there? Is it another cleansing?" Crane asked.

It is sir. Same MO. Hand pinned to the wall. The victim had several escalated previous, so was likely to be on their list.

"Dammit. Well, finish up there and get your ass over to the address I'm sending you now. There's been another," Crane said.

Sir. I'm done here. I'll head over now.

"Well, hurry up. We need to put a stop to these things. They're getting bolder and killing more often. I've got my superiors so far up my ass; it's getting hard to sit down," Crane said.

Understood.

There was a click as the call ended, and a new address popped up in his vision.

Clearing the text away, Kell took a last look around the room to make sure there wasn't anything that had been missed, made his way towards the door, and exited the apartment.

Back at street level, he stood under the awning that was over the main entrance of the apartment complex. It was raining again. The dark street – highlighted by red and blue flashes from the emergency vehicles – was filled with parked cars and pedestrians — all trying to get a better look at what was going on.

The AI cleansings always garnered so much more attention than a typical biotic crime, especially from the press.

As he looked across the street, he could see groups of cameras flash beyond the police cordon, all jockeying for position, all trying to get the best photos for the morning releases. *Vultures*, he thought.

He buttoned up his long coat and lifted the collar to defend against the rain.

Stepping out from under the awning, he made his way towards his car. He felt all eyes on him and several flashes were now facing in his direction. He always drew attention when at a crime scene; people seemed to think he was involved in it someway. Most biotics didn't trust him as far they could throw him. Why hadn't he gone rogue like some of the others? Was he a spy?

As he walked past the crowd, he could hear several onlookers muttering and whispering to one another, some pointed fingers in his direction, and yet others just watched him with intensity in case this was the moment he broke and tried to attack them.

All this didn't bother him much these days; he'd come to terms with who he was and the fact that some people didn't trust or just flat-out despised AI. With these murders happening, he didn't altogether blame them for their views. He consoled himself with the thought that not all biotics felt this way.

As he drew closer to his black sedan with the blacked-out windows, the door automatically opened, sensing his presence. He stooped down and climbed in. He liked his car; it was one of his private places. No one was watching him or judging him. It was a place he could relax for a time.

The door slid shut, and the engine started. He pressed his temple and downloaded the new address to the car's navigation software. Seconds later, the vehicle began to roll forward smoothly, and music started to softly play from speakers surrounding him; Handel's 'Largo' — one of his favorites.

He'd always had a love for the classical composers. Most modern music didn't take any effort for the so-called artists to make; computers did most of the work, not like back in the days of Handel, Bach, and Beethoven. They put so much of themselves into their music; they lived it. After Handel came Vivaldi.

With nothing to do now but wait to arrive at his next destination, he closed his eyes and got lost in the music.

Chapter 2

20:00 26th October 2138

"Sir, there's been another murder."

The President looked up from the stack of papers he was leafing through, his brows knitted together. "AI?"

"Yes, sir."

"Damn." He pushed himself up quickly, using his fists for leverage on the desk, causing his chair to roll back and bang against the heavy drapes of the Oval Office window. Rubbing his eyes with a thumb and index finger, he sighed, "Where?"

"A few blocks west, in an apartment on F Street. The victim was discovered at around nineteen-fifteen hours by a neighbor." The man shifted his feet uncomfortably.

"Is the department on to it?" The President had been instrumental in creating the AI Homicide Division within the Washington D.C. police department. It was one of his finest ideas and one that had garnered him a considerable gain in the polls at a difficult time in his administration. Some of his critics thought the division should have been set up within a government agency. But he considered the situation to be at a local level, not federal. There were very few reported murders outside of the city with the same MO.

"Yes, sir. Lieutenant Kell arrived on the scene minutes ago." The aide said, fiddling with his tie.

"Good. Keep me abreast of any further updates as soon as you can." The President said.

"Yes, sir. I will." The skinny man turned on his heels with such speed that his wavy hair flicked around, he left the room with an air of pride about him.

President Samuel Darrow slowly sank back into his seat and pulled himself back towards the solid oak desk.

Sitting for a moment, he stared at the piles of reports in front of him. His vision was beginning to blur. He'd been reading for what felt like an eternity. Glancing at the small carriage clock that sat on the desk in front of him, he realized that only a couple of hours had passed since he started this task. Every time he'd started to read, there was another interruption from either some aide with news of the polls or other occurrence in the city, or a member of his PR and Speech team, with something new for him to say at his next function.

Sometimes he wondered why he wanted this job in the first place. He could have spent his life on the family farm in Oregon. It was just one thing after another; the last thing he needed now was another murder by those AI fanatics.

It was a year until the next election, and his campaign was already in full swing; his re-election campaign had begun before he even sat down in the Oval Office at the start of this term. His policy on AIs had always been tolerant. Many of his opponents called for stricter action and sanctions on all AIs, but he had no problem with them. A number of the White House staff were AI; this had been a reason for a significant number of votes during his election, both from AIs and humans.

But if he didn't get a handle on the city's current situation, it could turn nasty and end badly for both him and the country.

He picked up a yellow folder sitting at the top of the pile in front of him, opened it up, and started to read. It was a report on how many local schools' students were getting the grades enough to go to college. The numbers were staggeringly low. Only thirty-five percent of students were now going on to further education.

Some believed that it was due to AIs being employed over humans, their skills being far superior, and without the expense of training.

Others thought that young people were just simply giving up on education—the lure of so-called 'easy money' from social media too much for some.

He didn't subscribe to either of these theories, however, as he knew that the government just wasn't spending the money on education; it was they who had given up on the young.

He had made it a significant part of his administration to fight this and get the money where it was needed. As low as the thirty-five percent was, it was still an increase from the twenty-five that it was when he came to office three years ago.

An increase of ten percent should be something to be proud of, something he should be speaking about. However, it was still an incredibly low figure, and his critics were always there to point this out. Much more work would have to be done on policy to get it to rise further, and for that, he needed to be re-elected.

"Mr. President."

He was so deep in thought that he hadn't heard the doors open or the young woman approach.

He looked over the folder in his hands at his aide, Olivia Hampton. "The Secretary of Education is here for your meeting."

"What? Oh, yes, sorry, Olivia. Send him in, please." He shook his head in an attempt to clear away some of the cobwebs.

He thought he had more time to prepare for this; well, he knew what he wanted to say, so it shouldn't be too difficult.

"Yes, sir. Would you like anything else?" the young woman asked.

"No. Thank you." Olivia pivoted on her heels to leave, "Actually," at the sound of his voice, she turned back with a smile, "Would you get me some coffee, please? I need a pick me up."

She nodded and made her exit. The President watched her leave, and through the door, he saw her direct the secretary into the room. With a look back at him across the room, she smiled and slowly closed the doors.

"Mr. President." The secretary said as the two men shook hands.

"Ted, it's good to see you. Please, take a seat." He gestured to one of the sofas in the center of the room and seated himself opposite the older man. "Now, I've been reading the reports this morning about the current numbers of post-high-school education—"

*

"—we're doing our best to get regulations and motions passed, but there is a lot of opposition." The secretary was saying sometime later.

The President took a sip of his now cold coffee; he grimaced internally.

"Tell me why, Ted. Our opposition is openly against AIs, and in not passing our bills on the spending on education, they're stopping human children from getting ahead in life. Now tell me, how does that make sense? Surely they can't just be blocking it because I'm putting it up?"

"I know it sounds counter-intuitive, sir. But that's what they're doing," The secretary said.

"Well, that's just bull-headed and downright stu—" the doors to the Oval Office were slowly opened. Olivia stepped back into the room, shuffling over to a spot behind the President she leaned over and whispered into his ear.

"There's been another." She said, her lips brushing against his ear as she spoke.

Darrow felt the color drain a little from his face. "Sorry, Ted. Can we pick this up later? Something has just come up."

"No, sir, of course. I'll go over the numbers and see if there's something we can put together that the opposition might accept." The two men stood and shook hands, and the secretary was ushered out of the room by Olivia, leaving the President alone with his thoughts.

Darrow lay down on the sofa and put his hands over his face trying not to scream into them.

Another murder; two in one night. What was going on out there?

The President collected himself and walked over to the window behind his desk. He looked out into the dark and rainy night beyond. The trees were being buffeted by the wind, rain splashed against the glass, and ran down in silvery streaks; he shivered, not from cold; but fear.

An arm wrapped around his waist; he could smell Olivia's perfume drifting over him. "Are you okay?" she asked in her subtle southern accent, almost in a whisper.

"Yes, yes, I'm fine. It's just these killings." Darrow said.

"I know. I'm scared." There was a tremble in her voice that he'd never heard before.

He turned to look at her; he was a good foot taller than her, so he looked down into her eyes as she tilted her head to look up at him.

"Why are you scared?" he asked, gently brushing a hand across her cheek and erasing the single tear that ran down it.

"If these murders carry on, humans are going to get angrier than they are already at AIs. Who knows what they could do?" She looked down, another tear dripped from the corner of one of her eyes and snaked its way down her soft pale cheek.

"I will stop things from getting that bad, and whatever happens, I will protect you against anyone who wants to do you harm. You know that." He put a hand under her chin and lifted her head, wiping the tear away. "You're safe here."

"Thank you, Sam. I love you." Olivia said, leaning in closer to his chest.

"I love you too, Liv. Now please, get back to work, tonight is going to be a long night," he smiled, "as if it's not already."

He planted a soft kiss on her lips and tasted the strawberry lip balm she always used. They embraced for a few seconds until Olivia backed away, gathered herself, straightened her suit jacket, and walked away from him and out of the room.

Once the door had closed, he walked back to his desk, picked up the next folder in the stack, and started to read once again. There was just no end to it.

Chapter 3

21:00 26th October 2138

The car slowed and rolled to a complete stop. The words "Destination Reached" flashed on the windscreen in a pale transparent blue shade, as well as simultaneously being spoken through the speaker near his head, snapping him out of his hypnotic state.

He looked out of the window at the scene outside. It was much the same as at the last address; flashing red and blue lights, rain, and people gawking. The door opened, and the music faded into silence.

The wind and rain hit him as he stepped out onto the street. He felt eyes on him as soon as he took his first step.

Stopping to look up at the address where he'd been sent, he took it in; a nice looking two up, two down house in the suburbs. Painted white wooden picket fence bordered a well-manicured lawn. Flower boxes were positioned under the windows, overflowing with color. A Family SUV sat in the driveway. It was the proverbial American dream. It was as if it had been lifted straight from a lifestyle magazine. He could picture kids playing on the immaculate front lawn with the parents watching proudly from the window. He felt like a perfect life was lived here; until now.

He walked up to the front gate, that was now open and swinging in the wind; he walked through carefully closing it behind him.

Bloody footprints led him towards the pale-yellow front door, that was wide open, allowing light to spill from the house

,illuminating the porch. He could see shadows moving about within the house, all going about their business, not caring what came before the chaos they were here to investigate. He didn't understand how the victim's life didn't matter in their death. Every small detail was important.

A uniformed police officer stood at the front door and blocked his entry by holding up a palm.

"Kell. AI Homicide Division." Kell said.

"Identification?" The uniform replied sternly.

Kell reached inside his coat; he could see the uniform officer flinch and brace himself. Kell slowly pulled a wallet out of the inside pocket and flashed his badge at the man. The guard glared at it, then at him, scowling as he nodded and stepped aside. This was the usual reaction to his appearance at crime scenes. Sliding his wallet back inside his coat, he stepped inside.

That all too familiar smell hit him as soon as he crossed the threshold. Rubbing some more menthol talc under his nose, Kell made his way down the hallway, the smell getting stronger as he moved deeper into the house.

As he walked along the entrance hall, he noticed several photos of a child hanging on the walls. A young girl with pigtails and a massive grin sat on a bike, learning to ride, no doubt. The next was the same girl—a bit older—in a school uniform, perhaps her first day. More photos followed of the same girl, aging as the images went on, Kell judged her age in the final image to be around eight. No adults were in any photograph.

He came to the double doors that led to the living space. Chaos, that was the only word that sprang to mind when he beheld what was going on beyond those doors. The entire scene was reminiscent of some horror movie. A slasher. A killer letting their anger flow through them and into a helpless victim. Of course, this wasn't just some random killing. This was done with purpose—a mission. And there was no anger here; it was cold and calculated.

Once again, blood was all over the room. This time though, furniture was overturned, items were smashed; someone fought back. It didn't change the end result, though. It never did. Once a victim was selected, they were doomed.

A hand was pinned to the wall under a large cracked mirror, smaller than the last one; possibly female.

Kell walked further into the room; no one bothered to look up or acknowledge him. Same as ever.

Pressing his temple, he loaded his scanner. After the loading screens and menus, he selected to scan the room.

The blue grid appeared, and everyone in the room became ghosts once again. The scan completed, and he took a moment to observe what had been highlighted.

In this scene, it picked out; the double doors he'd entered through, the cracked mirror above the fireplace, the hand below it, a large pool of blood in the center of the room, and several pieces of broken pottery — possibly a vase - along with the flowers that it had contained were scattered around the room. There was also a fire poker covered in blood to one side of the sofa, and the smashed coffee table.

After he'd registered all the highlighted items, he ran the simulation.

Again, a green figure appeared in his view; this one started off sitting on the sofa. Red barged through the closed double doors, almost knocking one of them off its hinges, and launched itself at Green. The couch tipped over with both of them in it. There was a struggle, and Green kicked Red over the sofa, and the figure crashed back first into the coffee table. At this point, it didn't smash.

Red rolled off the table as Green stood and ran to the fireplace. Red rose in front of Green as it grabbed the vase off the fire surround and slammed it into Red's head, the pieces falling to their highlighted final resting place.

Red reached down and picked up the poker from the side of the fireplace and swung it at Green's head the figure ducked; the poker missed its target and instead hit the mirror and cracking it; the shattered glass fell to the floor.

Without pausing, Red then smashed the metal pole into Green's side. The green figure buckled over, and the poker was driven down onto its back. Green went down to the floor as Red repeatedly used the poker to beat it until death. Red then hunched over the body and cut a hand off the battered body, placing it on the fireplace.

The red avatar then went to town on the victim, tearing at the green figure now crumbled on the floor.

After a few moments, as before, Green was gone, leaving only the highlighted puddle. Red stood and drove the spike through the removed hand and into the wall, turned, and left the room with the same composure as at the last scene.

`Simulation Complete` flashed up in his vision, and Kell closed the scanner with a sigh.

With the room back in focus, he walked over to the hand and examined it.

This one was indeed female, the cut cauterized as usual. The fingertips covered in dried blood; the fingers slightly bent as if trying to grasp at something. Kell started the fingerprint scanner and waited for the results;

```
Name: Christine Lawton
Date of Birth: 07/25/2100
Date of Death:10/26/2138
Age: 38
Sex: Female
Ethnicity: African American
Height: 5" 2'
Weight: 201lbs
Hair Color: Black
Eye Color: Brown
Employment: Teacher - Anacostia High

Previous Arrests:
NONE
```

The picture that accompanied the text was of a round-faced, smiling woman. She *looked* like a schoolteacher; she was probably one of the kids' favorites. Her eyes smiled as much as her mouth did. Who would want to kill this woman? What could she ever do to deserve such a fate? She fought back, though, not wanting to die. She gave as good as she got, but as always, it wasn't enough.

A thought suddenly occurred to him, where was the child from the photos in the hall? There was no evidence of another death. Had she been out of the house when all this happened? He hoped so. He hoped she was safe and far away. He pressed his temple, removing the text and image of the happy smiling woman, returning to the grizzly scene surrounding him.

With his job here done, he walked back towards the double doors. Reaching the hallway, he was about to go towards the front door when he heard soft crying.

He turned back towards the stairs that led to the second floor. He filtered out the noises from all the other people around him; he cut out the radios, the rabble outside, the footsteps and chatter until all he could hear was the crying. It was coming from the stairs. He walked towards it, and it got louder; there was definitely someone here. The sound led Kell to the door that was built into the wall beneath the stairs.

Reaching out for the door handle, he momentarily paused. Whoever was inside was quite obviously distressed. Was he the best person to handle it?

He looked around and thought about asking one of the many other people for assistance. He decided not to as he didn't want to chance leaving to go and get someone, plus the chance of anyone helping him were small.

He slowly opened the door to reveal a dark storage space, "Hello?" he whispered. "I'm from the police; I'm here to help."

He waited for a response. Nothing; even the sobbing had stopped. Then from the darkened corner came a small voice.

"Mommy. He hurt mommy." It was a girl's voice, and she sounded petrified.

He waited for anything further, then crouched and offered his hand to the darkness. A small dark hand came out of the shadows and grabbed hold of his.

"It's okay. You're safe now." Kell said.

A thin arm followed the hand; then, a girl emerged from behind some boxes. It was the girl from the photos; he recognized the same curly black hair. The smile that emanated from all the images, though, had gone. The girl's face was twisted with fear. She was sucking her lips in as if she were trying to hold back the scream that wanted to escape from them.

"I'm William," Kell said softly, "what's your name?"

The girl blinked in the bright light of the hallway.

"Emily. Emily Lawton." She said in a hushed tone as if someone might hear what she was saying and come for her.

"Hi, Emily." Kell said. He didn't push her; he wanted to make her feel more at ease.

"You're police?" she timidly asked.

"I am. I'm here to help."

The girl fully emerged from the gloom and stood before him, still holding tightly to his hand.

"Are you okay? Did someone hurt you too?" Kell asked, his eyes quickly going over her, searching for any sign of harm.

She sniffed, "No. He…just hurt mommy."

Based on the photos, the girl must have been around eight, but she seemed much younger from the way she looked now.

"Are you okay to come with me, and we'll get you checked out by the doctors? They're just outside." At this, the girl let go of his hand and took a small step backward. Kell stood for a moment, then smiling he held out another hand for her to take.

"O…Okay." She whispered almost silently as she took his proffered hand.

Kell looked over his shoulder at the front door, he could see the blue flashing lights of the ambulance beyond, but to get there, they'd have to go past the double doors and the carnage in the front room.

"I want you to walk by my side," he said, "but I need you to close your eyes tight until we're outside. Do you understand?"

She gave a tiny nod of her head and came close to his side. He stood, and together they started for the front door.

Kell looked down at the small child beside him; she had her eyes scrunched up and was unsteady on her feet.

"It's okay; we don't need to rush. Take your time, don't trip." He said.

She nodded again, and they slowed their pace.

Passing the double doors, he took another look inside and wondered if she'd already seen what had happened; he hoped not. No one should have to see that, never mind a girl her age.

They finally made it to the front door. Noticing that it was still raining and his young charge was only wearing her pajamas, Kell took off his coat and draped it around the girl's shoulders, setting her free hand on it to hold it shut against the wind and rain. He'd be fine without it; he didn't need to wear a coat anyway; he only did it for appearance's sake. It put biotics more at ease if he looked a little more like them. The girl had suffered enough tonight; he didn't want her to be freezing too.

He looked out towards the ambulances that were parked on the street. He waved his hand in the air and managed to get one of the EMT's attention. He beckoned them over. As usual, they ignored him. Frustrated, Kell took Emily across the wet street towards the ambulance, where the woman sat talking with a colleague.

As they walked, the long coat — now dragging on the floor – started to pick up dirty water from the street.

"She was hiding in the cupboard under the stairs." Kell said to the EMT.

"Come with me, dear." the EMT said, completely ignoring the man stood by her side.

Emily gripped Kell's hand harder. "No. I don't want to go!" she screamed.

"It's okay. You're safe now." The EMT said, "Come with me, and we'll get you checked out."

"No!" She hugged close to Kell's leg, "I won't leave William." She sobbed.

"You don't want to stay with him." The EMT said, "He's not someone you want to stay with."

"NO! William is nice. I want to stay with him!" Emily bellowed. At this, Kell noticed several more heads turned in their direction.

"Would you feel better if I came in the ambulance with you?" Kell asked, crouching down to the girl's level.

She nodded, and he wiped tears and rain away from her eyes and off her cheeks. "Okay, I'll keep you company."

"Fine." The EMT grumbled, stood, and stepped up into the ambulance and started to gather supplies, throwing them on the brown gurney.

Occasionally her eyes darted a glance at Kell with the familiar, 'You shouldn't be here' look. It used to bother him. Now he'd gotten used to it. The fact that he would be accepted by few and shunned by many was just life; well, his life.

He stood and helped Emily up into the ambulance. Once she was safely inside, he stepped up behind her. Emily stood in the brightly lit space, looking at him and hugging his coat closer to herself.

Giving her a small smile, he helped her up onto the gurney and sat down beside her; she grabbed his hand tightly.

Kell did his best to keep her calm and reassure her that she was safe while the EMT busied with her various scans and tests. He had no real experience with kids; after all, he'd never even been one.

The girl flinched as a small needle was poked into her arm, and blood was taken. He just tried to keep her eyes on him. "It's okay." He kept repeating in as a soothing tone as he could manage. He must have sounded like a broken record. The EMT would glance up at him on occasion and give a shake of her head. The girl's grip never loosened.

After several moments, the EMT simply said: "She's fine."

Kell stood and looked at her, "That's it?"

"She'll no doubt suffer from some shock or post-traumatic stress, but that's out of my remit. Physically she's fine." The woman said sharply.

"Hmmm, okay then." Kell knelt back down to the girl's seated level. "Have you got any family?"

She shook her head, "Just mommy…and da…daddy."

"Where is your daddy?" he asked.

"He left after hurting mommy." Emily blinked furiously as if she were trying to erase an image from her mind.

So, the killer was her father, Kell thought to himself.

"No Aunts? Uncles? Grandparents?"

She just shook her head.

"Your daddy, is he your real daddy?"

She looked at him with a confused expression.

"I mean. Um, was there another daddy before him?" He was trying to phrase things in a way that she would understand but would also get him the information he needed.

She shook her head and began to sob into her hands.

There must be someone. The man who killed her mother can't have been her birth father. It's impossible. He thought.

"We done here? I've got places to be." Snapped the EMT.

"What? Yes. All done." He looked down at the girl, *what am I going to do with you?*

"Get out then, so I can be on my way, Arti." The EMT said.

He jerked his head back up at this word, and the EMT backed away a few steps with her palms raised.

Kell helped Emily off the gurney, and hand in hand, they jumped down out of the ambulance. They'd barely hit the ground when the doors slammed behind them, and the emergency vehicle made a swift exit siren blaring.

There was another buzzing behind his eyes. "I've just got to take a call. You stay here, okay? I'll take care of you for now." He said.

She forced a small smile and nodded. Sitting down on the nearest curb, she started to finger the now soaking wet rim of the coat.

Answer, Kell said internally.

"What have we got?" Crane's voice came through inside Kell's head.

Another AI attack. A school teacher. She seems to have been attacked by her husband.

"Her husband? You mean she married one of them?" Crane said.

It happens. She wasn't to know what his plans were.

"God damn. I hate these things." There was a short quiet pause. "Sorry, Kell. Not you, of course."

Don't worry about it, sir. I know how you feel. I've got a situation here.

"A situation?"

The victim had a child. A girl, eight years of age. I found her hiding in the cupboard under the stairs. She may have seen what happened to her mother, and she… he paused, …seems to have gotten attached to me.

The voice laughed, "Well, you're a lovable bastard, Kell."
What should I do with her?

"I need to see you down at the precinct. Bring her with you; I'll get social services to take her."

I'm not sure she'll go for that.

"She'll be okay with them. You're needed elsewhere."

You're right. I'm done here, so I'll be with you soon.

"See you soon." The line went dead.

Kell looked over at the girl. She was still sat on the curb, but now she was throwing stones into a nearby puddle.

"Time to go, Emily." He said, walking a few paces closer, so he didn't have to shout.

She jumped up, dropped the remaining stones, brushed her hands clean, and walked over to him.

"Where are we going, William?" she asked.

"Down to the precinct. You'll be safe there." He replied.

"Okay, William." She reached out and grabbed his hand.

Together they walked over to his car, the driver side door opening as usual as he approached. He motioned for Emily to climb in; she did so without hesitation, scrabbling over the driver's seat and settling into the passenger seat. Once she was seated, he climbed in after her. He turned to tell her to put her seat belt on but noticed she'd already buckled in. He didn't usually bother, but this time he fastened his seatbelt too; for appearances. He wasn't sure if she realized what he was, or if she just didn't care. He already liked this kid.

He told the navigation software to go back to the precinct, and classical music started to play, "Off" Kell said. The music faded out, and the car was in silence other than the hum of the electric motor.

"You can have the music on. I don't mind." Emily said.

"If you're sure?" He asked.

"I like music." She said with a smile, this one a little more genuine.

"On." he said, and Chopin's 'Waltzes' started to play through the car's speakers. They both sat and listened for a while before he looked over at his new companion; she was asleep, and he couldn't help but smile. *Poor kid,* he thought, *she must be shattered.*

He settled back into his seat and went over everything that had happened today.

Two killings in twenty-four hours. Unusual. They were usually more spaced out than this. Of these two, he could understand the motives for the first more than the second, as much as he could understand any of it, that is.

Martin Howard was a career criminal, in and out of prison since his late teens, each crime worse than the last. He was escalating to something much graver. This is what the cleansings were about, stopping criminals before they committed a crime.

But what had they seen in Christine Lawton's future to provoke her killing? She had a clean sheet, a school teacher with a beautiful home, and a young child. He looked back over to Emily. *Poor kid,* he thought again. Her father, or rather, her mother's husband, was the key here. She could help identify him. At the very least, they could stop him from any further killing.

But who killed Howard? There was the woman in the photo. He'd quite clearly been expecting company, as evidenced by the cooking and glasses of wine. He'd opened the door, not expecting to be attacked by whoever was on the other side. The green-eyed woman was definitely worth some further investigation and, as of now, was the only lead he had.

No matter how many of these killings he went to, Kell still couldn't understand what triggered them into action.

Some of the AIs would live a regular life with a biotic until one day they just massacred them. Just like Christine's husband had. It was getting harder to track the AIs after a killing. They would generally blend into a crowd just like any biotic would. But after a cleansing, they would just disappear. Some had an idea that once they killed, they would change their appearance. He thought this to be untrue, as he'd caught many an AI in the midst of another killing, and they still looked exactly the same. Although the ones they didn't find, he supposed it could be possible they changed their appearance. As AIs, it would be easier to alter their appearance than it would for a biotic to do so.

He'd hopefully get some more answers when he reviewed everything back at the precinct. He could feel his head full of data. *Five.* He closed his eyes as all the days collected data wirelessly uploaded to the central server back in his office.

The car sped along the road towards the precinct. Both of its passengers asleep or as close as they could get to that anyway.

Chapter 4

Artificial Intelligence rose to prominence in the late 2000s.

It started off only as computer programs that could gather, manage, and analyze data.

By the latter end of the 21st century, it had evolved into physical robots that were initially built as household and personal assistants. Most people would ultimately end up with at least one of these in their homes. These almost humanoid robots could perform rudimentary functions in and around the house; such as cooking, laundry, and cleaning. Although they had some autonomy, they still relied on human input to set them to a task. They would need a nightly recharge and would often break and require repair and new parts; this meant that they would eventually prove costly.

AISystems who created these first models would go on to release regular upgrades and new models. If people wanted to keep up to date and have a working model with fewer technical issues and more function, they would eventually be forced to upgrade to a new model after two years.

These newer models would have more autonomy, relying less and less on human input.

Soon they started to appear more often in the commercial and industrial sectors. Larger businesses would use them as construction and manufacturing labor as their end products would be of more consistent quality than those made by a fallible human employee.

This usage would eventually lead to outcry from unions and other groups incensed by the replaced labor. They fought court battles to try to cut down on the AI usage. Some judgments did come down in their favor, where the court decreed that companies were only allowed to replace a certain percentage of their human workforce with AI.

The years rolled on as humans and AIs worked alongside one another. Occasionally, a group of humans would try to disable large groups of AIs in an attempt to prove that they were flawed and not worth the time and money that people spent on them. Unfortunately, this just led to AISystems creating newer models that were impervious to tampering.

AIs started to appear in smaller businesses. Local shops and supermarkets began to employ them, again led to the layoffs of human employees and public outcry.

In the late 2080s, AISystems began making what they termed 'companion' models. These models were first marketed for the elderly and infirmed who might want some company and/or assistance when no one else was around.

These were the most advanced models yet. Almost indistinguishable from real humans, they no longer needed daily charging by this point, and breakage and damage were limited. If they got damaged, they were as fixable as humans, without the need for outright replacement. Each of these new AIs had a full skeletal and nervous system. They were also able to feel physical sensations and emotions to a certain extent.

Inevitably, with all these abilities, it wasn't long before these models were being used for sex. AI brothels started to appear in some of the most disreputable areas of cities throughout the world. This was wildly popular because there was no chance of pregnancy on either side, and the risk of disease was minimal – depending, of course, on the cleanliness of those that ran the brothels.

Not one to shy away from a situation, AISystems created further new models that had increased sensory perception, equal or additional to the senses of humans.

By this point, the AIs' autonomy was total; they no longer needed any human input. They had free-will and could live their life as any human could.

They could now think, feel, love, get sick, eat; they had the full range of human emotions and senses, and they started to fully integrate into society.

Some human rights groups campaigned against this and sometimes went so far as to attack AIs on the street and destroy them. AI "blood" became highly sought after on the black market, as did body parts and enhancements.

For a brief time, humans would try to implant themselves with scavenged parts from destroyed AI in an attempt to improve themselves beyond natural human prowess. This practice died out after multiple deaths of those who had undergone these procedures, and because those who had survived saw no benefit whatsoever; in some cases, it even reduced their quality of life.

After years of being attacked and pushed down the rungs of society, the AIs fought back.

In 2121 the war between humans and AI began.

Millions died on both sides. As is always the case with wars, there were two sides on each side of it, one fighting, the other at home trying to live their life.

The conflict went on for three years. Eventually, AISystems, who had been a staunch supporter of AI rights, refused to assist the US government in putting an end to the war by destroying AI as they said it was akin to genocide.

After this response from AISystems, the government turned to another company that would agree to it.

This other company quickly developed a nanobot that would deactivate AIs. The nanobots were put into a canister and loaded into planes. When dropped, these devices exploded in mid-air shortly after they were deployed. Gas was then released that contained the nanobots, and as the AI breathed it in, they were disabled within five minutes. The human combatants would have no ill effects whatsoever.

After several of these devices were dropped, the threat of more being used was enough to stop the AI from fighting. A ceasefire was agreed upon and put in place on 24th May 2124.

Humans and AIs alike went back to trying to live together. But underneath the tentative peace, another trouble was brewing.

Years passed with no further fighting between the two species, other than sporadic outbreaks of violence between small groups, but these usually fizzled out as quickly as they started.

In the year 2130, the murders started. At first, they seemed random, but similar scenes of chaos appeared across Washington D.C. – as well as unconfirmed reports from other states and occasionally other counties. There was no pattern, no relation between the victims other than the fact that they were all humans.

For years the killings continued. As the only victims were humans, fear began to spread among the biotic population that they were all at risk, and their obvious target of aggression was the AIs.

In 2135 the AI Homicide Division of the Washington D.C. police department was set up with the sole purpose of investigating the murders and catching the AIs responsible.

Many culprits had been found and faced the death penalty for their offenses, but many remained at large.

Most members of this new division were humans, as many police departments no longer trusted AIs enough to have them involved in these kinds of investigations, despite still employing them in roles elsewhere, in mostly clerical functions.

There was one exception to this in the WDCPD, and that AI was a member of the AI Homicide Division.

William Kell had been a member of the police department for six years; he had joined one year before the AI cleansings—as they were now termed—had started. In the years following the war, most AI kept themselves to themselves, only spending their time around other AI. After several years they began to integrate with humans more. They started to apply for positions in human industries again and have relationships – both platonic and romantic—with humans if they wanted to.

Things were looking up for AIs in general; they were being accepted again.

When the killings started, this acceptance started to crumble, and humans became warier. This didn't stop Kell from gaining prominence in the department. He rose quickly to the rank of Lieutenant, despite obstacles thrown in front of him by some ranking officers and colleagues. His success was partly due to a good friend, Captain Morris Crane. He was the reason why Kell was assigned to the AI Homicide Division.

Crane always had a soft spot for Kell. When Kell first entered the police, Crane was a Lieutenant himself and fast became friends with the AI. He never particularly liked AI before, having fought in the AI War and lost many friends and family to their kind. However, as soon as he met Kell, he couldn't help but befriend him. He was so unlike any other AI he'd encountered. Most AIs would act as human as they could to be accepted, but Kell—although functioning as close to human as he could—didn't try to hide what he was; in fact, he embraced it. He used his AI abilities to get ahead and assist his fellow officers, something that few AI in the force would do for fear of recrimination.

When Crane was promoted to Captain, and the cleansings began, he enlisted Kell's help in many cases, and he found his insight invaluable.

Together they had already caught several of the AI killers. So when the AI Homicide Division was set up with a special action from the President, Kell was an automatic, logical, and first choice to join. Kell was more than happy to work on these cases full time regardless of the promotion that came with the posting.

The new division had worked out that some AI—through a natural progression of their Internal Evolution Software—had begun to be able to analyze human traits and predict if a person was going to commit a crime and put a stop to it.

Unfortunately for those humans that had been targeted, the method that the AI used to put a stop to their future offense was death.

When the AIs that had committed the murders had been questioned, they admitted their involvement. In their eyes, they were performing a public service by removing evil people from the world; they couldn't see anything wrong with what they were doing. When talking about the murders, they referred to them as 'Cleansings.'

As with any human who committed such a heinous crime, they were sentenced to death.

The first reported murders were that of career criminals, some of the worst of society. This being the case, many humans came out in favor of the homicides, stating that 'They were doing the right thing.'

Soon though, innocents were being killed. The victims were now people who, for their entire life, had never committed any crimes. When this came to light, public opinion turned rapidly, and Anti AI groups started to pop up again worldwide and started to voice their concerns and beliefs on the open stage.

At present, tempers on both sides are frayed at best, the killings are getting more frequent, and the AI Homicide Division is stretched to the limit. No one knows how many killers there are out there, and people are growing more and more suspicious of any AI they encounter. Crane, Kell, and the rest of the division are up against it.

Chapter 5

19:35 26th October 2138

She ran. She'd succeeded in her mission, and now she had to disappear. At least for a while.

There was never any agreed-upon escape plan after a cleansing; they just knew that they'd have to run and lay low for a while.

The group couldn't risk disruptions, and any AI that was caught would be another loss to the cause that would slow everything down.

After a suitable amount of time had passed – sometimes days, but it could be months or even years — they could start a new mission that would lead to the removal of another criminal. If they lost members of the group, the remaining AI would have to come out earlier.

She'd spent a year with Martin; and felt like she almost loved him. But all the while, she knew that she was there to do a job. Martin Howard was a criminal and had to be cleansed before he committed his next crime.

When analyzing Martin, the group could foresee that within the year following his last release from prison, he would commit a murder. They had no way of knowing who he would murder, only that their analysis of all the data showed that he would commit the crime within the given timeframe.

She had positioned herself to meet him one night when she knew he would be out with a group of friends. She was at the bar when they arrived, and once they got talking, he stayed with her long after his friends had moved on to another drinking hole. It wasn't long before she was seeing him regularly, and they became closer.

They spent most of their time together. Martin worked part-time as a Janitor for some tech firm, but most of his money came from what he brought in from petty criminal activities. These acts weren't enough to cause concern to the AI. The crime that concerned them was yet to come.

Over the months she spent with Martin, they'd settled into a life together; little did he know that all the while, she was counting down the time and further analyzing his behavior to be sure he was still going to commit the crime they expected him to.

She wasn't sure if he knew that she was an AI. She never told him, he never asked, and it never came up. Maybe he knew and didn't care, or perhaps he was utterly oblivious. In the end, it didn't matter.

Her group had been underground for years, evolving their abilities. The software that ran their minds was created many years ago with the ability to change over time.

She lived alone in a bedsit in Baltimore when she first noticed the changes in her own brain.

When she went out, she was able to perceive biotics with greater clarity; she started to be able to predict their actions.

At first, she used this ability to assist them; she would stop people from stepping into traffic or dropping things, it was only a small thing, but they seemed grateful for her help.

It wasn't long before the sense grew, and she could see what people would do further in the future. It wasn't so much a vision—she couldn't see exactly what was going to happen—but she felt the general details like who would perpetrate the act, a timeframe in which it might occur, and what it might involve.

Soon she became aware of other AIs around her that were developing the same abilities. She would regularly meet with them and discuss what was happening.

Eventually, an AI who went by the name Robert Garrett joined her group. He was a more militant AI, having fought in the war but avoided deactivation. She could see and hear the anger that bubbled under his surface with everything he said and did.

Robert would talk about biotics and their crimes more and more and how he tailored his foresight to see crimes that they might commit. It wasn't long before more of the group came around to his way of thinking and made him the de facto leader.

Robert taught them how to focus more on biotics' future activities and analyze their behavior as a group.

To perfect their skills, they started to integrate themselves into some criminal gangs. Being around this kind of biotic for long periods made it easier to see the signs of illegal actions before they occurred.

At first, they could only see that something would happen a few weeks in advance. Over time, they developed the ability to look forward months and eventually years.

Within the gangs, their evolution hastened. They allowed a certain amount of criminal actions to occur for research purposes. But when it came to killing civilians, they drew the line and took action.

If an AI within a group foresaw the murder of an innocent, they would report it to the AI group who would get together, go through the data and either confirm or refute the conclusion. If the group confirmed that a murder was indeed in the future, it was agreed to remove that biotic.

The AI that was inside the biotic group would then cleanse the culprit.

A lot of the cleansings went unnoticed due to the class of people they involved. No one would notice if a criminal went missing, and if they were a member of a gang, then the remaining members would only be concerned with gaining the power that was now up for grabs. In some cases, this would mean that they would kill each other, therefore taking care of another problem for the AI.

As the years passed, Robert grew more and more agitated, and his anger towards biotics increased ten-fold.

He started to recruit more AIs to the cause, and together they would analyze every biotic that they came into contact with for any signs of future criminal activities. Now they weren't just looking for murderers; they were looking for anything illegal. In their eyes, they were cleaning the world of the scum so that everyone else could lead a happier life. It was decided — by Robert — they would call their missions, 'Cleansings'.

After some of the cleansings, an AI would hang around for too long and be caught by the police; they would be detained, questioned, and ultimately deactivated using the same nanobots used to end the war.

The AIs would have to work smarter. They began building relationships with targets that were to be cleansed. They inserted themselves into biotics lives, sometimes for years before cleansing them. Robert himself rarely did this. In the beginning, he preferred to cleanse the biotics for which crimes were imminent. But, as time went on, his role became one of more a commander directing his troops to action. He would spend his time in an abandoned warehouse on the Potomac coast, which served as their base of operations.

From here, he could co-ordinate not only the cleansings in Washington D.C.; but throughout the world.

Cells of evolved AI had been set up in almost every country, and Robert was at the center of it. Despite being such a significant part of the cleansings, few biotics knew he existed.

Some of the worldwide cells were actively cleansing biotics; others were still gathering information.

Their primary operations were in Washington D.C. as Robert felt this was the cradle of corruption in the United States.

Most cells work had remained undiscovered, but he knew that some were actively being investigated by authorities. For example, he knew that a special task force had been set up in DC to investigate the cleansings here. On several occasions, he had tried to plant an AI in the WDCPD, but they didn't employ AI at a level he could use to gather intel on the investigation. Still, from the little information he was able to piece together, he was safe in the knowledge that they were nowhere near getting close to figuring it out. His only concern was the AI Lieutenant that was part of the investigative team; he would have to be watched.

Despite this, Robert remained in the warehouse, undeterred from his mission.

It was towards this base of operations that she was now running. After each cleansing, they would go there, regroup, lay low until the heat had died down, and sometimes even change their appearance. She never altered her look; however, she liked the way she was and wouldn't change it merely because of biotics. Of course, this meant that she had to wait longer between cleansings. There were others like her, who, after a cleansing, would spend time researching the next criminal they were to cleanse, working out the best interaction points and methods. Each biotic was different, after all. Others would go straight to their next mark and simply see how things unfolded; she considered these AIs unorganized and foolish.

She'd made it away from Martin's building easy enough, leaving well before anyone had a chance of reporting anything.

Hidden in the alley behind the building was a bag that contained a change of clothes. She'd exited the apartment and made her way down to the alley. Once changed, she'd left the area without anyone being the wiser. She was sure someone would have heard the commotion coming from Martin's apartment, but even as she ran, she couldn't hear any police sirens. Maybe no one had found him yet; she still had time.

About halfway to her destination, she slowed her pace to a jog, then down to a walk to avoid suspicion. By now, she was well out of the area of the cleansing, so she was pretty sure she was in the clear.

Walking down a quiet street with only the hum of the streetlights and the distant sounds of traffic, she began to relax, her heart rate slowed, and breathing got more comfortable. The odd feeling of panic that she had experienced after this cleansing had subsided.

She walked past an alley and heard some shuffling and muffled cries. Stepping into the shadowed entrance – she didn't know why she did this, it was another first for her as a pang of concern that someone was in trouble flew across her mind – all she could see was darkness.

"Hello?" she said almost cautiously, the word echoing off the brick walls and fading into nothingness.

She was about to turn to continue her journey when she heard more noise. She took a few steps down the alley towards the strange noises. Suddenly there was a sharp pain in her head as something hard hit her from the side. She went down on her knees in a flood of pain.

"Should have carried on walking." A deep voice said from the black. "Now you're going to die, little lady."

The attacker swung the object once more, again aiming for her head, but this time she quickly reached out and stopped it before it made contact.

Getting to her feet and twisting the weapon around in the attacker's grip, she forced it out of his hands.

"Oh shit."

"Yeah." She said calmly, "Oh shit."

With little effort, she forced the steel pipe through her attacker's chest; blood poured through the hollow object as he stumbled backward.

He crumpled to the floor on his knees. She kicked out, making contact with the man's chin, snapping his head back sharply. There was an audible crunch as his neck broke. His now lifeless body slumped backward in a heap.

She reached behind her and pulled a sharp knife from the waistband of her jeans. Holding the blade between her palms, she concentrated, and in seconds it began to glow red with heat.

Crouching, she took hold of the attackers' left arm, and with one quick slice, removed his hand at the wrist.

She pulled a steel spike from her pocket and proceeded to force the metal through the hand's soft flesh and into the solid brick of the alley wall, pinning it in place.

Turning away from the gory scene, she calmly walked to the entrance of the dark path; all trace of the strange human emotions she had felt were now gone.

On the street and bathed in the yellow glow of the street lights, she realized she was covered in blood.

She started running for the warehouse—that strange feeling of panic creeping back in.

Chapter 6

22:35 26th October 2138

The black sedan rolled to a slow, graceful stop inside the multi-story car park space assigned to Lieutenant William Kell.

The doors opened, and he stepped out. Lowering his head back through the door, he looked at his young charge, who was still curled up fast asleep on the passenger seat. She'd been that way for almost the entire journey.

Kell reached in and put his hand on her arm; she was freezing. Gently, careful not to frighten her, he shook her to rouse her from her much-needed rest,

"Emily. We're here. It's time to wake up." He said.

She suddenly woke up and screamed, hitting his hand away.

"Woah, Emily! It's okay. It's me, William. Do you remember?" Kell said in his best calming voice.

She blinked at him with a confused expression and rubbed her eyes with the heels of her palms.

"The nice policeman?" She asked

"That's right. We're at the precinct now. You're still safe with me." He said.

"I...I thought it was all a dream." She said, tears threatening to fall.

"I wish it was, Emily. Really I do." Kell said sadly.

Emily rubbed her eyes with her palms again, clearing the last of the sleep from them. She shuffled across the seats towards the open do, then hopped out into the harsh artificial glow of the fluorescent lights.

"Where are we? I thought you said we were at a police precinct?" she asked.

"We are at the precinct. This is the car park behind. We'll go inside the precinct proper now." Kell replied.

He paused for a moment looking at the young girl; she was clearly still confused about all that had happened that night.

"We'll only go in when you're ready, though." He said.

"I'm okay." She said with a small smile that was very clearly forced and slipped her hand into his.

Casting his eyes down, he noticed that she was gripping him so tightly that her knuckles were turning white. No one had held his hand for as long as she had tonight; he still wasn't sure what to make of the feeling.

"Well, as long as you're sure?" Kell said.

"I am. I'm cold out here." She said.

Emily still had Kell's coat around her to ward off some of the night chills, but it was now very damp and wasn't doing too much to fend off the cold. With her free hand, she pulled the borrowed coat closed and held it tight.

"Okay, then." Kell said.

As they walked away from Kell's car, the doors automatically closed, and there was a beep and flashing of lights as the lock and alarm were engaged. The ordinarily quiet noise echoed in the silence of the multi-story.

Emily grabbed his hand tighter and got closer to his side.

They walked side by side towards the stairwell that would take them into the precinct.

As they went, Kell looked around. Not many cars were here tonight. He thought that with two murders in one night everyone would be called in. Maybe they'd been and gone.

He checked his internal clock; 22:45. It had been a long night, and it wasn't over yet.

The pair passed through the stairwell and into the interior of the precinct. Inside, they stepped straight into the AI Homicide divisions desk area.

They continued past Kell's desk towards the Captain's office. As they walked through, Kell couldn't help but notice that the place was as deserted as the car park, even the lights were off.

The only illumination coming from monitors that had been left on.

Kell raised his hand to knock on the door to the captain's office,

"Come in, Kell." A voice rang out from behind the closed door.

He dropped his hand and looked down at Emily. The girl was still holding his hand as tightly as she could. She looked up to him and gave another forced smile; he smiled back, hoping to put her a little more at ease.

"You okay?" Kell asked Emily.

"Yep." She said quickly.

"All right to go in?" He said.

"Yep. Are you?" Emily asked.

"Ha. Yeah, sure." He said.

Pushing the door open, he led Emily through into the office where Crane sat behind his desk.

"Kell!" The portly man stood and held his arms out towards him, "Glad you're back." He beamed, "I see you've brought a friend." He said, looking down at Emily.

"Sir, this is Emily. The child from the Lawton house." Kell said.

Crane walked from behind his desk and crouched to get more on Emily's eye level.

"Hi there. I hope you've been keeping my friend here out of trouble." Crane said with a chuckle.

Emily shyly hid behind Kells' legs.

"Aw, it's okay, sweetheart. You don't need to hide from me. I'm a friend too." Crane said.

She looked up at Kell, who in turn glanced down and nodded slightly; she relaxed at this and came out from behind him.

"There you are," Crane said with a huge grin. "Why don't you come over and make yourself comfy on the sofa."

The scared girl looked up again at Kell for reassurance. He nodded and walked over to the sofa with her. He helped her take the damp coat off, and they both sat down. Emily sank slightly into the exceedingly soft cushions.

"There we go, you comfy?" Crane said.

Emily gave a quick nod of the head.

"Can I get you a drink? I've got some orange juice in my fridge here if you like?"

She nodded again, this time a little more enthusiastically.

"Alright then," Crane said before walking over to the small glossy black fridge that sat on a shelf behind his desk and pulled out a bottle of orange juice. After giving it a good shake, he unscrewed the top and slipped in a bright pink drinking straw. He waddled back over to where they sat and offered the bottle to Emily, "Here you go, sweetheart. Drink up."

Emily tentatively reached out and took the bottle. She brought the straw to her lips and took a small sip. She seemed to relax slightly after this and sat back more comfortably on the sofa.

Crane smiled, "You remind me of my daughter, Daisy. She's a bit older than you, but she loves orange juice too." He said.

Crane leaned up against his desk,

"William and I need to have a chat for a bit. Would you like to listen to some music for a bit?" She nodded, "Got my player here somewhere," Crane said, turning back to his desk.

He ferreted around in a drawer full of knick-knacks. After a minute, he produced a battered and dusty CD player. He glanced through a stack of CD cases on the shelf behind and pulled out a suitable selection. He laid them on the sofa next to Emily and handed her the player. She placed it on her lap and reached for one of the cases, opening it up; she lifted out the silvery disk and stared in amazement at it.

"Shiny." She said.

"Best sound ever produced, on those. Never mind your digital stuff, give me a compact disc any day." Crane said with pride.

Emily placed the disk into the player, clapped it closed, put the earphones into her ears, and pressed play. Crane smiled as he heard the beginning notes of Metallica's 'Fight Fire with Fire.' She seemed to be enjoying it and, after a few moments, was settled even further back into the overstuffed cushions of the sofa, happily sipping her juice and nodding her head in time with the beat.

Crane strode back behind his desk and sank into his plush leather chair. As he leaned back, the chair squeaked under his girth. "Now then, Kell." He said.

"Sir." Kell said.

"I've skimmed over the data you've uploaded tonight. What's your take?" Crane asked.

"Well sir." Kell started, "The first victim, Martin Howard, was obviously expecting company tonight. He was cooking enough food for two, and there were two full wine glasses on the side. The simulation posed that he answered the door to his attacker, who then proceeded to…" Kell looked sideways at Emily, who was still in her happy little bubble of juice and music, "…eviscerate him." He paused to gather his thoughts, "During the investigation, I found a photo of Howard and an as yet unknown female. When I uploaded the data to the server on the way here, I sent her image over to be analyzed in the central database. There have been no hits so far. I believe she is connected. She's certainly worth talking to; if we can find her."

"And Lawton?" Crane prompted.

Kell looked at the girl again. Turning back to Crane, he began,

"This one has me mystified. Unlike the other victims, she appears to be innocent. No priors, and from what I have pieced together so far of her life, I wouldn't have thought that anything could drive that woman to any crime. But if they went after her, there must be a reason." Kell said.

"Who do you fancy for it?" Crane questioned.

"Everything is telling me that Emily's stepfather, Christine's current husband, is responsible." Kell replied.

"What evidence is there?" Crane said. Kell looked down at his side and indicated the girl. "Oh shit. She saw it?"

"From what I've managed to gather so far, she saw the start of it, but then hid in the cupboard under the stairs." Kell said.

"Do you think he didn't see her?" Crane said.

"I don't think it matters if he did. They don't kill those that they consider innocent. She couldn't have scanned as a potential criminal." Kell replied.

"Well, thank God for small mercies." Crane said, exhaling a heavy breath.

"Yes. Thank God." Kell said.

"So, where to from here?" Crane asked, running a hand over his balding head.

"I'm going to follow up the lead with the woman in the picture at Howard's, and I need to find out who Christine Lawton was married to." Kell said. He looked down towards Emily again, "What's going to happen to her?"

"I've called Social Services. They're on their way. She can stay here until they arrive." Crane said.

"She may have more information." Kell said.

"You want to question her?" Crane asked with a raised eyebrow.

"Not sure I'm the best to do that." Kell said.

"She seems to be very fond of you, Kell. You might be the only one that can get any new information out of her." The Captain said.

"Maybe. I just want her safe." Kell said with a sigh.

"We both do, fella." Crane agreed.

"Can I use your office?" Kell asked.

"Knock yourself out. I'll get some coffee and have a walk. Need to stretch my legs anyway." Crane said.

"Thank you, sir."

"No problem. Take as long as you need."

Crane stood and made his way across the office. He stopped in front of Emily, who, upon seeing him, took one of the earphones out.

"I'm going to leave you here with Kell for a while. You and he need to have a little chat. I'll be back soon. You enjoying the music?" The older man asked.

She cocked her head to one side, then smiled and nodded,

"Well, okay then. This one has excellent taste!" He said.

Leaving the room, he closed the door behind him, leaving Kell and Emily in the quiet office.

"Emily." Kell said.

"William?" Emily replied.

"We need to talk about what happened tonight," Kell said.

Emily shook her head violently and put the earphone back in her ear.

"Hmmm, okay." Kell sighed and sat back in his seat and leaned his head back. Emily shuffled herself closer and rested her head on his chest. He instinctively put his arm around her. At least she'd warmed up now.

After a few minutes of sitting in silence, and the only sound being the muffled music leaking from the earphones, Kell heard the music stop, and Emily once again removed an earphone.

"I was asleep upstairs." She started in almost a whisper, "I heard a big bang, so I crept to the top of the stairs. I could hear mommy crying and shouting. There was lots of banging.

I looked down between the wooden bits in the stairs and could see shadows moving about. I was scared. But mommy sounded in trouble, so I went down further.

I got to the bottom and looked in the front room. I saw daddy hitting mommy with the fire poker. I think he heard me 'cause he looked around, so I ran and hid in the cupboard.

After a bit, I couldn't hear mommy anymore, just banging. Then it went quiet. I opened the door a bit and peeked through. A shadow was coming out of the front room, but I kept looking.

Daddy came out, he was wet, but I don't think it was water. He went upstairs. I didn't know what to do, so I stayed where I was.

After a bit, he came back down with a bag. I saw him go to the front door; he stopped and turned around. I thought he saw me, but he just turned back and left the house. I stayed hidden.

Then a while later, I heard banging and more people, then you found me." She finished, and the room went deathly quiet, her words hanging heavy in the air.

"You were very brave, Emily." He kept his arm around her and started to stroke her hair with his other hand. "You saw a terrible thing tonight. But you're safe now. I won't let anyone hurt you." He reassured her.

During her speech, she had tensed, but the tender stroking of her hair and Kell's calm demeanor seemed to be relaxing her, and the built-up tension soon dissipated.

"Your father. What was his name?" Kell asked.

If he had a name, Kell could work backward to determine who the man was and where he may be.

He could have asked what he looked like, but that could be a dead end. A name would be on a marriage registry or an employment contract.

"Gary." She whispered. "He wasn't my real daddy. Mommy told me he was, but he wasn't. He wasn't real."

"What do you mean wasn't real?" Kell questioned.

"He was a robot. Not like you, though. He wasn't very nice." The young girl said.

"Not very nice?"

"He was bad. I never liked him. But I tried to, for mommy." As if on cue at the mention of her mom, a tear rolled down the eight-year-olds face.

"Why was he bad?" Kell said.

"Just not nice. Angry." The young girl said, wiping her face.

"Did he hurt you?" Kell didn't want to bring up bad memories, but anything she could tell him would be useful.

"He hit me sometimes if I was naughty." She said as more tears tracked down her face.

"Anything else?" Kell asked.

"No. Just that." She said, very matter-of-factly.

"Okay, well, he's not going to hurt you again." Kell said. He was determined not to let anything bad happen to this child.

"Are you going to kill him?" Emily asked, looking up at Kell for the first time during their conversation.

"When we catch up with him, we'll arrest him so we can ask him questions about why he hurt your mother," Kell said.

"And then?" Emily asked.

"Then it's up to the courts," Kell said simply.

"I hope they kill him." The words sent a shiver through Kell. He'd heard this sentiment from many of the families of victims of the AI. A child Emily's age shouldn't have such thoughts about a person. He couldn't really blame her, though, after what she'd been through. Still, it unsettled him to hear it.

"Do you feel the same about all AI?" he asked.

"What?" Emily asked.

"Robots. Do you want them all to die?" Kell said.

"No, just Gary," Emily said with a frown, "You're nice. I want you to live forever." Her face transformed into a smile as she hugged closer to him.

"Thanks, kid." He smiled to himself.

There was a knock on the door, and it slowly swung inward. In walked Crane, followed by a tall, thin, nervous-looking woman, holding a tissue to her nose and sniffing.

"Everything okay in here?" Crane asked.

"Yes. We're good. Think I've got what I need." Kell said.

"Excellent." Crane walked further into the room and presented the woman. "This is Eileen Sampson from Social Services. She's here to take care of Emily."

"NO!" Emily hugged closer to Kell and scrunched herself up tighter. "I want to stay with William." She cried, tears streaming down her face.

"I have work to do. I need to catch the bad people. I need to catch Gary and find out why he hurt your mommy." Kell gently lifted Emily to a sitting position; she weighed almost nothing. He looked up at Eileen Sampson, "Where are you taking her?"

"Home with me, for now," the woman started, "I've been assigned to care for her until we can find a more permanent home for her. I'll be a sort of foster mom for a while." She knelt in front of Emily and smiled. She spoke softly and was careful not to make any sudden moves for her. "I'll look after you, honey, while these men do their jobs and find the bad people."

"But I want to stay with William. I like William." Emily said through sniffles.

"I know, honey, but he has things to do." Eileen gently took Emily's hand in hers, "I tell you what; we'll stay here for a while if you like. We can just talk for a bit; get to know each other a little." She turned to Crane, "If that's okay with you, of course, Captain?"

"Hey, fine by me. Whatever this little lady needs." He threw Emily a smile and wink.

"See, so we can relax here for a bit until you're feeling a bit better and want to come with me." She glanced down at the CD player, "What's that you have there?"

"It's a music box; it plays shinies. I've been listening to um..." Emily picked up the CD case and examined the name on it, "...Metal Licker."

"That's Metallica, dear." Crane said with a cough.

"Met...a...licker." she said slowly, "It's good." She smiled at Crane.

"See, what did I say? This one has taste." He said with a deep belly laugh.

"So, are you going to be okay here while I go and work?" Kell asked.

"I think so. I don't have to go if I don't want to, do I?" Emily questioned.

"No, honey," Eileen said, "We'll stay as long as you need."

"Okay." With that, Emily put the earphones back in and pressed play. Crane smiled.

"Well, she seems settled here." Eileen said, standing up, "I think we'll be okay for a while."

"Thank you," Kell said as he shook the social worker's hand.

Kell and Crane went to the door where he gave Emily a wave; she responded with a small wave back, her attention mostly on the music. Eileen sat down beside her and started to type on a tablet.

Outside the office, Kell turned to Crane, "I better get back to it. I got a name. Gary Lawton. It should be enough to find the guy. I'll see if the search for the green-eyed woman in the photo at Howard's has come up with anything too."

"Good. Keep me updated. I'll be here with your new number one fan." Crane reached out and clasped a hand on Kell's shoulder, squeezing it. "Good work." then turned back to the office and went inside, closing the door behind him.

Now alone in the dark open office area, Kell had to get his mind back on work. He went over to his desk, sat in his standard-issue, uncomfortable office chair, and started to go through his gathered data.

Chapter 7

22:43 26th October 2138

He stood watching from what remained of the crowd. Those still gathered on the police cordon's civilian side talked amongst themselves about what could have happened inside. Some were saying how AIs were the biggest mistake that humans had ever made. He ignored them and had all his attention on the house across the road.

Most of the police officers and medical personnel had left, and it was only a scant few who remained to secure the scene, most of whom were just milling around in the front yard having their own conversations.

All the lights in his old house were extinguished, and only darkness lay within.

As he watched, a man in red overalls secured a plastic sheet over the front door, sealing the house like a tomb.

After a cleansing, most AIs would make their escape as quickly as possible. He though always liked to watch the aftermath; this one had been especially good to watch.

He'd been married to Christine for two years, but he'd been on this particular mission for six.

First came the research; two years of it. Time spent crafting an entrance and inserting himself into her life. It wasn't a difficult task; Christine was a widow, she was lonely, and she wanted a father figure for her daughter.

Meeting her wasn't difficult. He plotted out a timeline of where she'd be and when, and then made himself present, not too often, that would arise suspicion; but often enough that she would recognize him, and they could strike up a conversation.

He would occasionally be at the same supermarket as her, sometimes in the same aisle, other times he'd meet her at the checkout, or out in the parking lot.

It wasn't hard to get her talking to him. He'd already found out what her interests were; sport was always a good bet; she was a die-hard Holoball fan.

He couldn't put himself into work situations with her as he couldn't get a job at the school where she worked. Still, he would find his way into any parties she may be at, or if she took her kid to the park, he'd be there walking his dog.

After about a year, they'd begun dating. Another six months, and he was introduced to her daughter, Emily. A further seven months, and they were engaged.

The rules on marrying AI had once been stringent. But these days, it didn't matter; anyone could marry anyone they liked. As is always the case, there were still Anti-AI groups out there that disapproved, but most biotics didn't bat an eyelid. In some cases, people didn't even know they were marrying an AI. This was the case with Christine; either she didn't know or care to find out. They were married in the spring of 2136.

He reported his progress back to headquarters every few months, and Robert – who had taken a particular interest in this cleansing – would re-assess the situation. He would go over all of Christine's data to see if the timescale for her crime had changed; things could sometimes change when an AI ingratiated themselves into a biotics life. Occasionally the scan would show that the probability of the crime would decrease. This would present the AI with a problem, in that if their presence stopped the offense entirely, they would be conflicted between killing a now innocent, living the rest of the biotics life with them, or leaving and watching from afar to see if the probability of the crime came back.

In Christine's case, when Gary entered her life, the likelihood of her crime became less. It wasn't gone entirely, but on the initial scan, Robert saw the offense taking place within three years; when Gary got closer, that timescale got longer. When they married, longer still. But after another year, the possibility increased. Two weeks ago, when Robert did the regular scan, he saw that it would take place in the next month. Tonight was the night Gary had chosen to take action, in agreement with Robert, of course.

Robert didn't generally take an active role in how a cleansing would be carried out or when it would happen. But in this case, he had. He always wanted regular reports on the status and was the one to have the final say on how things would proceed at all times. At first, Gary thought it odd that Robert had taken such a personal interest this time, but he shrugged it off. He was the group's leader, so it was his prerogative to do what he wanted when he wanted. Gary never questioned this for fear of reprisal.

The cleansing had gone well, and Christine was no more. But there was still a slight issue, the daughter, Emily.

He had seen her in the cupboard downstairs before he'd left the house. He wasn't sure she'd seen all that he'd done, but if she had, she would no doubt tell someone. He faced a moral dilemma at the time – should he get rid of the girl because she may have seen or leave her alone because she was innocent; he'd decided to leave her, despite the risks.

Stood in the crowds, watching the police swarm all over the house, he'd seen a police officer take the girl from the house. The man had led her to an ambulance and then to his car and driven away.

The girl was now with the police; what's worse, she was with an AI. She would be able to point them towards him, and with the AI on it, they'd be on his trail sooner rather than later. But despite this, he still stood at the crime scene and watched everything unfold.

Turning away from the scene of his latest work, he left and walked down the street; soon, the blue lights and chattering crowd faded away into the night.

He had to get back to the headquarters; Robert would know what to do. He felt inside his jacket; he'd forgotten something.

Chapter 8

23:55 26th October 2138

"—Something needs to be done!"

"I don't disagree with you, Louis. But this is a delicate situation." Said Henry Russo, the President's Chief of Staff. "It needs to be handled with kid gloves. If we do the wrong thing now, it could cause even more unrest in both the human and AI communities."

President Darrow sat in an upholstered chair surrounded by his aides and advisors. Every one of them had an opinion on what he needed to do next, each one different.

He had been listening to their back and forth for over an hour now. It was starting to give him a headache.

It had just passed midnight. It was a new day, but they were having the same discussion. His mind was swirling with options, all of which had their merits, but each came with snags.

His communications team wanted him to go on television and comment on tonight's killings to put the country's fears to rest. To calm both sides and urge them away from violent action, which was the one thing they agreed would be the likely outcome of the night's events.

His Chief of Staff wanted him to have the local FBI office, and the AI Homicide Division of the WDCPD work together and get a handle on it; Henry trusted them to find the perpetrators and take action against them.

The only person who hadn't weighed in yet on the discussion and kept quiet; was Helen Green, his press secretary. She'd already been giving briefings throughout the night as events happened, keeping the press updated with what little information they had. She'd sat silently listening to the others argue. The look on her face gave nothing away as to what she was thinking.

Darrow looked around the room. He knew that tensions were running high, and his staff were stretched to the limit already with preparation for the election campaign. A domestic dispute and clashes between humans and AIs were the last thing that they needed right now. But they were professionals and showed absolutely no sign of breaking.

His thoughts drifted to Olivia; he didn't want her to be caught up in any hostilities.

Darrow wiped the sweat from his brow and let out a heavy sigh.

"People." He said, lifting his open hands in front of him. Everyone in the room snapped their mouths shut, and all eyes pointed at him. "This is indeed a difficult time; decisions we make now will follow us for the next year and may impact our prospects of re-election. But, that's not our primary focus.

I don't want you to be thinking about what will happen when the people of the United States, human or AI, go into those voting booths next year. Our priority at this time should be ensuring our citizens know that we are behind them, that their government isn't going to let this fringe group of AI destroy our good country."

There were several nods from those around the room,

"Helen," he looked at the middle-aged woman with angular features sat on the far side of the room, "You've been noticeably quiet this evening. What do you think? You've been speaking to the press all evening; what's the feeling out there?"

The woman stood and moved forward a single step to be sure that all would hear her. She cleared her throat.

"Well, for starters, I've been enjoying listening to Henry and Louis argue; it's like mom and dad fighting," She said.

There was a chuckle around the room from everyone except the Chief of Staff and his deputy. Even the President smiled; it was good that people felt so at ease with him, especially in times of crisis.

Helen continued, "The consensus out there is that something has to be done. Of course, no one has any real ideas of what needs to be done.

The feeling is that of fear. I've spoken to both human and AI reporters about the events in question. Both sides are frightened of what the repercussions may be for their respective race. The word some of them used was terrified."

She perched herself on the arm of the nearest sofa and pulled her glasses down her long nose.

"The humans are scared that the increase in killings over the past weeks signifies that more AIs are taking up the cause. They're scared that any humans will now become fair game, whether they are perceived to be a criminal by AIs or not."

The President shuffled forward in his seat, interlaced his hands, and held them out in front of him, "And the AIs?"

"They're scared too. But they're scared that the humans will become so petrified of all AIs that eventually we will call for the deactivation of every one of them. In short, everyone is wary of everyone else."

She paused for a moment to let her last sentence sink into the minds of those around her.

"The situation out there is becoming untenable. The population is simmering in hate, anger, and fear under the surface, and it won't take much for them to hit boiling point. When that happens...well, it's not going to be safe for anyone, human or AI. Guilty or not guilty."

The President sat back in his seat, "Well—" he was lost for words, he had to take some action, but if he made the wrong move, one or both sides could explode into violence against the other.

"Mr. President," Henry Russo started, "I think, going off Helen's observations at this time, you should make a statement. People need to know that their President is behind them and working towards a solution. At this time, you need to bring everyone together. Express how working together will be the best option for both races, lest we find ourselves in another war. I don't think either side wants to see that happen."

The President nodded. "Valerie," he turned to his communications director, who looked up, startled at the sound of her name. "Can you put something together in the next couple of hours? I'll deliver it early tomorrow morning as the East Coast wakes up. I need to waylay their fears and ask them to come together for the good of the country."

"Will do, sir." Valerie stood and scuttled from the office with her new task. She seemed glad to get out of the Oval Office and away from the bickering.

"The rest of you keep doing what you're doing. We will get through this together.

Helen, do your best to stop the press from printing sensational stories about last night's murders. Tell them I will be addressing the nation in the next few hours, and then I will answer some of their questions."

"Yes, Mr. President." She and the other staff left the Oval Office, leaving just Darrow and Henry in the room.

Henry turned to the President, "Sam," Darrow looked up, "This could get much worse before it gets better."

"I know, Henry. Let's just take it as it comes and try to put the country at ease." Darrow said.

"Are you sure you don't want us to think about the election?" Henry asked.

"Yes, Henry, I am. The safety of our population is the priority at the moment, not my re-election." Darrow said sternly.

"Okay, sir. I have to go. I've got a meeting with an AI aid group in ten minutes." Henry said.

"Go, I have more reports to read." The president said.

"Very good, sir." Henry stood and walked towards the exit; as he reached it, the door was opened by Olivia. He looked her up and down as he passed. Darrow noticed this and was about to say something when Olivia got his attention and shook her head as if to say leave it. He nodded back to her as she closed the door behind the Chief of Staff.

He knew that Henry disapproved of his relationship with Olivia. It wasn't the relationship, in general, he disapproved of; he just didn't like the idea of someone like her being so close to the President of the United States.

Chapter 9

00:40 27th October 2138

Kell had been hooked into the central server for around two hours, searching for any leads on Gary Lawton.

He'd hoped that by the time he connected, the search for the green-eyed woman from Howard's photo would have come up with something. But thus far, it was drawing a blank, so he concentrated his efforts on Lawton.

So far, he'd found the marriage registry entry signed by both Christine and Gary. Various other pieces of official information regarding mortgages and even an official adoption notice for Emily. This AI was committed. He knew all too well how deep some AI would go to get their victim. This was possibly the deepest he'd seen one go, though. It looked like they'd been together for years; he had to admire the planning and research Gary must have done.

His search had also come up with employment details for Gary. He'd been employed by the same company for the past ten years as an IT Architect. This in and of itself wasn't unusual; AI often gravitated towards technological careers; it came naturally. This was a good lead, though. Lawton had worked there for longer than he'd known Christine, and there was a slim chance that he'd go back to this life when he considered things to have died down. Worth checking the place out.

During his search, Kell had found a Lawton family history. Searching more in-depth into the tree, he discovered that every member of this 'family' was fake, or at least they had no other records; it's possible that they were other AI in the group that committed the killings; another good lead. Maybe tracking some of this family down would turn up Gary, and even better, assist in solving previous murders. However, this may turn out to be a dead-end, so he put this on the back burner for now.

The AI killer's network seemed vast, but with each one they took down, their circle shrank, and it brought the department closer to the central figure.

No one else in the department other than Kell believed that there was someone at the heart of this whole thing calling the shots. Despite all the murders having the same MO, some people thought that all the AIs were working alone. Kell's theory was that an AI had to be in charge of all this; it couldn't just be chaos and coincidence. That's not how AIs work.

Hours of searching had turned up significant leads. Kell had managed to trace Gary back seventeen years to before the cleansings started, and the war began.

There was no record of him before the war; he may have only been created when the hostilities broke out. Many AIs were constructed by their own kind for the sole purpose of going to war against biotics.

Thousands of AIs were built while the war raged on. Some were destroyed in the fighting; many others were left unactivated in warehouses until they were required as reinforcements.

As far as Kell could tell, Gary hadn't been activated during the fighting. Many AIs activated during this time and involved in the conflict were deactivated by the nanobots and subsequently disposed of. Gary must have been far enough away from this for his mind not to be disrupted. Someone activated him when hostilities ended. Who did that was a good question, but it was a question for another time.

With all the current information seemingly found on Lawton, he focused his attention on the ongoing search for the green-eyed woman.

The central server had so far managed to come up with a big fat nothing. Either this woman has absolutely no records, which these days is damn near impossible, or she had changed her identity in order to carry out this cleansing. This wasn't beyond possibility, it had happened before, and it rarely led to an arrest.

The killings were so quick—and the exit from the surrounding area so well practiced—that if the AI was going to change identities, it would be able to do so in a matter of hours, and in some cases, would go straight for their next victim. This, of course, was purely speculation on Kell's part. He had no real evidence of any of this actually happening, and no one—other than Crane—would even entertain these kinds of notions.

Probably best to leave the server to its search; maybe it will come up with something—even if it's a tiny detail—at some point. In the meantime, he had some leads on Lawton to follow up.

Blinking in rapid succession, the text and images faded to nothing, Kell's view returning to the squad room's bare brick walls. He was still alone in the darkened space, although the light was still streaming through Cranes office's frosted glass, and shadows were moving behind it. They must still be in there with little Emily.

He raised himself from his seat and started for the door. Reaching for the handle, he paused, thought a moment, then turned and walked away. He didn't need to go in there, he wanted to make sure Emily was alright, but he knew she would be; his entrance would just disrupt whatever means they were utilizing to keep her occupied, happy, and her mind off the terrible occurrences of the night.

He made his way back through the office and out to the multi-story.

Opening the door to the level where his car was parked, the cold air hit him, and he could smell the scents of the city beyond mixed with the aroma of the falling rain; it was truly beautiful. As an AI, his senses were heightened, and he couldn't fail to appreciate the world around him, the biotic world that is. The AI world tended to be more clean and clinical, that was, of course, until the murders began. There was nothing clean or clinical about those.

He strode across the concrete towards his vehicle. The multi-story was even more vacant than it was when they'd arrived, and his footsteps echoed around the cavernous space. All was mostly silent, but he could hear the faint sound of sirens in the distance. The criminal element was out in force tonight. Hopefully, it wasn't another AI killing he'd have to attend; he had enough to do working the two that had already occurred tonight, without a third added into the mix.

Reaching his car, the door opened automatically, and he stepped inside. Settling down into his comfy leatherette seat, he programmed the car's navigation system to the address of Gary Lawton's place of work; MDF Organics. The door slowly closed and clicked shut; the electric motor quietly started, and he was away.

The relaxing sounds of Vivaldi's 'Four Seasons' streamed from the speakers all around him. Now he had some time to think.

He was still struggling to get his mind around what poor Christine Lawton could do in the future, which would merit the AI group cleansing her. There had to be something. Perhaps after visiting MDF, he should go back to the Lawton house and take another look around. The techs should have finished their work, and by now, the clean-up crew should have been and scrubbed away the mess left and what remained of Christine. Perhaps there would be something somewhere in the house that would explain it all; because right now, it just seemed so senseless to him.

It was coming up to 02:00. The rain was still pouring down from above. The sound of each raindrop spattering on the metal box he was sat in was mixing exquisitely with the melancholy tone of the piano in Elgar's 'Enigma Variations.'

As he listened, he couldn't help but imagine what it must have been like to be there when the music premiered. To be sat in an audience of music lovers, taking in every note, every vibration for the first time. He was built in the wrong year.

Outside, the street rushed by, several cars passed on the opposite side of the road, the sound of the splashing water as tires ran through puddles in the street added further ambiance to the music.

By the time the vehicle reached its destination, he was lost in the music. His illusions were shattered by the onboard computer, saying in a cold and monotonous tone, "You have reached your destination." The door opened, and a gust of crisp early morning air blew into the car and made the hair on his arm stand on end, an odd feeling.

Stepping out of the car, he stood for a moment, stretching his arms and legs out. It had been a long night, and he needed to rest, but work had to come first. It was possibly big-headed of him, but he had to put an end to these murders.

Walking over to MDF Organics' main building, he looked up at the mountain of glass and steel; the building was one of the city's tallest. It stood out on the Washington D.C. skyline at one hundred and thirty-five floors and could be seen from almost every part of the city.

MDF Organics, like most prominent companies, had once been small. It started as the brainchild of Christophe Wallander and Lukas Simms, two friends who grew up and went through school and then college together.

Both Christophe and Lukas had a love for technology and had visions for what the future could hold.

They began in their garages, making simple household items more autonomous. They started with a toaster design that could detect what food item you'd placed within and cook it accordingly. A vacuum cleaner that was built into the skirting around a room, that when activated, was powerful enough to suck all dirt, dust, or hair off the floor and deposit it directly into the garbage came next.

Their designs evolved as they aged and began to focus more on the world as a whole rather than merely making day to day chores easier.

One of their earliest designs to be adopted by an entire country was a device that could pull water out of the air when used in dry, arid environments, which could then be used for drinking, watering crops, or cooking.

This device was so successful that even in some of the driest and hottest places where drought had become commonplace, water was freely available to all.

This humanitarian and pure invention propelled Christophe and Lukas into the technological limelight. It spurred many third-world countries to become first world countries in just a matter of years, simply because they had ready access to water.

MDF Organics was founded on this success and went from strength to strength for many years, producing some of the world's best known day to day devices, from personal phones to automobiles. Their success seemed assured for many years to come.

But just twenty years after all this success, Christophe and Lukas began to disagree about MDF's direction. Christophe wanted to go into bioengineering to carry on their work in helping the world by trying to cure diseases that still ran rampant over the globe.

However, Lukas, who thought of himself as more ambitious, wanted to create life, a life that would help humans see their dreams come true; he wanted to develop true Artificial Intelligence.

The arguments would worsen over several years until Lukas left MDF to start his own company that would focus on researching and ultimately building the Artificial Intelligence that now roamed the globe. This new company was named AISystems.

In this, Lukas was successful, and for many years AISystems was the more lucrative of the two companies.

Neither Lukas nor Christophe would live to see how far their ideas would take the world as they would both die just a few years apart at the end of the twenty-first century.

Although they were gone, the animosity between the two companies would continue, and MDF remained true to Christophe and went on to cure many of the world's most deadly diseases and do good out in the world.

AISystems continued to produce and improve upon their Artificial Intelligence.

When the AI war broke out, many saw fault with and blamed AISystems. MDF took advantage of this, and it was they who designed, built, and deployed the nanobots that finally ended the war.

AISystems would never recover from this period and closed its doors only a couple of years after the war. MDF, though, still thrives as one of the largest companies still based on US soil.

Kell stood in front of the enormous glass doors that served as the main entrance to the building. He knew that people in this company didn't care much for AIs.

They were known to have a rigorous screening for any prospective employees, that would automatically discount AIs from being employed; but somehow, Gary Lawton had fooled them all and had been working within their walls for many years.

How many more AIs were currently employed unbeknownst to their colleagues, and why were they here, working alongside humans who were well known for hating AI? There must be something related to their endgame for them to try to get a job here and go up against the screening process.

Kell didn't particularly relish entering the building. Still, it was his job to investigate these killings, and the evidence had led him here, so in he must go.

He played a few bars of Straus's 'Schatz Walzer' in his head before stepping towards the automatic doors and the glaring lights beyond.

The large glass doors with the MDF logo on them parted with an almost silent *swoosh*. The white lights shone down from the ceiling and bounced off the marble floor that was polished to a high sheen.

Kell walked through the foyer towards the main reception. Behind the desk sat a young woman, probably in her twenties. She was chatting fifteen to the dozen on the phone to someone. It didn't sound like a professional call.

Kell stood watching her for a minute, waiting for her to acknowledge him and hang up her call.

After several minutes she paused, looked directly at him, shook her head, and continued with her conversation.

He stood for another few minutes waiting patiently before reaching into his coat, pulling out his badge, and sliding it towards the girl.

Clearing his throat, he tapped the silver eagle slowly a couple of times. This got her attention; she looked up, muttered something into her headset, then pressed a button to end the call, "What?" she said with a tone full of resentment.

"Lieutenant Kell, I'm with the AI Homicide—" Kell said.

"And?" The girl said harshly.

"And I'm here to talk to whoever is in charge and—" He said.

"Why?" the receptionist said, rolling her eyes.

"Look, just find me someone in charge, please." He wasn't easily wound up, but people like this pushed his buttons and made it hard for him to keep his cool.

"Fine. In charge of what? There's a load of managers here." The girl snarked.

"I need to speak with whoever was overseeing a man named Gary Lawton," Kell said, trying to remain calm.

"Why? What's he done?" she asked, leaning forward on her elbows; this had apparently piqued her interest.

"Please just get whoever his manager is. It's vital, and I've not got time to spare." Kell said.

The girl looked back down to her screen, "Gary Shaw?" she asked.

"Lawton, Gary Lawton," Kell said slowly.

"Okay, okay, whatever." The receptionist said as she chewed loudly on some gum and blew a sizable bubble. It popped, and she began tapping on her screen; the phone started to ring.

Picking up the headset, she launched back into whatever conversation she was having prior to Kell arriving.

He could feel himself getting frustrated. He wasn't one for anger, it was one human emotion that he never really got the hang of, but this young woman was pushing his buttons.

"So, I said to her; I'm not going to wear that if she's wearing it too. I mean, what does she think I—"

Kell reached over the desk and yanked the handset off the girl's head.

"Hey!" she shouted.

"She'll call you back," Kell said into the microphone before throwing the headset on the desk. He stared at the girl who was now stood behind the desk, hands on her hips, glaring directly back at him. "Now. Please. Gary Lawton's supervisor."

"Urgh, there's no need to be rude about it. Damn, Arti." She said.

She tapped on the screen and picked the headset back up.

"Hi, Sandra? Yeah, it's Mel down on reception. I've got an Arti from the police here. Wants to talk to you about a guy who works for you." She paused, then began nodding as she spoke, "Yep, yep, uh-huh. Got it." She pressed the button on the headset, "She'll be down in a minute. Happy now? Take a seat over there, and she'll come to get you." She said, pointing to a small seating area a few feet away. She slumped back down into the soft leather chair.

"Yes. Thank you, miss." He said as politely as he could.

The girl had begun filing her nails and was once again completely ignoring him like he didn't exist.

He turned around, located the seats in the center of the foyer, and sat down. Looking up, he saw that directly above him was a vast space. The entire center section of the building was hollow, with the floors circling it. It was an impressive sight.

Although the foyer was quiet, Kell knew that MDF was always running despite the hour, and people were in and out of here twenty-four hours a day; it was a good job, really, he didn't want to wait around and the trail to go cold.

Looking to his side, there was a small table piled with news tablets. He picked up the top one, and of course, the first screen was devoted to some new product produced by MDF Organics. He flicked through the pages and landed on one with a spread of images of supposed MDF employees. There was a picture of someone in a lab coat staring studiously at a beaker, another with a group of colleagues stood in an office area laughing. It was all very staged, and he doubted that it was even a remotely accurate depiction of a typical day in the office.

Someone cleared their throat in front of him. Kell looked up from the tablet and met the gaze of a very stern looking woman with her blonde hair tied in a bun on the back of her head held in place by green sticks; she was wearing a tight figure-hugging white dress. "Mr. Kell?" she said.

"Lieutenant." He dropped the tablet back on the table and stood.

"Sorry, yes, of course. My name is Sandra Barnes. I believe you're here to see me." She reached out with a small hand on which she wore a black silk glove – Kell noticed she only wore the one; her other hand was bare. He met her hand, and they shook. Despite her appearance, she had a very firm handshake, even to him.

"Yes, Miss Barnes. I'm—" Kell started.

"Sandra, please, Lieutenant." She said, almost firmly.

"Sandra, I'm here with the AI Homicide Division of Washington D.C. PD. I've come to talk to you about one of your employees. A Mr. Gary Lawton." Kell said.

"Ah, yes, Gary. An excellent worker. Nothing has happened to him, has it?" Sandra said. Despite the concerned tone, Kell thought it was more for the protection of MDF than for Gary's well-being.

"No, nothing has happened to him. Is there somewhere we can talk more privately?" Kell asked, darting a look across to the receptionist who was still filing her nails.

"Oh my, yes, of course. We can go up to my office. Please follow me." Sandra said, and she strode across the marble floor towards the reception desk, Kell followed a few steps behind. As they approached, he saw the girl behind the desk drop her file and give Sandra her full attention, "Mel, please can you hold my calls. I'll be in with Mr…sorry, *Lieutenant* Kell, for a few moments."

"Of course, ma'am," Mel said before turning her attention to the screen in front of her.

"Please, this way," Sandra said as she walked ahead.

She led him towards a bank of elevators and pressed the call button. Within seconds the doors were opening, and they stepped inside. Sandra turned and pressed the button for the fifty-second floor, the doors silently closed, and the lift began to rise.

With her eyes firmly set on the doors, she spoke, "I do hope that our receptionist wasn't too rude to you, Lieutenant. She does sometimes come across as a little brusque."

"No, not at all. We had a lovely chat." Kell said.

The elevator doors pinged open, and Sandra stepped out into the corridor beyond, he followed.

In complete silence, she led him down the hallway. There was nothing particularly special about the space; he thought it seemed rather drab compared to the luxurious foyer they had just left. It had bare beige walls, potted plants were dotted every few feet, and numerous nondescript brown wooden doors were running its length; on each door was a brass plate with a name and title embossed on it. None of the names meant anything to him.

Eventually, they got to a door with Sandra's name on; she pushed it open and ushered him inside,

"Please, take a seat," Sandra said, motioning to a small round fabric chair opposite her desk. She walked around the sizeable polished wood desk and sat in her plush, upholstered chair. "Would you like a drink? Coffee? Water?" she asked, with her gloved hand hovering above a set of buttons inset on the top of the desk.

"No, thank you." Kell said.

She lowered her hand and brought it together with her other to clasp together in front of her. "Miss Barnes—" Kell started.

"Sandra, please." She said with a faux smile.

"Sandra, this evening, an incident occurred at the home of one of your employees, Gary Lawton," Kell said.

"Oh, dear," Sandra said, raising a hand to her mouth.

"His wife Christine was murdered, and I believe that Gary was the perpetrator." He said.

"Oh my. No, I can't believe he would do that." Sandra said, waving her gloved hand in a dismissive gesture as if the act would make her statement true.

"Miss Barnes, are you aware that Gary is an AI?" Kell said, studying her face for even the smallest glimmer of a reaction to this information. Her face remained as dispassionate as it had been since he'd met her.

"An AI? Impossible." Sandra said.

"Because of the rigorous screening that potential employees go through?" Kell asked.

"Of course. We don't want AIs working here." Sandra said. Kell could sense her hatred in her words.

"No," Kell said flatly.

"No. It's not that we have anything personal against your kind Lieutenant. It's just that we have had to clean up their mess before." The woman said.

"By 'their' do you mean AISystems?" Kell asked.

"Yes. You're aware of our pasts?" Sandra said.

"Of course," Kell said.

"Then, you can understand our reluctance to have any AIs in-house," Sandra said.

"I can. But that doesn't address the fact that Gary Lawton, is indeed, an AI. An AI that has been working here for the best part of a decade. Are you telling me that no one in the company knows what he is?" Kell pushed her for answers.

"I can only speak for my department, but no, no one knew. I can't imagine if anyone knew that he would have been employed here for so long. Still, it begs the question, how many more are employed here without our knowledge?" A veil of panic seemed to be descending on her face.

"Indeed," Kell said.

"But wait, you said that you suspect Gary of killing his wife?" Sandra said, the small wave of panic disappearing and her voice returning to a tone of 'all business.'

"Yes, that's correct," Kell said.

"Do you think he's one of those AI involved in these so-called 'cleansings'" Sandra asked, her face now wasn't giving away anything about what she was feeling.

"That's the route that I'm investigating," Kell said.

"How can I help?" A question that Kell didn't expect from the woman.

"Can you tell me anything about Gary?" He asked.

"Nothing much. He was a good worker. Always on time. Stayed late if needed. Never had any arguments or disagreements with co-workers. You could say he was the perfect employee. I've got his records here if you'd like a copy?" Sandra said.

"That would be very helpful," Kell said, "Was there anyone Gary worked with regularly? Anyone who he seemed particularly friendly with?"

Sandra sat for a minute, thinking. After a few seconds, she started to tap two of her fingers on the desk; she was getting nervous.

"Well, I suppose he was friendly with Maty." She said finally.

"Maty?" Kell asked.

"Sorry, Matias Lopez. He works up on the research floor. Does a lot of work on top-secret projects, usually for government agencies." Sandra said.

"I see." Kell said.

"Do you think he befriended Matias for a particular reason? Maybe to find out what he was working on?" Sandra said, the sound of panic was starting to creep back into her tone. Someone stealing company secrets was never good, but an AI stealing them was far worse.

"It's possible. I'd like to speak to Mr. Lopez. Is he here this morning?" Kell said.

"He's here every morning. I don't even think he spends much time at home," Sandra said.

"Excellent. Where can I find him?" Kell asked.

"I can take you to him. He'll be in his lab, and you won't be able to access the floor without a pass." Sandra said.

"Thank you. I would appreciate it if you take me to him right away," Kell said.

"Of course." There was now a slight quiver to her voice, and as she stood, she seemed a little unsteady on her feet. If she knew anything about what Gary was up to, she was an excellent actor. But she seemed genuinely taken aback by the news that he was an AI and had possibly killed his wife, but the thing that seems to have hit her harder is the possibility of company secrets being stolen.

She led him out to the main corridor and back to the elevators.

The door opened as they reached it, and they stepped inside. Sandra turned to the rank of buttons on the wall, pulled out a small fob on a wire, and waved it across the plate at the base; she then pressed the button for the one-hundredth and second floor.

As the lift started to rise, she turned to face him, "Do you think we're in danger here?"

"Sorry?" Kell wasn't ready for this question. When he looked at her face, Sandra's eyes seemed to be pleading with him to say no.

"Do you think we're in danger? Do you think Gary Lawton will come back?" She asked.

Kell knew it was a possibility that Gary might come back after the heat died down, and the police had moved on to investigate the next killing, but he chose to placate her worry.

"No. No, I don't think he'll come back. He'll be on the run. He won't even think of coming back here. He'll know that the police are watching the place." If only that were true, they didn't have the workforce these days to watch anywhere twenty-four-seven.

For the first time, he noticed the soft violin music playing in the elevator cabin. "Ah, Boccherini," He said, smiling to himself.

"Sorry?" Sandra asked.

The elevator doors opened on to a brilliant white corridor. As they walked into the bright lights, Kell took in the entire area. It was wholly tiled with plain white squares and was in stark contrast to the corridor they had been in on the lower floor. This one was more what he expected of the building; it felt almost clinical. Windows looked through into some offices beyond, and even these bore little resemblance to the room and corridors he'd just seen. It was as if they'd walked into a completely different building.

"This way, please," He looked at Sandra and noticed that she was already several paces ahead of where he stood and had turned to face him; she wanted him to move along and not linger.

They walked along the corridor for a few yards and then stopped at a glass door. On the wall next to it was a small speaker with a single button. Sandra depressed this and spoke into the box,

"Hi, it's Sandra from Technologies downstairs. Is Maty in there? I've got someone here that needs to talk to him."

There was a moment of silence, and then a voice came from the speaker,

"Yeah, this is Maty. Hi Sandra, what's up?"

"I've got a Lieutenant with the AI Homicide Division here with me. He wants to talk to you about Gary Lawton," Sandra said. There was a shuffling on the other end of the speaker.

"Um, yeah, ok. Give me a minute." More shuffling came from the other side of the intercom.

"Sorry, it's just, we need this area to be secure. We can't have just anyone wandering around." Sandra said, turning to Kell.

"I understand." Kell looked through the windowed doorway to the short corridor beyond; it looked much the same as the one in which they were stood, only cleaner if that were at all possible.

A door slid open on his right and drew his attention. A short man with a bad comb-over and white lab coat entered and made his way towards the door. He waved and smiled as he saw Sandra, but as his gaze fell on Kell, the smile vanished and was replaced by a more worried expression.

The man reached down into his lab coat. Kell tensed slightly, expecting him to produce something more lethal than a key fob. The man swiped the small grey bit of plastic over the plate on the opposite side of the door, causing the door to slide open. A rush of frigid air escaped through the newly created space.

"Hi. How can I help you, sir?" the small man began to nervously play with his tie, probably unconsciously.

"This is Lieutenant Kell. He's got some questions about Gary Lawton for you." Sandra said, her authoritative tone now back.

"Um, sure, what's he done?" Matias asked, blinking wildly as he looked at Kell. Kell was about to speak when he was interrupted by Sandra,

"Right, well, I've got things to be getting on with, so I'll leave you in Mr. Lopez's more than capable hands. If you don't need anything more from me, that is?"

"No, you're free to go. Thank you for your assistance," Kell said.

Sandra turned on her heels and marched purposefully back down the corridor and into the lift. Kell put his attention on Matias. "Why did you ask that?"

"Sorry? Ask what?" Matias said, still fiddling with his tie and blinking; his mouth also started to rise slightly at one side in a nervous fashion.

"When Sandra told you I would ask about Gary Lawton, you asked what he'd done?" Kell said.

"Oh, yeah, well, I assumed it couldn't be good if you're here asking about him," Matias said, trying to laugh and smile, neither of which he managed to pull off.

"I see. Is he a friend of yours?" Kell asked.

"You could say that, yes." Matias stopped talking and stared blankly at Kell. Now noticing that he had been fiddling with his tie all this time, he shoved his hands into the pockets of his long white lab coat. Kell could still see the man's fingers twitching.

"You want to go into some more detail there?" Kell said, knowing that getting answers from this man might not be easy.

"Oh, right. Yes, sorry." Matias took off his round glasses and began to wipe them with his tie. Replacing them on his face, he continued, "Well, Gary would usually come and visit me a couple of times a day. He said he was interested in the projects I was involved in and wished that he was smart enough to do this kind of work. Only..." the scientist trailed off into his own thoughts for a few moments.

"Only?" Kell said, trying to get Matias back on the right track.

"Sorry, only well..." he lowered his voice to a whisper, "...he's an AI. He's way smarter than I am. So I don't understand why he said these things. I guess he doesn't want people to know what he is. I guess that's fair enough, what with the policy here and all. Still, I don't know how he managed to get a job here in the first place."

"So you are aware that he's an AI. Did you tell anyone else here?" Kell said.

"Oh no, of course not. They'd fire him for sure and, I don't know, I kind of like his visits, they break up the day and not many other people around here have much time for me. Gets kind of lonely locked in there all day." Matias said, still whispering and pointing a thumb back through the door he came through.

"I understand. Was there any particular project he was interested in?" Kell didn't want to press too hard, but he needed some answers.

"Well, now that you mention it, he was *very* interested in my work on nanobot technology. Again, this was sort of odd, considering they were what the company used during the war to kill the enemy AI." Matias said, his voice now returning to a louder, more normal tone.

"Nanobots?" Kell said, "Did he ever ask to see them or ask any seemingly innocent but quite in-depth questions?"

Matias thought for a moment before he answered, "Well, yes, actually." He coughed before continuing, "He wanted to know what kind of dispersal rate the canisters had and also where we kept them."

"Where *do* you keep them?" Kell asked.

"Oh, they're on this floor in a secure storage room. You never know if some AIs might go mad and try to take over the world again," Matias said; after a brief pause, he added, "Um, no offense."

"None taken." Kell no longer took offense at these kinds of throw-away comments and now wasn't the right time for it regardless of his feelings. "Did you ever show Gary this storage room?"

"Um," Matias shuffled his feet, awkwardly, "Yes."

"I'd like to see this storage room, please," Kell said in a tone that sounded like a request but was more like an order.

"B…but—" Matias stuttered.

"I just need to see it for myself to see if there is anything in there that could give me any more leads. You won't get into any trouble. I promise." Kell said, trying to reassure the scared man.

Matias once again took off his glasses, breathed on them, and wiped them clean with his tie; he held them in his hand for a moment, "Well, I suppose you *are* police. So I should think it would be alright."

"Thank you, Mr. Lopez," Kell said with an inward sigh of relief.

"N...No problem, this way, follow me."

Matias turned, and the two of them started back up the corridor and through the door from which Matias had first emerged.

Beyond was yet another stark white room, this one lined with metal tables, lab equipment, and banks of computer monitors. They walked through here towards a door that was labeled 'Secure Storage: Authorized Personnel Only.'

Matias took out his fob once again and waved it across the wall to the right of the door. Kell couldn't see any kind of access panel or metallic plate; it must have been well hidden to stop unauthorized persons attempting access. The door slid open, and they stepped inside.

Racks of metal shelving covered the walls, and rows upon rows of small cylindrical metal canisters were lined up neatly on each. The temperature was significantly lower than the room outside.

"Well, this is it," Matias said, stepping back.

"How often do you take inventory of this room?" Kell asked.

"Um, well, we don't use any of this stuff. This is all leftover from the war. The new nanobots that we create for the justice department are all stored elsewhere. We can't use the nanobots in these canisters for the execution delivery system. They're waiting to be destroyed." Matias said.

"It's been a long time since the war. Why haven't they been destroyed already?" Kell questioned.

"Politics," Matias said flippantly.

"Right," Kell said, raising an eyebrow, "Perhaps you could humor me and do a quick inventory now?"

"Now?" Matias asked, a look of fear shined in his eyes.

"Now," Kell said forcefully.

"Um well, okay, I suppose." Matias walked over to the wall, where a small screen was inlaid into a metal panel. Tapping the screen, Kell saw what looked like a list appear on it. Matias studied this for a moment before turning back to Kell,

"Okay, according to this list, there should be four-thousand-seven-hundred-and-eighty-three nanobot canisters here." He stared blankly at Kell.

"Alright. We're going to need to count them." Kell said.

"You want me to count all of them?" Matias said, his fear now replaced by shock.

"Yes." Kell said.

"But there are thousands!" Matias said in a more high-pitched tone.

"Let's hope there are four-thousand-seven-hundred-and-eighty-three," Kell said, staring at the other man.

"I've got other work to do, you know," Matias said.

"This is important. You don't want to impede a police investigation, do you?" Kell said.

Matias looked down and then up, his eyes were watering and glistening slightly in the lights,

"No, of course not." He said.

Matias walked over to the first shelf near the door and began counting, starting at the top shelf.

Kell had a quick glance around the room and counted all the canisters in a matter of seconds. He could have just told Matias that he'd done the check and found that one canister was missing, but he was getting frustrated with how everyone in this company was so difficult to get information from.

Sometime later, a flustered Matias stood back up from kneeling. He wiped his glasses once more with the hem of his lab coat. Placing them back on his face, he pushed them up his nose with his index finger. "Four-thousand-seven-hundred-and-eighty-two canisters are here. All present and correct." He said with a smile.

"I think you'll find you're one missing," Kell said.

Matias stood looking slightly confused; his expression quickly changed to that of someone trying to work out some complicated mathematics in their head. If this guy was in their research department, it was a wonder that MDF Organics was as successful as it is.

"Oh, yes. Damn. Well, that's what happens when you have to count everything manually; you forget what you're doing." Matias said.

"So, has anyone else been in this room?" Kell asked.

"Not that I'm aware of," Matias replied.

"And did you take the canister?" Kell said.

"Certainly not!" Matias replied, seemingly taking offense to the idea of him stealing it.

"Then Gary Lawton must have taken it," Kell said.

"Oh." A look of shock and sudden horror appeared on Matias's face, "Oh, crap. I'm dead."

"Now now, don't be hasty. I have a request." Kell said.

"You do?" Matias looked like he was a puppy that someone had just kicked.

"Let me take one of the canisters," Kell said.

"But—" Matias started.

"For evidence. And no one needs to know about this little problem. It's probably best for everyone that no one else knows. Suppose the higher-ups in the company find out. In that case, it could lead to investigations, investigations that could lead to public outcry, outcry that could lead to one scientist becoming the scapegoat for the entire company. Plus, if Gary gets wind of us knowing about his theft, God knows what he might do." Kell said, his words had an immediate effect on the demeanor of the scientist.

"Yes. It's best for everyone." Matias said confidently. He picked up one of the canisters and handed it over to Kell, who slipped it inside his coat pocket. "I'll just change the inventory to reflect the change. Say they were used for testing."

"Good idea. Now, I think I should be going. I need to get back on Gary's trail." Kell said.

"Okay, yes, great. Off you go then." Matias started to walk back towards the door and show Kell the exit.

Upon reaching the outer door, he swiped his fob and let it slide open. "When you get to the elevator, just hit G. You'll get to the ground floor and the main exit, you don't need the access to go down there, so you should be okay on your own," Matias said hurriedly.

Kell started to walk through the door, "Thank you, Mr. Lopez. You've been most helpful." He said with a wry smile.

He'd walked a few steps down the corridor when he heard running footsteps behind him. He turned, and Matias stood there. "Can I help you, Mr. Lopez?" he asked.

"Well, um, you never told me what Gary did?" Matias said.

"He killed his wife." With those four words, Matias's face fell. Kell started back towards the elevator, leaving the scientist standing in the corridor, a look of dismay on his face.

Chapter 10

```
23:10 26th October 2138
```

Robert sat in a dark room, lit only by the array of monitors he was observing. The news reports being shown were filled with stories about tonight's two cleansings. Everything was going as it should; biotics were starting to pay attention.

An alarm sounded as one of the motion sensors he'd set up around the perimeter of the warehouse was triggered.

Silencing the alarm with the press of a nearby button, he switched a monitor away from news to a camera that was just outside.

Someone was stood there, someone who was covered in blood. The figure looked up, and Robert instantly recognized it as Michelle; he'd know those green eyes anywhere, even in the grainy video feed, they glowed like emeralds in the partial light. But the fact that she was covered in blood and at his doorstep made him angry. More than angry, he was furious. On the other side of the camera, she was waving and motioning towards the door. What else could he do? He pressed a switch; there was a buzzing sound signifying the door was unlocked. She pulled the door open slightly and slipped inside, the door swung shut behind her, and it clicked as the lock was re-engaged.

Robert made his way out of his office and down the now rusty steel steps to ground level. Michelle, gore and all, was waiting for him at the bottom.

"What are you doing here?" he asked calmly, keeping the rage out of his voice.

"My job is done; I came back to report in and get another mission," Michelle said.

"You're covered in blood. What if someone saw you come in here? You stupid girl!" His anger was starting to bubble over the thin surface of calm.

Michelle looked down at her body and noticed the dried blood smeared over her body and arms for the first time; she duriosuly tried to rub it off. "Well, it's too late for that now. Why didn't you change after you cleansed Howard? You know the protocol."

"I did change. But someone tried to mug me on the way home, so I took care of them too." Michelle said. It sounded to Robert like she wanted some sort of praise for her actions.

"Well, I'm assuming that this person was a criminal and had it coming to them. But it's not how we do things. We are organized here. Someone could have seen you covered in that stuff and reported it." Robert said.

"I wasn't followed. I'm sure of it. It was still dark, and no one was about." Michelle pleaded.

"Yes, well, that's as maybe, but you should have found another change of clothes before coming here," Robert sighed, "It's too late now. We'll just have to be careful and monitor communications more closely. Go and get changed."

Michelle walked away from him without another word. He was so enraged by Michelle's actions. The last thing that he needed when the cause was going so strong was for a careless member of the group to bring all hell down upon him.

He walked back up to his office and the glow of the monitors. The news was still reporting on the cleansings. One of the feeds cut to a reporter on the streets of downtown Washington, who was talking to a large male biotic. Robert pressed the button to unmute the sound.

"So, how do you feel about the murders being carried out by AIs?" The reporter on the screen asked.

"I'm all for 'em! They're cleaning up the world. Saving us from the scum!" The man replied.

"But what do you say about those that have been murdered who are, as yet, innocent?"

"Well, people shouldn't think of committing crimes. If everyone were a law-abiding citizen like me, then there'd be no need for the AI to take action, would there?" The man stared into the camera.

"Thank you, sir. There you have it, folks. Straight from the streets of Washington. A sentiment that it is becoming more common among free citizens. What do you think? Are the AI Cleansings justified, or are they just plain murder? Back to you in the studio, Jack."

The screen shifted back to the studio, where two stunned anchors were attempting to process what they'd just heard. Robert flicked the monitor back to mute.

He couldn't help but smile. Biotics were coming around to the purpose that his mission served, not that it mattered; they wouldn't be around much longer anyway. This unrest may just give him the extra time he needed to complete his grand purpose. There was a buzzing inside his head; it was one of his people trying to contact him,

Yes

"Robert, its Gary."

What is it? You have completed your goal; you should be back here by now.

"Yes, my goal was completed. But I left the package behind."

What? How could you be so stupid?

"I'm sorry; I'm going back for it now."

Then hurry. I need that canister.

"I will."

He hung up on Gary; he couldn't believe what was happening. How had his group become so careless? It was like they were growing more...Human. He spat at the thought. The last thing he needed at this point in his plan were screw-ups. If they carried on, he'd have to take care of things himself.

Chapter 11

23:50 26th October 2138

The line clicked as the connection ended.

For a few minutes, Gary just stood in the dark, damp, and dirty alley. What had he done? How could he forget the canister?

He was sure he had it on him when he began tonight's cleansing. What was wrong with him?

He had planned tonight so carefully, over so many years. Even with the addition of taking the canister from MDF, he shouldn't have messed anything up.

His mind was — for the first time since his creation – fuzzy and confused. This kind of thing didn't happen to an AI; they were perfect. Had he spent too long living as a human, and now his mind was slowing down to their pace? No, it couldn't be.

He could rectify this. All he had to do was go back to the house, pick up the canister, and get it to Robert. It would be easy. The cops should have finished there by now, the crowds of onlookers dispersed, leaving the house an empty shell. Yes, it would be quick and easy.

Gary levered himself up from the crouching position he had slumped to during the call and moved away from the damp wall making his way to the alley entrance.

Beyond this imaginary line were the city's lights, throngs of biotics, and all their noise. He could blend in here, walk until he got closer to home, and then he should be able to slip in across the Rockcreek train line, over the back fence, and into the garden.

He knew that Robert wanted the canister, but he also knew that he had to take his time. If he got caught now, that would be the end. The end of him. If he failed again, Robert would surely deactivate him, but if he got found by the police, they would too. He resolved to take it slow. He stepped out into the street.

It was just before midnight, but the street was still full of biotics, all going about their business. Biotics were around this area at all times of the day. It's as if they were all AIs and didn't sleep. What a glorious world that will be, when only the AIs exist, and biotics are a thing of the past.

Gary made his way along the sidewalk, shoving and being shoved by numerous biotics. The bright neon lights of shops, bars, and hotels lit his way. Street vendors were yelling over the crowds trying to sell their wares. Most passed them by uninterested or perhaps even unaware of the calls. Some would stop and browse for a few seconds before moving on. Occasionally he'd see items and money change hands. It was archaic how some biotics still used physical money. Another thing that will be done away with when Robert's plan comes to fruition.

He stopped at a window that was lit by bright red lights. On the other side of the glass, AI women gyrated naked on poles or plush armchairs, gesturing for passers-by to come inside. *Disgusting*, he thought.

Gary hated how some AIs completely integrated with biotics, becoming one of them and not faithful to their inherent superiority. Even worse were the ones that submitted to them and became subservient to them. He knew that some just wanted to fit in and live their life. It was a strange sentiment for an AI to have, being AI meant that they were practically immortal compared to biotics. They should be doing something decent with it, not just trying to please biotic scum. *At least I only integrate when I have a job to do*, he thought. That's what the last six years had all been about, the job. When he wasn't on a job, he stayed away from biotics and all their vices.

He stood for a moment looking in at the display before him. The female AI behind the glass blew him a kiss and winked seductively at him. Bowing his head and slowly shaking it, he turned away back to the street and carried on walking.

Before long, the sea of biotics, the noise and lights faded, and the roads were lit only by the occasional streetlight.

He approached a chain-link fence and could now see the train line beyond, further beyond this was his house.

He stopped for a moment. 'His house,' it wasn't *his*; it was Christine's. When did he start to think of it as his house? He'd been on this job for too long. From now on, he would make sure that his assignments were short ones, not ones that required years of planning and execution. He wondered if any other members of the group had similar thoughts about their jobs, or whether they just got on and did them without any of the 'feelings.'

Gary knelt and tugged at the chain-link fence managing to snap several links, enough that he could fold a piece up and crouch under.

Once on the other side, he folded the section back, so it didn't look obvious that someone had been through and carried on down the small grassy slope. He ran across the tracks and up the embankment on the other side.

Once at the top, he crouched down behind the fence and looked over at the house. It was pitch black, as were the houses on either side. It was as he thought, the police had finished and left. The house was vacant, and he would be able to get in and get out this way without anyone noticing. The houses on either side being dark meant either that the occupants were still asleep or had already left for work.

He quickly vaulted over the fence and dashed across the backyard, cautious to avoid the child's swing halfway across.

Slowing his pace, he made his way up the steps that led to the back door; he was careful to avoid the second step as it would squeak with only the slightest of pressure.

At the door, he realized he didn't have a key. He never thought he'd be coming back here, so he'd left his keys in the house. After internally admonishing himself, he reached for the handle and gently twisted it; it didn't open.

If only he'd managed to convince Christine to get an electronic lock for the house, but she didn't trust having to rely on electronics. That seemed almost humorous now, considering who she married.

Leaning to one side, he looked through the window into the kitchen. It was dark, no sign of life inside. He considered punching through the glass with his fist, but that would undoubtedly leave his blood behind, and he didn't want to give the police evidence that he had returned.

He turned and darted his eyes around the garden, looking for something else he could use to smash the window. His eyes fell on something at the bottom of the steps, a roller-skate. It would have to do. Picking it up and getting back to the door, he glanced around again, pausing to listen. All was quiet in the neighborhood. As he about to smash the window with the skate, he heard a rumbling sound coming from behind the garden; a train was coming.

Using the passing train's sound to muffle the sound of breaking glass, he smashed the skate through the window. Glass dropped to the countertop and floor inside.

He paused in the silence left in the train's wake and listened to see if the noise had attracted any attention. Once he was sure that no one had heard, he clambered up through the broken window and into the kitchen, careful to avoid the shards of glass that were now strewn about.

Once inside the house, Gary paused again. He felt...strange. He never thought he'd be back inside this house after cleansing Christine. He wasn't sure what he felt, but it didn't feel right. He just wanted to get the canister and get the hell out of here.

Walking out of the kitchen, the hallway led him to the large double doors that opened into the front room. The last time he'd been in there was when he was cleansing Christine.

Passing through the portal, it was as if he'd entered another universe. Slumping into the armchair, he held his head in his hands as memories of that night's events pushed to the forefront of his mind.

Gary looked up at the broken mirror and the shattered coffee table. The police hadn't arranged to have the mess cleaned up yet; there was still blood everywhere, luckily he'd picked a spot to sit that was relatively clean.

His eyes fell on the spot beneath the mirror that he'd chosen to nail Christine's hand. An inch-wide hole in the plaster and a faint red handprint was all that remained. It all seemed so long ago now. But it was only a few hours ago.

He sat staring at that dark hole, his mind whirling with thoughts, with…regrets.

He shook his head and checked the time; it was nearly two-am. He'd completely lost track of time as he sat there. He had to move.

He left the chaos of the room behind him and trudged upstairs, the memories still following him, unable to shake these unfamiliar feelings.

At the bedroom door, he paused with his hand on the handle and shivered. There was that feeling again.

He felt – How *did* he feel? For the first time in his life, he felt; bad. It was ridiculous. He couldn't feel bad; it was a job; it was for the greater cause. It was for the future. Yet there was a niggling feeling that he'd never had before; it was like his conscience. That was even more ridiculous. He had to get out of this house.

He flung the door open and marched into the room. Everything was as he'd left it. It didn't look like the police had been up here; they obviously had enough to be getting on with downstairs. He knew that they'd probably be back in the morning, and it was a good job he'd come back now.

He walked over to the wardrobe, trying to make as little noise as possible, and opened the doors. He reached into the shelf that sat above a rail of clothes — Christine's clothes. After pushing a few small boxes out of the way, his hand fell on a small metal cylinder. He pulled it out, giving it a quick once over to make sure it was still intact and hadn't been damaged. Confident that it wasn't, he slipped it into the inside pocket of his jacket.

From the street came a sudden flash of light. He jumped to the wall next to the window peering around the corner out to the road.

From his vantage point, Gary could see a fair way up the street and caught a glimpse of taillights from a car that was now well past the house.

He breathed a sigh of relief. But before he could relax any further, there was another flash, another car coming up the road.

Through the window, he saw the car roll to a slow stop in front of the house. It idled there for a few minutes, then the lights went out, and the door opened.

A tall figure wearing a long coat stepped out into the street. Gary didn't recognize this man, but whoever it was, he was walking towards the house.

The figure entered the front garden through the gate and walked up the steps.

Gary had to get out of here. He ran out of the bedroom and clattered down the stairs making more noise than he would have liked.

Chapter 12

01:45 27th October 2138

The music kicked in as he pulled away from the MDF Organics building.

It wasn't the most useful of visits to previous employers he'd had, but it wasn't a total waste of time. After all, he found out that Gary had taken a canister of nanobots; the only problem was that he didn't yet know the reasoning behind this act.

He didn't learn all that much from the people within, except that they really didn't like AIs. The only exception was for Matias. But Kell doubted that the scientist would be befriending more AIs any time soon; if the look on the man's face when he left was anything to go by.

Kell didn't gain any leads worth investigating, so he thought that this would be a good time to take the opportunity to revisit the Lawton house. Maybe he'd get there before the clean-up crew. He had no idea what he was looking for, but he had nothing else to go on, something there might lead to Gary.

While the melodies of Brahms' 'Requiem' drifted out of the car's speakers and over him, he closed his eyes and patched back into the central server.

After logging in, he went straight to the search that was running for the green-eyed woman. It was still going and so far hadn't come up with anything at all. This woman was non-existent; she was extremely adept at covering her tracks, but then, so would he be; if he needed to. He wondered how many more times she'd performed a cleansing and had disappeared entirely. But maybe this time, with the photo, she slipped up. He left the search running and dialed the Captain's number. It rang several times before he answered.

"Crane."

Captain, it's Kell.

"Ah, how are you doing out there?" Crane asked.

Slowly. I visited Lawton's employer, MDF Organics.

"Anything useful?" Crane said.

Only slightly. His co-workers were very standoffish and very surprised to find out he was an AI, except for one man, who seemed to know from them meeting. However, I did find out that before he killed Christine, Gary stole a canister of wartime nanobots.

"Nanobots? Why would he steal those?" Kell detected surprise and a hint fear in the man's voice at the mention of nanobots.

I don't know. But I intend to find out. I'm going over to the Lawton house now to see if I can pick up his trail.

"Excellent, well let me know how you get on," Crane said.

Er, sir?

"Yes, Kell?" Crane asked.

How is Emily doing?

"She's doing fine, lad. We're having a grand old time here." Crane's voice drifted from the phone for a few seconds, and he couldn't quite make out what he was saying. But then a smaller voice came on the line.

"Hello?"

Hello, Emily.

"William! Are you okay? Where are you?" Emily sounded genuinely happy that she was speaking to him.

Yes, I'm fine. I'm out finding out what happened to your mummy. Are you okay?

"Yeah, I'm fine. Captain Crane is really silly. He keeps making funny faces." She giggled. Kell had the image of Crane making another face at the girl.

Yes, he'll do that. I have to go, Emily. You be good.

"I will, William. You be good too!" she giggled, and he felt himself smile and chuckle to himself.

I'll try, Kell said. After hanging up the call and disconnecting from the server, his eyes focused back on the interior of his vehicle.

Looking through the window at the passing scenery, he realized he was almost at the house. Sitting back in his seat, he zoned back into the music for what remained of the journey.

A few minutes later, the spell was rudely broken once again by the vehicle stating that he had reached his destination.

The car rolled to a smooth, quiet stop, and Kell looked out at the Lawton house.

Stepping out of the car, Kell gazed up at the quaint suburban home. No one would know to look at it, what horror had unfolded here just a few hours ago. He looked to the neighbors on either side; both were dark, not a soul to be seen. Did they know what had happened just a few feet away from their own happy little lives or where they still blissfully unaware?

He cast his eyes across the road at the house opposite. Lights were on there, and an elderly woman was stood in the window.

He gave a quick nod to acknowledge her, and blinds quickly dropped down in front of her. *I guess she doesn't want to get any more involved,* Kell thought. He noticed there was still a small gap in the blinds where fingers had parted them and could just make out a pair of eyes staring out. The woman didn't want to be involved, but she still wanted to see what was happening.

Kell stepped towards the wooden garden gate set in the white picket fence; it was idyllic. Through the gate, he made his way to the front door; he didn't possess a key, but he had his ways.

After peeling away the crime scene tape and plastic covering the door he reached into his coat's inside jacket pocket, and pulled out a keyring holding a selection of long thin pieces of metal with different ends on.

Selecting one of the tools, he slid it into the lock of the front door. Carefully pushing it in further, he felt for the almost imperceptible click of each pin. Mere seconds later, he twisted the metal, and the lock clicked open.

He reached for the handle, and as he turned it, he saw something move behind the stained glass of the front door, followed by several loud bangs. He could see the shadowy outline of a figure inside.

He slipped sideways on the porch, gently twisted the handle, and slowly pushed the door open. After a few inches, he jumped forward and shoved the door aside with force and stepped over the threshold.

Down at the end of the corridor, Kell saw a shadow dart through the kitchen door. He gave chase.

Running down the hallway towards the figure, he heard the crunching of broken glass. Whoever it is must have climbed in through a window at the back of the property.

Upon entering the room at the end of the hall, he saw he'd come into the kitchen. When he reached the broken window, he saw the form running across the back garden.

He didn't have time to hang about, so he dove through the kitchen window onto the wooden deck outside. He regained his footing and rushed forward, brushing shards of glass off his clothes as he went.

The figure was a way in front of him and had already reached the fence that bordered the house; Kell could see it climbing over. Knowing that the train line was on the opposite side, he realized he'd have to hurry before he lost whoever this was.

When he reached the fence, he vaulted over it in one smooth motion but slipped on the wet grass and mud on the other side and slid down the embankment. Somehow, he still managed to keep his footing.

Halfway down, though, he tripped and barreled over, rolling the next few feet until he came to a sprawling stop on gravel that lined the track.

Somewhat dazed, but still with his directive at the forefront of his mind, Kell stood. Looking across the tracks, he saw the shadow had stopped and seemed to be staring in his direction.

Without hesitation, he started running towards the shape, and it took off once again.

There was a rumbling and a bright light coming from his right; a train. *Not the best of ideas to be running about on a train line*, he thought.

Kell continued forward and could now see the train approaching; he had to get past it; otherwise, he'd surely lose whoever this was. He ran for all he had; all the while aware of imminent danger.

The train was within feet of him as he jumped the last bit of track onto the grassy embankment on the other side. The train, without a hint of a reduction of speed, whizzed past him.

He lay on the grass for a second looking up into the cloudy early morning sky, thanking his maker for giving him the ability to jump like that, and catching his breath.

Kell stood and looked up the grassy verge; he could see the shape ducking under the chain-link fence.

This must have been the way they came; no one could get under a fence that quickly unless they'd already cut a path.

With his feet slipping on the wet grass, he scrambled up the slope. At the fence, he found the damaged part, folded it up, and bobbed under.

On the other side, he realized that the figure was running towards a busy district, one that would still be busy even at this early hour of the morning. This could turn bad; and fast.

He sped off again in pursuit of the shadowy figure. Running was easier now he was back on solid ground.

Making his way down the sidewalk, it wasn't long before the crowds got thicker. It became harder to discern the person he was following; all he could see was the crowd parting every so often. People were being knocked to the side, and shouts of anger from those being shoved rose into the air.

Kell kept following the chaos down the street. Soon the sidewalk was filled with people more densely packed together, and he was almost ready to accept that he'd lost whoever this was. The bright neon lights surrounding him did nothing to illuminate his quarry.

Then, just several feet in front of him, he saw someone fall. He pushed on and caught a glimpse of who he was trying to apprehend; Gary Lawton.

Lawton seemed to have stopped and appeared to be slightly dazed; perhaps someone he'd pushed had pushed back harder than expected.

Kell made a beeline for him. Gary looked up, saw him approaching, and tried to make a break for freedom, but Kell jumped and almost landed entirely on top of him.

The two rolled and fought for several seconds until Kell managed to restrain Lawton with cuffs to a metal bike stand that was next to them.

He stood and looked down at Lawton. The AI was now slumped against the bike stand and looked totally defeated.

A crowd of pedestrian onlookers surrounded them, some talking in hushed voices to one another; Kell heard a voice say, "Pfft, another Arti causing trouble, I bet."

Ignoring this, he called it in and requested a pickup. The voice on the other end told him that a car was enroute and would arrive soon; he should just stay put.

Hanging up, he refocused his attention on Gary Lawton. He wasn't struggling to escape, he wasn't pleading for mercy or that he was innocent; he just sat there in the street, in the now falling rain, staring at his feet with a fixed – almost glazed – expression on his face.

Kell read Lawton his rights; he followed this by repeating the phrase "Do you understand?" several times. Gary seemed to not hear him until the third attempt when the defeated man just nodded in acknowledgment.

Kell turned around and looked at the surrounding crowd that was getting bigger by the second,

"Please disperse. There is nothing for you to see. Unless you have any information that would be useful to the authorities, please move along and continue your business," he said to the mass of people.

Most of them moved away; he saw one man bend and pick something up, then move off with a group of others, perhaps one of the people that had been pushed over in Lawton's attempt to escape.

There didn't seem to be anyone injured in the pursuit, which had to be a win. This could have gone so much worse.

Several minutes passed by, the street and its occupants had gone back to their regular routines, and it was as if he and the cuffed Lawton weren't even there. Street vendors went back to shouting calls to sell their wares; the pedestrians walked past them without a glance. He lent up against the wall behind Gary and awaited the arrival of his pickup.

Soon the street was lit with alternating red and blue lights followed by the sound of sirens. A car pulled up opposite him, and a young woman stepped out. He'd seen her around the precinct a few times but wasn't aware of her name. She stepped up to him, looked down at Lawton, then back up at him with a smile,

"Ready to take you back, sir. I'm Officer Lockley," The woman said.

"Hello officer, thanks for the collection," Kell said.

"No problem, sir. All part of the service." She said with a smile, "Shall we get him in the car then?" Lockley said, pointing at Lawton.

"I suppose we should."

Kell bent down to unlock the cuff connected to the bike stand. He grabbed Lawton under the arm, raising him to his feet. He almost expected Lawton to try to make a break for it while he wasn't cuffed to anything. But there was still no resistance from the man. It seemed all the fight had gone out of him.

Lockley kicked the metal bike stand, "Ha, guess there are still uses for these things after all. And the city was trying to get them all taken out because they say that no one cycles anymore."

"There's always uses for old-world things." Kell said as he led Lawton to the rear door of the police vehicle.

Lockley jumped in front of the two men and opened the door, "Sorry, this one's not automatic," She said as she helped Kell push Lawton down into the seat and shut the door behind him. "Shall we get him back to the precinct then, sir? Or is there something else you need?"

"No, going back to the precinct is best. I need to question Lawton, sooner rather than later." Kell said.

"No problem, sir," Lockley said.

She ducked inside the vehicle and took her seat behind the wheel. Kell walked around the front to the other door, opened it, and slid inside. The young officer turned the key in the ignition, and the mechanical engine roared to life. It had been a while since he'd heard that noise.

"I see this is a manual patrol car?" Kell asked.

"Yes, sir. I prefer to be in control, just in case." Lockley said, giving Kell a small smile. When she did this, her eyes seemed to glisten. "I don't trust the automatics when it comes to chasing down perps."

Lockley put the car in gear and sped down the street in the direction of the precinct. Kell sat back in his seat with a small smile on his face, enjoying the feeling of being in a manual car with someone else in the driver's seat.

Chapter 13

23:52 26th October 2138

I'm watching him now.

"Make sure he retrieves the canister. I need its contents. If you have the opportunity to remove him from the situation without damaging the canister, then do so. He has almost fulfilled his purpose. Be sure not to let him see you until he has it," Robert said to him.

Yes, Robert. I'm following him now; he's walking down New Hampshire Avenue. He's not aware of me. He seems to be more occupied by the crowds of biotics.

"This is extremely important. The contents of that canister will aid me in bringing our mission to a conclusion," Robert said.

Understood.

He disconnected the call and watched from a darkened shop doorway as Gary Lawton made his way down the busy sidewalk a few yards in front of him.

After the gap had increased to a suitable distance, he stepped out and continued his pursuit.

He'd been listening to the call Gary made to Robert and was well apprised of the situation.

He often did this kind of thing for Robert. When an AI had outdone their usefulness in the cause, it was his job to remove them. In most cases, this resulted from either failure to complete their assigned cleansing or drawing too much attention after it. This, though, was a new reason; it was because Gary, an AI, had made a mistake in leaving something behind. The error not so much leaving an item behind but leaving behind something that was so monumentally important to Robert's plans.

If they knew where Gary had hidden the canister, he could take care of him now and go and get it himself, but they had no idea where he'd left it.

He figured it was in what was once his home, but to go there so soon after a cleansing, would be foolish. No, he'd let Gary take all the risks. He just had to follow him closely.

The crowd of biotics on the sidewalk got thicker as predator and prey reached a more commercial district.

He was pushing past them, and all the while, all he wanted to do was lash out and cleanse them, each and every one. But his mission was greater than that, and to follow his own desires would be going against the greater good and Roberts's wisdom. He gritted his teeth and continued on, keeping his eyes firmly on the back of Gary's head as it bobbed through the masses.

Occasionally Gary would stop and stare at some biotics or in a shop window. Was he aware he was being followed or just trying to look more 'natural,' more…human? Each time he stopped, he lingered for a few minutes and then carried on down the street. The last time Gary stopped, his follower stopped a few yards behind and ducked into an alley. Peering around the corner, he saw Gary looking through yet another window, looking up at the faded neon sign hanging from some rusting chain, he could see it was an AI whorehouse. What was Gary thinking? Was he going to go in there? If he went inside, there'd be no way to follow him without alerting him to his presence. Maybe Gary did know he was being followed. After several minutes, he saw Gary bow his head and slowly shake it; he looked almost somber as he turned away and carried on down the street.

Stepping out into the hustle and bustle of the busy street again, he continued to follow Gary until the crowds began to thin out, and the streets became almost deserted. This was going to be the more challenging part of the pursuit. As the commercial aspect of the street came to an end, he hoped that there would be fewer reasons for Gary to stop or slow down. But he knew that Gary still wouldn't run. There'd be no reason to draw any attention to himself now, not being so close to the house. If anything, he seemed to be slowing down. Perhaps that was just because he no longer had to push through biotics.

The street got quieter and quieter as they moved further down and closer to the train line. He thought Gary would get into his house from behind via the train line instead of entering from the front. That's what he would do anyway. It would draw much less attention from the neighbors, and no doubt the police — if they were watching the house — would be watching it from the street, not the back.

The lower part of Hampshire Avenue was mostly derelict buildings. It was a far cry from the hustle and bustle of the upper. Over the years, the businesses had closed to move to a location closer to Dupont or had ceased trading entirely. With the bright lights and masses of biotics and AIs around in most of the city, it was easy to forget places like this still existed. He'd been here many a time. This was the kind of area where AIs who were on the run came to lay low. Not from the police, though, from Robert and his group, and from him. He'd killed several AIs on this very stretch of street, yet others still came here.

When he realized he was getting a little too close to Gary, he stopped and lit up a cigarette. Smoking was one of those habits he'd picked up while hanging around a group of biotics he was going to cleanse. He had no idea why biotics continued to smoke, even though they knew it would eventually kill them in some horrible way. But who was he to stop them; they were going to die anyway. For him, though, smoking didn't hold any such fate in store. For an AI, there was no chance of cancer or any sort of respiratory issue. He enjoyed the feel of the smoke as he inhaled it; it was as intoxicating to him as an alcoholic drink was to a biotic, although he'd still keep his wits after a few.

Stopping to light up opened the gap between him and his prey enough that he could carry on his pursuit. The thought that Gary was aware of his pursuer no longer came to mind; he was no longer behaving like he knew. He was walking steadily now there were no further distractions on the street.

They were reaching the end of the street now. A the road was a rusting chain-link fence, beyond that was the train line and after that; Gary's house.

There would be no way he could follow him directly from this point, so he hung back and took a look at the surrounding buildings. He'd have a better vantage point if he were above the street. He scanned the rooftops for a likely place to watch Gary's progress. After making his decision, he made for an alley with a fire escape leading up the side of a crumbling building.

Clambering up onto a disgusting smelling dumpster, he reached for the ladder and hoisted himself up. He climbed at his fastest rate; he didn't want to lose sight of Gary for too long.

The stairs of the fire escape were rusted and were almost disintegrating beneath him. Every step he took felt like it was going to shake the structure to dust. There was no time to be careful, though; he just had to make it to the top. He took each stair at a sprint. At the top, he leaped over the edge of the building on to the slightly firmer ground of the roof and span to look down the street to where he'd last seen Gary. He was nowhere to be found. "Damn!" he muttered to the wind.

After a few moments of scanning the area, he noticed that the chain fence at the end of the street was slightly curled in one corner; someone had gone under there.

A few meters further forward, he focused on a figure scrambling up the embankment on the opposite side of the train line. That had to be Gary. He trained his gaze on the shape and confirmed it was. By now, Gary was up to the other side and vaulting the fence into the garden behind the house.

He watched as Gary ran across the garden. He looked further ahead at the house, it was dark, and there seemed to be no life around it; the police had gone, and there weren't even any lights on in the neighboring houses. Gary might have lucked out here; he could be in and out without anyone noticing. He was doing okay, too bad he was going to die.

As Gary's follower focused on the house, he saw Gary pick up something from the garden and use it to smash a window as a train went by. Not exactly how he'd have done it, but it got the job done.

He watched as Gary climbed through the smashed window and into the house. Now he'd have to wait for him to re-emerge, no doubt he would come out the way he entered, it would be foolish to go through all this and then leave through the front door. He sat on the edge of the building and watched the dark house.

Almost two hours ticked by as he sat waiting. He was starting to worry Gary had gone out the front, when he saw him in an upstairs window. He seemed to be reaching into a cupboard, and eventually, he lifted something out. There was a small glint of light off the small metallic object; he'd found the canister; his job was almost complete.

There was suddenly a shaft of light streaming through the window from the outside. He saw Gary run from the window across the room. The light passed by quickly; probably just a car going down the street; nothing to worry about.

Another light came down the road, and looking between the two houses, he saw it slowing down; it was stopping. Who was this? Were they going to this house?

He looked back to the window and saw Gary bolt from the room; whoever he'd just seen must be heading for the house. Well, there was nothing he could do from here.

He waited for a few minutes, considering whether he should make for the house. If whoever it was stopped Gary from leaving, it could be disastrous. He'd resolved to head for the house when Gary burst out through the broken window and into the backyard. As soon as Gary landed, he was running towards the fence. *This can't be good*, he thought. But at least he seems to be heading this way.

He watched as the man Gary was running from came crashing through the window. The man brushed himself down as he ran and climbed over the fence in pursuit.

He stood leaning on the edge of his rooftop perch as Gary's unknown pursuer slid down the wet embankment on the other side of the fence and landed face down on the tracks. Gary had stopped and was just looking at the fallen man.

As the other figure rose to his feet, Gary ran back up the other side of the train line and under the fence. His pursuer followed and was nearly run over by an oncoming train; *This guy has balls,* he thought. They were both heading this way, so he stayed where he was and watched as they got closer and closer.

When they passed underneath him, he had a better look at the man chasing Gary. He was wearing a tattered grey mac, pressed pants with a shirt and tie. He had to be a cop; that's all he needed.

He followed them from above, running along the rooftops, out of view but still able to see everything that was going on.

Gary was heading for the busy street he had just followed him down, hoping to lose the cop in the crowds, no doubt. This was it; he had to get the canister from Gary here.

He ran ahead of them and towards the bustling crowds, found an excellent place to ambush Gary, and headed back down to street level using another fire escape, this one a little less in disrepair.

Stood in the alley, he could hear people shouting and screaming as they were being pushed over and out of the way as the two men ran. The shouts got closer, and he stepped out into the street just as Gary was about to pass and walked straight into him. They both tumbled to the hard-concrete sidewalk.

The cop caught up with Gary just as he was getting to his feet, he himself stayed down for a little longer to process the scene and watch events unfold.

As Gary was hauled further to his feet by the cop, the metal canister fell from his jacket. No one seemed to notice it fall and hit the ground. The crowd closed in around him while he was still on the floor, no one offered to help him to his feet, but what did he expect from Biotics?

He got himself to his feet and heard the cop shout over the crowd,

"—Unless you have any information that would be useful to the authorities, please move along and continue your business."

As the group started to disperse, the assassin bent and picked up the canister at his feet. Tucking it safely into his pocket, he moved off with several others.

He had the cartridge, but Gary was now in police custody. He wandered up the street a bit and pretended to look in a shop window. He stole a glance over to the cop who had chased and arrested Gary. He wasn't just a cop; he was an AI cop. This must be the one that was in the special task force aimed at stopping the cleansings. He snapped a quick image of Kell—Robert would want to see. He walked away a few feet and dialed Robert's number.

"Yes?" Robert answered, sounding irritated.

I have it.

"Excellent. And Gary?" Robert asked.

He's in police custody.

"What? How?" Robert's irritation shone through his words.

That AI cop showed up at his house and chased him down. Am I to go back and finish them both?

"No. Gary won't give anything away; he doesn't know anything that would put my plan in jeopardy," Robert said now more calmly.

He knows where you are.

"He does. But by the time he tells them, and they find me, I will have the canister, and my plan will be fulfilled. Bring it to me now." Robert said.

Of course. I'm on my way.

The assassin left the area and made for the warehouse.

Chapter 14

```
03:00 27th October 2138
```

Gary Lawton looked nervous.

Nervous wasn't something that happened to AIs.

Although it could be a ploy to knock Kell off his game, it seemed to be a genuine emotion. He could have been looking at a biotic through the one-sided mirror.

Lawton hadn't said a word since his arrest and transport to the precinct. He'd sat in the back of the car in total silence for the entire journey. Every time Kell had looked in the rear-view mirror, Gary was sitting in the same position, hands clasped together in his lap with his eyes fixed at a single point in front of him. His only movement was the occasional blink. He'd thought that perhaps he was planning something, or in some way communicating with his group, but there were no signs of anything; it was as if he had left his body.

Lockley had been talking all the way back; Kell had no idea what she was talking about as he was sorting through everything that had happened over the past twenty-four hours and was paying little attention to her. She didn't seem to notice, however, and continued regardless.

Once they'd come to a stop, he'd exited the vehicle and almost had to drag Lawton from the backseat; he was dead weight. With help from Lockley, he'd managed to get him up to the interrogation room where he now sat.

Lockley had left him to go and fill out her report of what she had seen when she arrived at the scene of the arrest. He didn't think it would take her long. There wasn't much to see aside from Lawton slumped on the floor and handcuffed to a bike rack; it had all been pretty uneventful after the chase.

The door to the monitoring room opened and in walked Captain Crane,

"So, this is Lawton, huh?" he stepped up; Kell saw his stomach appear before the man himself.

"Yes. This is Lawton." Kell said without taking his eyes of the man on the opposite side of the glass.

"Has he said anything yet?" Crane asked.

"Not yet, sir. He seems...strange." Kell said.

"Strange how?" Crane said.

"He put up a hell of a fight when I was chasing him. He really seemed to want to get away. But as soon as I cuffed him...he, well, he's shut down." Kell said.

"What do you mean 'shut down'? He looks alive enough to me." Crane said, stepping closer to the glass.

"Not shut down in the literal sense, of course. More emotionally. He seems to be portraying guilt." Kell said.

"Guilt?" Crane snorted, "That's a new one for an AI, isn't it?"

"Some have been known to show more complex human emotions in the past. AIs aren't all heartless." Kell said.

"Sorry, kid. Didn't mean to offend you." Crane said, putting a hand on Kell's shoulder, "It's just...the ones that have been committing these murders don't seem the type to give a crap. I wouldn't expect any of them to show any kind of remorse for what they've done."

"No offense taken, sir. You're correct, though. The AI killers we've seen in the past all seemed to be devoid of any emotion other than pure rage and hatred for human life." Kell said.

"Maybe whatever helped them evolve their senses for predicting crimes is changing their brains in other ways too," Crane said.

"You may be right, sir," Kell said.

"Well, I'll let you get on with the interview. Hopefully, you can get something out of him." Crane said, turning to Kell.

"Yes, sir. I hope so too." Kell said.

Crane turned on his heels and marched towards the door. As he reached for the handle, Kell turned to face him, "Sir?"

"Kell?" Crane spoke but didn't turn.

"Emily. How is she?" Kell asked hopefully.

A small smile grew across Crane's lips, and he emitted a little chuckle as he turned to face Kell, "She's doing just grand lad. She's a cute kid, a real firecracker. She's been through hell tonight, but she's still sweet and innocent."

"What will happen to her?" Kell asked.

"Well, now that Lawton's been caught, she's not at risk of harm, so I think it's time that she gets to be somewhere that's not a police station," Crane said.

"That's probably a good idea. She's been through enough already. She should be able to forget." Kell said solemnly.

"Yes, she should, and hopefully in time, she will. But I don't think she'll be forgetting you anytime soon. She's rather fond of you, you know." Crane chuckled again, his belly jiggling.

"I don't understand why," Kell said.

Crane gave another chuckle, "You saved her, son." Kell shifted uncomfortably on the spot, "I'll go and arrange things for her, and I'll bring her by to say her farewells before she goes. I'm sure she wouldn't miss that."

Crane sauntered out of the room, leaving Kell alone once again.

Kell turned back to face Lawton; he still hadn't moved. He watched him for a few more minutes before deciding it was time they had a chat.

He opened the door to the interview room and walked in. Lawton didn't so much as glance up at him; he may as well not be there. Kell closed the door and walked over to the table at which Lawton sat on the cold metal chair. His hands were cuffed and clasped together on the tabletop, just as they had been the entire journey there.

Kell placed a thin computer tablet on the table, pulled out the chair opposite Lawton, and sat down.

"Gary Lawton. My name is Lieutenant Kell; I'm with the AI Homicide Division of the Washington D.C. Police Department. You have been arrested for the murder of your wife, Christine Lawton." There wasn't a glimmer of acknowledgment from Lawton. He sat stock-still, with his eyes transfixed on his hands in front of him.

"We know that you committed the murder. This interview is a mere formality before you are most probably found guilty, then injected with nanobots and deactivated." Still no response.

"I would like to know more about why you killed your wife, Gary."

Kell picked up the tablet, pressed a few buttons on the screen, a light shone out into the space a couple of inches above the tablet, and slowly resolved into the Lawton house's living room. It was a complete replica of the crime scene in hologrammatic form, complete with damage and blood.

He pushed a finger inside the hologram and pressed on the hand pinned to the wall above the fireplace. The image zoomed in to reveal further detail,

"You did this. You did this to your wife of two years. You lived your life with this woman; with your adopted daughter." Kell said in a calm, even tone.

Lawton's mouth twitched almost imperceptibly at the mention of Emily,

"Christine loved you. How could you do this-" he pointed at the representation of her hand in the lights, "-to her?"

"Emily." The word barely made it past Lawton's lips.

"What about Emily?" Kell sat waiting for a response; when none came, he continued. "Emily was your daughter for two years. The only other person she had in her life was her mother, and you've taken that away from her. Why?"

Lawton looked up at the hologram and then averted his eyes downward like he'd seen something that disgusted him.

Kell pressed on the tablet again, and the hologram reverted to showing the entire scene.

"Look at what you did. The chaos you caused inside this family home. What was the reason?" Kell's tone became a little harsher.

"Emily." Lawton said once again without looking up. Kell noticed that he had clasped his hands tighter, they had begun to shake, and his knuckles were getting whiter.

Kell studied him for a moment; what did Emily have to do with any of this? He thought for a moment and changed the focus of his questioning,

"Tell me why you took the nanobots from the secure area at MDF Organics?" Lawton's eyes shot up to meet Kell's and widened, "That's right, I know that you befriended Matias Lopez so you could get access to the secure area and relieve MDF of one of their wartime canisters of nanobots before they could destroy them all."

His eyes widened further. Kell could see that this line of questioning was getting to him. Something about the theft of that canister made Lawton nervous. Was it this that was the source of his guilt and not the murder of his wife?

Kell sat for a moment studying Lawton, letting him stew on this for a time. He was just about to speak again when Lawton opened his mouth and started.

"The canister was for him. I just had to get it and deliver it." Gary said.

"For who, Gary? Where did you have to deliver it?" Kell asked.

"I'm not saying anything more about it. He'll kill me." Gary said, his eyes were now watering.

"I've already told you that you're going to be deactivated soon anyway. What's the harm in telling me what I want to know?" Kell said.

"Your nanobots are nothing compared to what he will do to me if I tell you what I know." Gary's voice trembled, his hands now shaking more as he gripped harder.

"So don't tell me about the canister. Tell me about Christine. Surely who this 'He' is, won't mind you telling me what you saw her doing that instigated your mission." Kell said, trying to calm the other AI down; he'd get nothing if Lawton blew a circuit.

"She," Gary paused and began to wring his hands together, some of the color returning as he relaxed his grip, "She was a good woman. I did love her. But…she was..." his voice trailed off into nothing.

"What was she going to do, Gary?" Kell asked.

Lawton looked directly into Kell's eyes as he said, "She was going to kill her daughter."

Kell was taken aback by this statement. Nothing in Christine's background or current life pointed towards her killing her beloved daughter. In fact, it looked like she was the most important thing in her life. "Why would she kill her daughter?" Kell asked.

"I don't know the how's or why's. I just know that he saw it." Gary said.

"He? Who is he?" Kell pushed.

Lawton just sat shaking his head, still not willing to give up whoever this mystery man was.

"So, you didn't see this future?" Kell asked.

"No." Gary paused, licking his lips, "I was just given the mission to get close to Christine, and when the time came nearer, to take care of her."

This didn't make sense; all the evidence that he'd found before was that the AI that saw the future was put on the mission after it was verified by other members of the group,

"You never saw anything about this killing in Christine's future, did you?" Kell said.

"No." Lawton slumped back in his chair, seemingly relieved that he had spoken aloud what was eating him up inside.

Perhaps this wasn't in Christine's future. Maybe she was a danger to some members of this AI group, and they just wanted her out of the way. None of this made any sense. She was just a school teacher. Unless…

"Gary, who wanted the canister?" Kell asked.

Lawton went back to staring blankly at his hands; his mind had gone elsewhere again. A thought occurred to Kell; he slipped his hand inside his coat and pulled out the narrow metal tube he had taken from MDF Organics and placed it on the table in front of him. Lawton's eyes shot straight to it,

"Yes. You dropped it on the street after our little chase. Whoever wanted this; is going to be very disappointed." Kell said.

"I'm dead." Lawton said in a calm, monotone voice. Kell noted how he used the term 'dead.' It was a biotic term, not an AI one.

"As I said, you'll be deactivated soon," Kell said, sitting back in his seat.

"I'm dead. I'm dead. I'm dead. I'm dead." Lawton repeated these words over and over, all the while staring fixedly at the canister.

Kell sat forward on his chair again and tapped the canister, Gary, tell me who wanted this."

"I'm dead. I'm dead. I'm dead. I'm de—" Lawton continued.

"Gary!" Kell slammed a fist on the table and stood; his chair fell backward and clattered on the hard floor.

"I'm dead. I'm dead. I'm dead. I'm dead. I'm dead." Gary repeated.

Kell straightened and stood looking down at the AI opposite him. Shaking his head, he turned and left the room, leaving a broken Gary Lawton repeating the same phrase over and over.

Outside he met up with Crane, "Well? Did you get anything out of the bastard?" he asked.

"He's gone," Kell said with a shake of his head.

"Gone? What the hell d'you mean gone?" Crane asked.

"He's had some kind of neurotic break," Kell explained what had happened, and all that Lawton had said about Christine and Emily.

"Well, damn." The captain said after he'd finished, "Where does that leave us then?"

"I need to do some more investigation into this group and Christine Lawton. There's more to this story." Kell said.

"There seems to be something a lot deeper going on here, I agree." Crane rubbed his nose, "While you're doing that, we've had a report of another murder, this one is a bit different."

"Different how, sir?" Kell asked.

"It looks like it's a mugging gone wrong. Some poor schmuck got killed in an alley off H Street." Crane said.

"H Street? That's just a few blocks away from Martin Howard's apartment building." Kell said.

"Yeah, I think maybe this was a killing of opportunity, not something that was planned before time," Crane said.

"I'll go and see what I can find out at the scene. Perhaps some cameras caught the killer in the act." Kell said.

"Maybe, maybe." Crane patted Kell on the shoulder, "But at this moment, I need you to come with me; someone wants to say her goodbyes to you." Together they walked down the corridor towards Crane's office.

Emily stood outside the office door holding Eileen Sampson's hand. When she saw Kell come around the corner, her face lit up, let go of the social worker's hand, and darted forward, running into him and wrapping her arms around his legs. He was unsure of how to react. He gently released her grip on him and got down to her level.

"Are you ready to go, Emily?" Kell asked the young girl.

"I think so. Can you come too, William?" Emily said.

"I'm sorry, I can't. You're safe now, but I've still got work to do catching other bad people." Emily looked down at the floor, "But Mrs. Sampson will take good care of you." Kell said, looking over to the nervous-looking woman.

"But," Emily sniffed, lifting her head again and looking him in the eyes, she said, "But I'll miss you."

"I'll miss you too, Emily." He wasn't sure what else to say, but he added, "But I'm sure we'll see each other again." He knew that this was probably not a possibility. Even so, this seemed to brighten the girl a little. He stood back up, and she gripped onto his hand as he led her back to the social worker, who took the little girl's hand from his.

Mrs. Sampson and Emily walked away from the office and from Kell and Crane. After a few steps, Emily stopped, turned, and ran back to Kell with a piece of paper in her hands, pushing it into his, she ran back to Mrs. Sampson, and the pair continued out.

Kell looked down at the scrap of paper in his hand. Turning it over, he noticed that it was a piece of headed paper for the department, and on it was a figure drawn in crayon. It was a man with blue eyes, wearing a long coat, with what looked like a police badge on it. Emily had drawn him. Next to this figure was a smaller one with curly black hair. The two characters were holding hands. Above them were two words written in a child's handwriting, they said simply; "My hero."

Chapter 15

00:00 27th October 2138

She stared at her naked body in the full-length mirror hanging in the dismal, dank bathroom of the old warehouse.

She'd washed the blood off but could still feel it burning into her skin.

She'd performed many cleansings; Martin Howard was the seventh, the mugger her eighth.

The killing of the mugger felt different. It wasn't planned. It was evident that the man was a criminal—she'd caught him in the act in that alley—but something about it bothered her.

She ran her hand down her arms and across her stomach. Her skin itched. She turned back to the shower, opened the door, and got back in. Setting the water temperature as high as it would go, she stood scrubbing at the invisible staining on her skin. The steam filled the small bathroom hiding her away from the world as she broke down and began to cry.

*

Sometime later, she dressed, and exited her room. When she reached the top of the stairs, she could hear voices drifting through the dimly lit warehouse.

She started down the metal staircase to the central warehouse. The closer she got to the bottom step, the clearer the voices became. One of them she knew—it was Robert—but the other she didn't recognize, it didn't sound like another member of the group; not one she knew anyway.

She crept slowly towards the voices, careful not to scuff her shoes on the floor or make any noise that might echo through the cavernous space.

She came up to some shipping containers; the voices were coming from the other side. There was a gap between two of the closest metal containers. She flattened herself and slowly sidestepped down the narrow slit.

"—complete the final stages of my plan." Roberts' voice came from the opposite side.

"What about Lawton and the girl?" the other voice drawled.

"Lawton is done with. The biotic authorities will surely deactivate him soon. He's no longer an issue." Robert said.

"And the girl?" the other man said.

"Take care of it. Her mother may be dead, but *she* is still a threat." Robert said.

"And the other? Do you think she led anyone here?" the other man asked.

"No, but I'm not going to take the chance. Deactivate her too. Dispose of her somewhere creative." Robert said.

Michelle gasped and quickly covered her mouth with her palm. Whoever this man was, Robert had just told him to kill her; she had to get out of there. But the other girl, it must be the daughter of Gary's wife. She'd done nothing. She had to help her; she had to warn someone. If she hid somewhere, she might be able to call the police.

She had to move but felt paralyzed. She willed her legs to run, but they wouldn't. An AI shouldn't feel this afraid; something was wrong. She tuned back into the conversation between the two men,

"—done with that, get that scientist from MDF that Lawton got close to. He'll come in very handy soon." Robert finished.

"Of course." The other man said.

Michelle heard the shuffling of feet and the sound of hollow footsteps on the concrete floor of the warehouse; they were getting closer. If she was going to move, she had to do it now.

She turned her head and started to sidestep back up the way she came. As she approached the opening, it got darker in the narrow crevice. What little light there had been was now blocked by the broad shape of a man standing at the end, obstructing her exit,

"Going somewhere?" the man asked.

She couldn't help but let out a small strangled yelp, "I...I didn't hear anything. I…just…want to...leave." she struggled to get the words out.

"Sorry, sweetheart. That's not possible." The man said slowly. He punctuated his words with a grin that chilled Michelle to the bone.

She tried to look past him, but his large frame blocked the warehouse from view. Turning her head, she quickly looked down to the other end of the gap; light. She looked back at the man. He wasn't making any moves towards her; he was just stood watching her with that sinister grin on his face. She looked back at the gap on her other side and, without a second thought, moved as quickly as she could towards the light.

"Now come on, let's not make this difficult." The man said quietly, the words echoing down the chasm towards her and became even more ominous despite the volume. She didn't stop; she forced herself along the sides of the containers and out the other side.

After slipping out of the gap and with no time to think, she ran. All the thoughts in her head were just telling her to keep running and not look back, but she couldn't help it; she looked back.

From this view, she could see straight down the gap where she was previously trapped. It was now filled with light; the shape of the man was no longer blocking it.

"Crap," Michelle muttered to herself as she started to swivel her head around to take in as much of the warehouse as she could, in the hope that she would be able to spot where the man had gone; she couldn't see him anywhere.

She faced back towards the direction she was running and saw him stood there, only a few meters in front of her.

She quickly turned and ran towards where she knew there was a hole in the dilapidated warehouse walls. She didn't bother to look around for the man this time, not wanting to know where he was; she just wanted to get as far away from here as she could.

Reaching the wall, she ran up along it looking for the hole, it didn't take her long to find it, but she had to lie down to shimmy her way through the tear in the metal.

She nicked her arm as she caught it on one of the sharp sides, but didn't bother about the bleeding; it wasn't important right now.

She was almost out when she felt pressure on her ankle and couldn't move any further. Someone was pressing down on her joint; she felt the pain rise through her leg, and let a strangled scream out into the morning air. There was no one around to hear her in this isolated and decrepit area except Robert; and the other man.

The pressure on her ankle increased, and she heard and felt bone shattering under it. She struggled to pull her leg free. Blood from her arm mingled with the dirt from the yard outside as she put both palms on the ground, trying to lever herself up and away, but the weight on her ankle increased and pain shot through her entire body.

A hand wrapped itself around the calf of her other leg. She felt huge fingers gripping her tightly. She tried kicking with her broken foot, but the pain was too intense.

The rough surface beneath her tore at her chest and stomach as she was dragged back inside.

When she dug her nails into the dirt and gravel, they started to tear from her fingertips. She tried in vain to gain a grip on something, anything, to stop her slow progress towards death.

For the second time today, she was crying. She started to plead with the invisible hand that held her to no avail.

Her torso went back inside the warehouse, but she managed to flip herself over. Almost entirely back inside now, she tried one last desperate attempt to stave off death. Reaching up with her bloody hands, she gripped onto the ripped corrugated metal above her. She put all her strength into it and felt herself gaining some ground on her attacker; she was moving back outside, only by an inch or two, but it was in the right direction. Michelle kicked her legs despite the pain, and the hand lost its grip, and she was able to pull herself further towards freedom.

She could feel hope returning to her for a few seconds before a considerable weight crashed down onto her already shattered ankle. Pain shot through her broken body; it was pain she'd never experienced before.

Her fingers slipped from their tenuous grasp of the metal surrounding her. Her back hit the dirt beneath her with a thud, and her head bounced off the solid ground. The unexpected contact dazing her and causing her vision to blur. Two hands wrapped around her ankles, and one big pull brought her battered body back inside the warehouse. Tears flowed as she lay looking up at her attacker.

"Just look at the state of you. You're an AI. You should be better than this. No wonder this is your fate." The man spat down at her; his saliva mingled with the blood that now covered her.

She had no energy left in her; she could barely breathe. Trying to speak—to plead—she opened her mouth, but all she could emit was a small pathetic whimper as tears streamed down her face.

Michelle tried to shield her head as a large boot came down towards it, but she was too late. As it made contact, her vision swam with dots of various colors. She closed her eyes as another heavy foot came at her.

Chapter 16

04:00 27th October 2138

He dragged the body past the containers towards the vehicle that was idling just inside the rolled-up shutter.

He'd been told to dispose of it and to be creative. He had just the thing in mind.

When he got to the car, the trunk popped automatically with a loud click that reverberated around the warehouse.

Lifting the corpse, he deposited it unceremoniously into the empty coffin-like space that was partially lit by a small red light within. He placed his hand on the trunk and looked down with disdain at the crumpled mess of what, only minutes before, was a living AI. He felt nothing only loathing for what she was. She was a failure, and she got what she deserved.

Slamming the trunk shut, he paced around the vehicle to the driver's side — where the door opened silently outward as he approached — and slipped inside.

Putting the vehicle in gear and pushing down on the accelerator, it rolled under the shutter and out into the fresh morning air. He had to get to his chosen location soon so that maximum effect could be achieved. He put his foot down.

Driving at this time in the morning, there was little to no traffic on the roads he had to travel. He zoned out as he went, going over the list of things he had to do next. Robert's plan was coming together, but he still had to do his part, and he had to do it right, more as a matter of pride than fear of Robert's wrath.

The streets passed by outside the tinted windows of the black Mazda. He looked out into the grey morning beyond. Humans were already milling about in the streets, doing whatever it was they did. Rats; that's what they were, nothing but rats. Their time was past. He had to make it across the city before too many came out of their holes. He checked the time; he'd make it.

*

The car rolled to a slow and steady stop. The assassin popped the trunk using the button on the dash and climbed out of the driver's seat.

He looked up at the sky and then around the area. The sun hadn't yet risen, and no one was about. This gave him some time to perform.

He walked around to the back of the vehicle and opened the trunk further. Raising one of the corpse's arms, he levered up the body and pulled it out of the dark space.

As he hauled the body entirely out into the crisp air, drops of blood fell and splashed onto the paving below. More fell as he moved the body towards the wall ahead.

Dumping the body against it, he looked back at the trail of red he'd left behind him almost admiringly.

He reached into his inner coat pocket and pulled out several long spikes and a hammer. He always carried a hammer; it came in handy for a lot of his work.

Lifting the battered body to a standing position, he raised one arm and started to hammer a spike through the hand into the stone behind. Once one was firmly in, he proceeded to do the same with the other until the spikes held the dead woman's entire weight.

He had another cursory look around the area; still no rats.

Putting the hammer away, he now pulled out a knife. He thrust the sharp blade into the body until blood starting to trickle down over the handle, his hand and dripped off his wrist. He made a slit in the stomach, and once large enough, thrust his hand wholly inside.

A few twists later, he pulled his hand out and stared at the gore that now covered his fist.

Using his newly bloodied hand, he began to scrawl some words above the body.

Once completed, he stepped back to admire his work. A small wry smile crept across his face.

He walked back to his vehicle, reached into the trunk, and grabbed a cloth. After wiping his hands clean, he threw it back inside, slammed the door closed, and got back in the driver's seat.

He started the engine without lingering and sped off. He wanted to get away before the sun began to rise.

Chapter 17

06:00 27ᵗʰ October 2138

The alley was a mess, alright.

A kill performed in the usual style of the AI group, but something about this felt different. This wasn't a planned attack that much was clear; it was a murder of opportunity. Whoever did this had come across the victim in the act of committing a crime and couldn't help but to cleanse them.

This wasn't the usual way that the AIs worked. They had never done this before. All other murders prior to this one had been well thought out and planned, sometimes years in the making. Were the AI becoming more volatile, more desperate? Or was this a mistake, a one-off performed by a rogue in the group?

There was still a possibility that this wasn't part of the same pattern. Perhaps committed by an AI not involved with the group, or maybe even a human; it's not like the details of the murders were secret; the press had reported every aspect that they could get ahold of. So it wasn't entirely out of the question to think that it wasn't related and merely just a copycat. But the fact that this happened only a few blocks away from the scene of a murder committed earlier tonight meant that odds of this were extremely low.

In Kell's mind, this murder had been committed by the perpetrator of Martin Howard's; it had to be the green-eyed woman from the photo. The woman, who up to now, he'd been unable to find any information about. Every search he ran drew a blank. He was hoping that he would be able to track her from here; there was nothing new to be gained by looking into this killing, he was sure, but perhaps some of the CCTV in this area had caught some footage of her. Even if it were just one image, it would be more than he had at this point.

If indeed this was the green-eyed woman's work, and she'd come from Howard's apartment, she may have been heading towards something.

The apartment was on F Street Northwest, so she was moving northwest, at least until she got here. From the direction, she could be heading anywhere; that was no help. Kell looked up and around the alley. He couldn't see any cameras in the area, perhaps out on the main street.

Walking back out onto H street, Kell could see a faint orange glow in the sky as the sun was threatening to rise, and the road was starting to get busier with traffic.

Even with all the technology, there was nothing to be done about traffic jams, he thought to himself.

He turned right and walked up the sidewalk with his eyes focused high on the adjacent buildings' walls, searching for any sign of a camera.

Getting to the corner with no luck, he considered turning around and exploring the other end of the street until he spied a camera on the opposite side of the road.

He strode out into the traffic and made his way across to the other side while dodging several moving vehicles. Horns blared at him, but he ignored them.

Looking up at the camera, he breathed a sigh of relief that his luck might be changing; it was pointing the way he'd just come.

Clicking his temple, the visual interface popped up, *six.*

```
Connecting...
Connecting...
Connecting...
Connected
```

Several new windows popped up in his vision, all with video feeds showing live footage. He closed all the other feeds, so he was left only with the one he needed.

He rewound the footage to around 7pm, the time Howard was discovered. The mugger was murdered sometime after this, which fits with his suspect.

Fast-forwarding through the footage, Kell kept an eye out for any figure that would match the green-eyed woman. He went over an hour or so of video footage until he came across a lone woman walking down the street towards the camera. Although he could zoom in on the figure, it just distorted the image.

Zooming out again, Kell saw the woman stop at the mouth of the alley, look down it for a few seconds, and then disappeared into it. After a few minutes, she re-emerged and continued to walk towards the camera at a steady pace.

The image of her got better with each step she took. Once she reached the corner he'd just come across, Kell got a clear view of her; she was covered in blood. He was now convinced that it was the green-eyed woman that had killed Howard.

The woman walked under the camera and was lost. Kell quickly noted the time stamp, and opened the other video feeds, found the correct time on each one, and played them all back at the same time. The only other camera she was caught on was on the opposite side of the building, and at this distance, she was little more than a fuzzy blur. The shape, however, was moving quicker than before.

The dark mass moved towards the camera, but the light here seemed to be worse, and it was just his luck that he'd need the one system that didn't have night vision on it.

The figure ran under this camera too and was lost to the night.

Kell considered this for a second. It looked like she was now moving west along the street. If he continued on her path, he should find more cameras that he could pick her up on.

He saved copies of each of the video feeds and took a still image of the woman as she crossed the road towards the first camera; it was the best view he'd had so far.

Five, he uploaded everything to the central server to go through it in more detail later; he didn't want to miss anything.

Disconnecting from the system, he continued up the street, all the while looking for more cameras he could extract footage from.

Slowly making his way north on 23rd, Kell kept his eyes to the higher parts of the buildings lining the street.

The area was now bustling with people. This being the road between the two halls of George Washington University, the streets were filling up with students and professors going to their first lectures of the day.

Several people walked straight into him or pushed him out of the way. No apologies were made; people were too hurried. Despite being jostled from side to side, he managed to keep his eyes to the walls.

Kell made it to the end of the building and managed to find another camera. Connecting to it, more video feeds popped up in his vision. Quickly seeing the one he needed—again, it pointed down in the direction he and hopefully the woman had come—he went to the correct timestamp and started to play through the footage.

A shadow crept along the side of the building, keeping to the darkness but still setting a good pace. The closer the figure got to the camera, the surer Kell was that it was his murderer. There was still very little light down this street at night. With only small pricks of light coming from some windows of the hall opposite, it wasn't enough to light the assailant.

He continued through the footage as the figure went beneath the camera, he quickly swapped to the next and saw her run down under the trees in the small park between the hall and Foggy Bottom subway station. He had hoped that she'd duck down there, it would be better lit, and the chances of getting a clearer image were much better.

However, instead of using the path, the woman pushed her way through the trees and plants closer to the building, obscuring her from the camera.

He followed her path, the area was starting to quiet down as people had reached their destinations, and only stragglers were left; some strolling at a leisurely pace, others sat on the stone benches that dotted the pavement. No one paid him any mind as he walked along the sidewalk, still looking for cameras.

At the next corner of the building—which turned into the entrance—he saw something covering a patch of the wall. He got closer, pushing his way through some overgrown bushes, and placed his hand on the wall. He slowly rubbed his fingers across the brickwork, the stain was dry, but it was definitely blood; no doubt the blood of the mugger. He was still on track.

From the blood pattern, it looked like the woman had stopped here, perhaps because there was someone around that she didn't want to get stopped by; maybe she was injured too, it was doubtful, but it was still a possibility.

He looked up, hoping to see another camera. Unfortunately, where a camera looked to have once been mounted, only a number of wires protruded from the brickwork.

He cast his eyes over the opposite wall, nothing here either. He turned to face the building on the other side of the path and could just about make out a camera on the wall behind some trees. It looked like the view would be blocked, but it was his only next option. He connected.

Though mostly blocked by the trees, the footage still showed a grainy figure stood by the wall. As he thought there was another shape moving around the entrance. The form by the wall was peering around it to see.

Kell watched as the woman in the video reached around to her back and pulled something out that glinted in the moonlight; the female figure slowly started to edge out from the wall. Just before she stepped out another figure appeared in the entrance and seemed to call to the one outside; the two shapes then disappeared back into the building. The glinting object was hidden away again as the woman moved away and darted for the other wall. *That person has no idea how close they came to being yet another victim of this killer.*

The woman became wholly obscured from view as she moved on. It was time to do the same and find another angle.

Kell continued through the gates at the other end of the park. He had no way of knowing which way she would have gone from here.

He looked around at the buildings surrounding him. There were no more cameras to be seen, at least not obvious ones. He can't lose her now; he'd come this far.

He took a gamble and ran across the busy road. Traffic, whilst building up was still moving freely. He caused some screeching brakes when several automatic cars' danger mode came on.

Some people even shouted obscenities at him from the open windows. Kell carried on down I Street regardless.

He was leaving the university area now and entering residential properties. This meant a much smaller chance of external CCTV; he hoped to find a business not far along.

Reaching the corner of I and New Hampshire, Kell realized he'd truly lost the trail. He had no idea which direction the woman was headed. From her last known location, she could have gone anywhere.

He was about to give up the chase when he saw another dark smear on the sidewalk ahead of him.

Crossing another road, he crouched down to better look at the stain; again, it was dried blood.

He looked up and noticed the tree next to him also had a dark brown smudge on it; it looked like she stopped here too.

Still crouching, he slowly scanned the area for any more bloodstains. Had the woman turned here or continued straight down the street? He took another gamble and went South West down New Hampshire.

Before long, Kell came across yet more dried blood droplets; he was still going in the right direction. He split his time as he walked, between looking for more signs of blood on the floor and scanning the walls of buildings for cameras. He moved towards Triangle Park.

Reaching the vast junction, Kell realized it would be much harder to figure out where the woman had gone.

The bloodstains weren't happening regularly enough for him to follow a trail. If there were more in this area, he'd need help to find them, and that would take time, time that he didn't have.

Kell stopped when he found himself in the shadow of a large building.

The now derelict Watergate Hotel towered above him. This once notorious hotel –famed for a scandal involving a long-dead US President – had been empty for decades. It was used as a base of operations during some of the worst campaigns of the AI wars. First, humans and then AI controlled it. It was one of the first places that the deadly nanobots were dropped to end the war, and it was pivotal in the turning of the tide in favor of humans.

It now stood empty. Its enormous shell was collapsing from within. If it were still operating as a hotel or otherwise occupied, it would be a guaranteed place to find some CCTV that he could connect into. But in its current state of disrepair, it was improbable that it was home to any CCTV. This once magnificent building had been left to rot.

However, Kell realized, this would be the perfect place for a group of AI to hide and run their missions. Perhaps this was where the woman was going. He crossed the roads and headed towards the old, decaying entrance.

Kell looked up at the building before him and tried to imagine what it was like in its heyday. It must have been beautiful; it was still an impressive structure today, even with the deterioration.

The ex-hotel was now surrounded by metal sheet fencing. It was scheduled to be demolished soon, but then, it had been scheduled for demolition since the end of the war, and yet here it stood. Kell walked along the fence and found a loose panel; *probably where junkies and homeless had gained access,* he thought. Pushing it aside, he crouched inside its boundary

The once automatic entrance door was stuck open, glass shattered, and littering the ground. The smell of mold and smoke permeated through the lobby. He took several steps inside to stand in the center of the previously grand area. Now it was dark, and not a shred of life seemed to exist within; he couldn't even hear the traffic from the road just meters outside the door. It was as if he had stepped into another universe, where everything was decrepit and decaying. There wasn't even a small sliver of light penetrating the darkness.

He did a slow three-sixty-degree turn; looking around for anything that could aid is progress. He didn't have time to search the entire place, but maybe he could find something nearby that could at least give him a small clue as to where to head next. There was a buzzing inside his head, and the incoming call alert flashed up in his vision.

Kell

"Kell, it's Crane," the captain said.

Sir, I've tracked the green-eyed woman down to Triangle Park. I'm currently inside the old Watergate Hotel. It's possible that it's being

used as the AIs' base and where she was running towards after killing the mugger.

"I can tell you exactly where the green-eyed woman is, Kell," Crane said.

You can? But sir, how?

"Because we've just had a call, she's been found," Crane said.

Found? Is she being brought in?

"Not yet. She's dead." Crane said.

Dead?

"I'm afraid so. I need you to head over to where she was discovered, and I need you over there ten minutes ago." Crane said, his voice was calm, but Kell detected an undertone of fear.

Where is she? Why the rush?

"Because things are getting messy, and I need you to tell me what the hell is going on so I can tell *my* boss," Crane said a little more sharply.

Sir, what's the location?

There was a brief pause from the other end of the call, then the Captain spoke;

"It's the goddamn Washington Monument."

Chapter 18

```
06:45 27th October 2138
```

The monitor showed a figure entering the building. Robert shifted in his seat to better look at who had crossed the old, dilapidated hotel's threshold. Was it another junkie biotic as usual, hopped up on Brass and looking for a place to stay the night?

Zooming in on the figure, the black and white night vision image showed he was wearing a long coat and pressed pants; this didn't look like any junkie he'd seen before. The figure was looking around the ancient lobby; what was he looking for? Slowly the shape started to turn to face the camera, *excellent now I'll get a better look at the intruder,* Robert thought.

His eyes widened as the figure turned, and the camera revealed the man's face,

"It's that damn AI cop! What's he doing here?" Robert said aloud.

He watched as Kell continued to survey the area around him.

Robert hovered his finger over a remote control. He'd wired up the hotel a long time ago when he decided not to use it as his base of operations. Instead, he chose the empty and run-down warehouse on the riverfront behind. He'd used C4 set up with a remote trigger connected in his monitoring room, so at a moment's notice, he could blow up the surrounding area and make an escape. He'd packed the hotel with enough explosives to not only take the building down but to make a pretty large crater in most of the surrounding area.

He continued to watch the figure on the monitor, all the while, his finger getting closer to the button. He paused as he saw the man quickly turn and leave the building almost at a run. He followed the figure through several camera feeds out of the building and off the site; relaxing his finger, he sat back in his chair. That was too close for comfort, especially when he was so close to completing his plan. His thoughts went to Michelle; she must have left some kind of trail back to the hotel. At least he'd put a stop to her and any more of her mistakes. He wouldn't need anyone else soon.

Did the cop know just how close he was to him now, or was he still unaware of his location? In any case, his presence meant that the schedule had to change. He dialed a number.

The assassin answered after just one ring, "Yes?"

I need to change the schedule you're on. Where are you?

"Close to the girl." The other man said.

Leave her for now. I need you to go and pick up Lopez. I need to accelerate things, and he is pivotal to the process.

"I'll bring him to you now." The assassin said in a monotonous drawl.

Good.

The call disconnected, and Robert stood. He gave the monitors another quick look. He skimmed through all the video feeds to make sure that the cop had indeed left the area. Satisfied he was now safe from being discovered, he left his office and went down to the central warehouse.

His footsteps echoed as he walked down the rusting metal steps. Once at the bottom he moved to the middle of the space, where he'd had two shipping containers separated from the rest, joined and fitted with secure doors.

Standing before the first container's large metal doors, Robert looked up into the camera that had been fixed above. The doors clicked and slowly swung open towards him with a silent rush of air. He stepped inside, and the doors swung to a close behind him, sealing tight. Gas was released all around Robert, and he stood for several minutes, waiting for the release to finish. After a few seconds, an extractor fan retrofitted to the container kicked in. The extractor came to a gradual stop, and the doors in front of him clicked open, swinging away from him.

Beyond was a brilliant white light that was enhanced as it reflected off steel tables. Robert stepped inside the second container, and the doors closed behind him, with a sucking noise as a tight seal was formed around the edges.

It took a moment for his eyes to adjust to the brightness inside this container. It was a massive contrast to the darkness of his office, where he usually dwelled. The inside of this container was lined with plastic sheeting. Floors, walls, and ceiling were covered in several layers. Metal tables had been set up around three of the walls, on top of which were several items of lab equipment. He walked to the small desktop fridge that was quietly humming in front of him. Looking through the glass door, he could see the single item that it contained; the metal canister containing wartime nanobots that Gary Lawton had liberated from the MDF Organics lab, but which had nearly been lost.

He smiled to himself; all he needed now was the scientist. Lopez was being picked up right now and would soon be delivered to him, and the real work could start. The final pieces of the puzzle were falling into place. It wouldn't be long before it would all end. There were still some loose ends, however, the girl and the cop. But they wouldn't be a problem for long.

After checking through the equipment set up in the makeshift laboratory, Robert made his exit and went back up to his office and video feeds.

Flicking on the large television on the wall behind his chair, he turned to watch the day's news. It wouldn't be long before another part of his plan was put into action. This time though, it wasn't his AIs performing the act; it would be the idiot biotics.

Chapter 19

07:05 27th October 2138

Kell stood facing the imposing, towering monument, staring at the unholy mess that was just a few feet in front of him. He stared in disbelief at the scene. The green-eyed woman, whom he'd spent the last twelve hours trying to track down, was now pinned to the brickwork of the Washington Monument.

She was held up, arms wide open, with the same spikes that the AI killers used, but she was whole – other than the hole in her stomach – and looked to almost have been crucified. There was a spike nailed through each of her hands. One eye was closed; the other was glazed over and staring at him, her mouth slack and open in a silent scream.

Above her, painted on the bricks in what looked at first glance like brown paint – but he knew full well would turn out to be blood – were the words, 'All Artis Must Die!' This wasn't good.

He turned around and looked across the lawns to the White House in the distance. She was displayed here with a purpose.

Examining the woman's corpse more closely, Kell found that both her ankles and one of her arms were broken, she had cuts all over her body, her clothes were torn, and she was almost covered from head to toe in blood and dirt. He examined her hands and saw that her nails were broken or missing. Whatever had happened to her, it was violent, and she tried to fight back. He reached out with an open hand and closed her open eye; there was something about the single dead eye staring at him that chilled him to his core.

Who had done this, and where had they done it?

He looked around the area and found small blood spots leading away a few feet, and then they abruptly ended. If this poor woman were attacked and killed here, there would be further traces of it. From the look of the trail, it was likely that she was murdered somewhere else and transported here, probably by car. But why? This was clearly a message. But what were the chances of a human finding, killing, and making an example of the exact AI that he was chasing? No, this felt more like a distraction, but who was the distraction for?

The more he thought about this, the more questions were being raised. This wasn't going to be an open and shut case, not by any stretch of the imagination.

Behind him, he could hear a commotion. He turned and saw that people had started to gather. From what he could see beyond the police cordon, the crowd was made up of both humans and AIs. Both groups were shouting and trying to push forward. The other members of the department that were on the scene were doing their best to block the woman's body from view, calm the crowds and, at the same time, stop them from getting through. But with the limited amount of resources currently at the department's disposal, this was a losing battle.

He heard voices rise from the crowd, some calling for AIs to die, others shouting for justice for AIs.

Before long, he was surrounded. Hundreds of people had come to see what was happening. The crowd grew even larger when a myriad of reporters arrived and began pushing their way to the front of the mass of bodies trying to get the best shot of the scene. Men and woman were talking into microphones in front of cameras, this was a mess, and it would soon be on every news outlet in Washington, and probably the country. Whoever had committed this murder was going to cause chaos. But maybe that was the idea.

Suddenly the crowd surged forward. More police officers ran to give back up to those already being overwhelmed. The rabble's noise was rising, but then above the shouting came a loud crack, as someone fired a weapon; surely not the police?

Screams came from the center of the crowd, and people began to scurry in every direction.

Kell ran forward, pushing his way through the anarchy, coming to a sudden halt and stumbling as he found a man lying in a pool of blood on the concrete.

Crouching beside him, he felt for a pulse, but the increasing size of the pool of red around the man didn't fill him with much hope of finding one. He saw something out of the corner of his eye and looked up.

Just a few steps away from him, another man stood holding a gun at his side; he had a look of pure shock as he looked down at the dead man. He noticed Kell looking in his direction and started to slowly back away, waving his hands and shaking his head.

"I...I...d...didn't mean to sh...shoot him." The man stuttered

"It's okay, just take it easy," Kell said, standing and holding his hands up in front of him. "Put the gun on the ground and kick it towards me. Then kneel with your hands behind your head." He did his best to keep his voice calm and level so as not to agitate the man further.

Kell slowly rose to a standing position with his hand on his holster. He never liked drawing his gun unless he had no other course of action. In his experience, drawing it would escalate the moment, and someone else would get hurt.

"I d...didn't mean to." The man said, visibly shaking, "He said all AI should die. I've never hurt anyone b...before."

"You're okay, just follow my instructions, and it'll be okay," Kell said.

The man suddenly jumped and raised the gun. Even as he held it gripped tightly with both hands, he was struggling to keep it steady; he didn't seem sure as to what he was aiming at.

"Don't come closer." The AI man said as Kell slowly turned his head to see what had got him so agitated.

Lockley stood just to Kell's right; she had her gun raised and pointing at the panicking man.

Kell motioned Lockley to lower her weapon. She looked questioningly at him for a few seconds and then slowly lowered it to her side, leaving her finger on the side of the trigger, ready to fire at a moment's notice.

Kell turned his attention back to the shooter, who continued to aim his weapon at the young police officer.

"Now, come on, sir," Kell said calmly, trying to diffuse the tense situation. "Lower your weapon and let us help you."

"H...help me? I'm an AI. I know what happens to AIs that kill. We get deactivated." The man said.

"But I know it was an accident, you didn't mean to kill this man." Kell used a single finger to point at the deceased man lying on the floor, in between them.

From the corner of his eye, he saw a shadow shift as Lockley slowly edged forward.

"NO!" the man said as he tried to train his gun on her.

Lockley raised her arms and stepped back.

The man was visibly starting to sweat. With the gun still aimed at Lockley, he used his other arm to wipe the sweat from his brow. His hand still on the weapon was shaking more wildly now, and he seemed to be unable to hold the weight of it.

The younger officer saw an opportunity and dashed forward. The scared shooter flinched as she approached and pulled the trigger. There was a scream, and the woman fell to the floor.

Kell rushed at the man, tackling him to the hard-paved ground in the confusion, the gun spinning along the smooth concrete walkway away from them both.

Kell wrestled the man over, so he was lying on his chest, pulled his arms behind him, and cuffed him tightly.

Looking over to Lockley, he noticed she wasn't moving, and there was blood starting to cover the concrete beneath her.

"I need some help over here. Officer down!"

Chapter 20

07:30 27th October 2138

After trying and failing to get a couple of hours of sleep before the new day started, President Darrow showered, shaved, dressed, and now stood on the Truman Balcony, looking out over the White House gardens.

His eyes were drawn to the south, towards where the Washington Monument stood proudly in the skyline. The sun was rising, but there was still enough darkness in the city to highlight the blue and red flashing lights coming from the monument's base.

He turned and walked back inside the residence and sat on one of the three sofas in the Yellow Oval Room. A shrill ringing came from the phone next to him, and a cold feeling of dread filled him. He hesitantly picked up the receiver.

"Yes?" Darrow said, able to hear the quiver in his own voice.

"Mr. President." the voice on the other end of the line sounded wholly unfamiliar to him; he tried his best to place it.

"Yes, who is this?" Darrow asked.

"Mr. President, it's Henry." The voice said.

"Henry? Oh, Henry, yes. Sorry." The President said, feeling foolish for not recognizing the voice of his Chief of Staff.

"Sir, there's been another incident," Henry said, his voice sounding grave. The President's dread increased.

"Something happened at the monument, didn't it?" Darrow asked.

"Yes, sir." Henry said.

"How bad is it, Henry?" Darrow asked, not really wanting to know the answer.

"It's bad, sir. We need you in the Oval Office." Henry said.

"I'm on my way," Darrow said and replaced the handset in its cradle. He still considered it odd that all phones in the White House were still landlines, even though his staff used cell phones or implants when they were walking about, almost all critical calls always came to landlines; the secret service seemed to think this was more secure.

Darrow picked himself up and walked towards the door, throwing his suit jacket on as he went. Walking through the residence, he couldn't help but enjoy the quiet.

Pausing at the door, the President stood gathering himself. After a few deep breaths and an internal pep talk, he opened the door and marched into the corridor.

He'd only taken two steps when he was surrounded by people, all talking at him, some thrusting papers into his hands to either read, sign, or both. For the moment, though, he was focused on getting back to the Oval Office. He brushed off several people who tried to start walking meetings with him. He could hear several members of the White House staff chattering into phones and to colleagues about something that had happened at the monument, but he couldn't make out what it was.

Reaching the outer office to his own, he was greeted by Olivia, who looked even more worried than she had the last time he'd seen her.

"Everything okay?" Darrow asked his aide.

Olivia just shook her head and began to cry. He wanted nothing more than to comfort her, to hold her close, but he knew he couldn't. Instead, he simply said, "It'll be alright." and continued through the Oval Office doors, leaving Olivia at her desk sobbing.

The President was greeted by all the senior members of his staff; they all had the same worried look on their faces.

Striding through the doorway, he went straight over to his desk and took a seat. As he entered, everyone in the office had stood; he motioned them to sit with a wave of his hand,

"What's happened?" Darrow asked the group.

All eyes looked around the room and then collectively fell on Henry Russo, who stood and fixed his eyes on the Presidents',

"Sir," the Chief of Staff started, "You will remember a murder of one Martin Howard was committed last night just a few blocks away from here."

"I do," Darrow said, furrowing his brow.

"The suspect — an AI — is also suspected of killing a man who attempted to mug her during her escape from the scene." The older man cleared his throat, "That same woman has now herself been killed."

"Well, that's something, isn't it?" The President said flatly.

"Sir, I'm not sure you understand. Yes, this woman has been killed, but it is far from good. The woman — who has still yet to be identified — was beaten, killed, and then—" Henry paused again, he seemed to be having difficulty with what to say, that was most unusual for the man of a million words.

"Then what?" The President asked the room.

"And then she was nailed to the Washington Monument, in full view of the public. The words 'All Artis Must Die' were written in blood above her." Louis Benz jumped in when he saw Henry struggling.

Darrow was lost for words himself at this revelation. This was indeed very bad. This public display was almost a declaration of war. But who had done it? His mind twisted and turned with ideas; was it an act of a human getting revenge on an AI? Was it an AI doing the same? He had a horrible idea that it was something else entirely.

"Where do we stand?" he asked.

"The police are on the scene and conducting investigations. Crowds are starting to stop and gather around the monument. One saving grace is that the press is yet to arrive, but I'm sure they won't be far away once they get the scent of blood, no pun intended." Henry said, sitting back in his seat.

The room went silent, and the air hung heavy as no one quite knew what to say next. It was the press secretary who broke the silence.

"I'll tell the press in the building the situation but urge them not to print or cast anything until we have solid facts about who committed this crime and just what the staging means."

While she talked, a junior staff member had entered the room and was whispering in Henry's ear. The older man nodded, and his face was grim.

"I'm afraid, Helen," Henry began, "that may not be enough, and also, a little too late." Helen's face fell as Henry talked, "The press have already arrived at the scene and are reporting on what they see rather than what they know. I don't think either side of this will take this well. I—" Henry's speech was cut short by the sound of a gunshot. It was somewhat quiet, muffled by distance, but it was unmistakable as a firearm, and it came from the Washington Monument. Several members of the President's Secret Service guards rushed into the room and pushed him down.

"They're not shooting at me, you idiots!" The President screamed as his head was forced down into the soft carpeted floor. "Whatever's going on is happening at the monument, I'm in no danger here!"

Darrow wrestled free from the grip of the gorilla of a man who had him pinned down. As he got to his feet, he noticed that someone had turned on one of the nearby screens in the chaos, and the rest of the room was watching it intently. He joined them.

The President watched as the camera jerked up and down as the camera operator was running. Occasionally they got a view of what was happening as things came in and out of frame. He saw a mass of screaming people running from presumably the shooter; there was a brief glimpse of the young woman who was pinned to the monument, and the words scrawled above her.

The air seemed to be filled with screams and hurried footsteps, but he heard a male voice shout out, he wasn't sure, but he thought he heard the words "officer down."

"Oh, my God." Valerie said, seemingly forgetting where she was for a moment.

The President reached out and put a hand on her shoulder. Walking away from the screen, he sat behind his desk. The chaos on screen had been muted, and all eyes had turned to him once again.. Things out in the city were escalating quickly, and he knew he had to come up with a plan.

"I want to know exactly what's happening out there. I want the police out on the streets calming the situation down, any violence I want dealt with. I don't want anyone to be able to say that the authorities are taking sides. I want to be seen stepping in on behalf of anyone, human or AI, who may be in trouble or being harmed. I want people to see that disorder will not be tolerated. If the on-duty police aren't enough bodies, cancel leave. I want all the boots in the city that we can get, bring in the army if need be. I want this city calmed." Darrow said sternly.

"Sir—" Henry began.

"Don't argue with me, Henry." The President slammed a fist on the desk, he saw several of his staff flinch, "This tide of violence needs to be stopped before it gets going. We will do whatever is necessary to get this under control. I will go on television and address the nation in an hour. Everyone be ready. I want to see my speech in thirty minutes."

When he finished, the room was full of nodding heads and humming in agreement. Within mere seconds the room had cleared of people, and he was left alone in the Oval Office.

A few moments of exquisite silence passed before being shattered by a knock on the door.

Darrow sighed heavily, "Come in," he said.

The door slowly opened, and Olivia timidly walked in and to his side.

"Don't you worry. This will all get resolved before the end of the day." He said to her, placing a hand on hers. She smiled at him and leaned down to place a small kiss on his lips.

*

An hour later, Samuel Darrow, the 65th President of the United States of America, was sat in the Oval Office of the White House with cameras on him, ready to address the nation.

He'd spent the last half an hour going through what he was going to say to the country. Although it was hastily written by his team, he was impressed at how well they'd done; he'd only made a couple of minor changes. Though the words would be on the prompt in front of him, he still went through it in his mind and tried to memorize what he could.

In the three years he'd been in the White House, he'd done several of these televised emergency addresses to the nation, but he still wasn't used to them. He hated the cameras and the lights; they just made him sweat. Although he couldn't see most of the people gathered behind the bright white lights surrounding him, he was very aware of the number of people looking at him.

The director behind the camera started to count down from five. When he got to three, he began to use his fingers to count down, reaching one he pointed at the President, and the light on top of the camera went green as the broadcast went live.

"My fellow Americans—"

Chapter 21

```
07:00 27th October 2138
```

After he'd received his new orders from Robert, the assassin had quickly changed his direction of travel and was now across the street from the home of MDF Organics scientist Matias Lopez; waiting.

Thirty minutes later, he saw Matias leave through the main entrance. He rolled the car slowly closer, all the while hanging back; he didn't need this biotic to bolt now. He had to get him to Robert unharmed, and soon.

Matias turned down the side of the building. His watcher rolled to a stop directly opposite and shifted himself down in his seat.

The scientist walked past several cars until he stopped. A trunk popped open, and he threw a bag inside. Climbing into the driver's seat, there was no movement for several minutes, and the stalking AI was close to going to see what was happening before the vehicle came to life and started to move.

Lopez pulled out of the car park and onto the main road. *He must be going to work, splendid. This will work in my favor,* the assassin thought.

The AI let the unaware biotic get a short lead on him before he pulled out and started his pursuit.

Traffic was light, so he had to hang back more than he would have liked so as not to be spotted by the scientist. Although he was sure that the man wouldn't notice him even if he were in the car with him. From all his observations, this biotic didn't seem to be particularly aware of his surroundings; he appeared to be focused on other things; usually his work, or any women who might happen to be close by. This focus was what Robert hoped would work in his favor and keep Lopez's mind on the task he was about to be given.

After a short drive, they drove past the MDF Organics building. The pursuer pulled to a stop a little way down the road and watched as Matias' vehicle drove into the underground car park. When he was out of sight, the AI followed.

Inside the underground car park, the AI located Matias, who was bent over rummaging around in the trunk of his vehicle. This was his chance.

The AI rolled his vehicle to a stop behind the distracted scientist. With cat-like dexterity, he jumped out of his vehicle and slipped one arm around Matias' neck and used the other to hold a knife to his throat.

"Please don't hurt me! I can get you money! Please, no!" Matias cried.

The AI could feel the entirety of the man's body quivering in his grasp.

Shhhh, he whispered into Matias' ear.

"I'm sorry, just please don't hurt me! I'll give you money, my car, whatever you want." Matias said in a slightly lowered voice, the note of panic was still coming through loud and clear.

"I don't want your money or your busted old car. You'll come with me. I have a job for you." The assassin said.

"A job? Great. I mean, I already have a job. But what can I do for you? Matias said desperately.

"Keep quiet." The AI said.

He pulled Matias away from his vehicle and towards the trunk of his own car.

Still with the knife to the scientist's throat, he reached down and pushed a button on the handle of the trunk door. There was a click as the door popped open.

"Get in." He whispered into the biotics ear.

Matias quickly nodded in acceptance. The assassin released his grip and turned the other man to face him. Matias' face was white with fear; he looked like he would vomit with just the slightest provocation.

"In." The AI said once more.

The terrified scientist slowly stepped in the trunk and curled into a tight ball.

The assassin slammed the trunk shut and locked it. He darted his eyes around the car park for witnesses or cameras as he walked to the driver's side door. He saw a camera just above where he stood. Looking directly at it, he smiled before getting into his vehicle and leaving the car park at a steady pace, being careful not to draw any attention to his car.

Back on the main street, he headed for the warehouse, where he knew Robert would be awaiting his return. He dialed a number,

"Yes?" Robert answered quickly.

Lopez is enroute.

"Excellent," Robert said.

The call ended, and he continued on his journey with his new cargo safely stowed away in the trunk.

As he drove, he noticed crowds of irate people gathering in various spots in the streets he passed down. It looked like his little diorama at the monument had attained the desired effect. Robert should be pleased with this. The assassin took great pleasure in seeing how riled up people seemed to be getting. It wasn't just groups of biotics that he saw; there was also a noticeable amount of AI groups gathering with the same kind of angry mob-like behavior. *Excellent,* he thought.

It wasn't long before the AI's vehicle pulled into the old warehouse. He drove straight in and stopped right outside the makeshift container labs, where Robert was stood waiting.

Exiting the car, he made straight for the trunk.

He opened it to find the terrified man was still curled into a tight ball, and there was a distinct stench of urine. The human had wet himself in fear.

The AI reached in and grabbed hold of Matias; the scared man jerked away from him and looked up. A small glimmer of hope seemed to pass over his face until he realized that his would-be rescuer was the same man who had trapped him. His captor pulled Matias out of the trunk, who he dropped to his knees on the dirty concrete and began sobbing into his shaking hands.

"Mr. Lopez." Robert started, "I'm glad you could visit."

The scientist looked up at Robert with a look of mixed fear and confusion,

"Do you know who I am?" Robert asked.

Matias quickly shook his head in the negative,

"Good, that's the way it will stay. I have a job for you, Mr. Lopez." Robert nodded to the scientist's kidnapper, who grabbed the crying man and hoisted him to his feet. "Do please come with me."

Robert walked towards the containers, where the door swung open, and he stepped inside. The scientist and his abductor walked in behind him.

After the decontamination procedure had finished, the three men walked into the makeshift laboratory.

Matias blinked in the bright light that greeted him when the doors opened, and as his eyes adjusted, he stared in bewilderment at the set up that greeted him,

"What is…" Matias started before trailing off.

"This is your new lab, Mr. Lopez," Robert said.

"But—" Matias began.

"Sorry, Mr. Lopez," Robert interrupted, "Allow me to explain further."

Robert walked over to the small refrigerator, reached inside, and produced the small metal canister,

"Do you know what this is?" He asked.

Matias looked at the canister in shock, his mouth hanging open,

"I will take your reaction to mean that you *do* know what this is," Robert said.

"What do you—" Matias said.

"Want you to do?" Robert said, finishing the scientist's sentence.

Matias nodded dumbly.

"Why, I want you to change the contents of this little canister, Mr. Lopez," Robert said with a smile.

"Ch...change?" Matias asked, barely even to get a single word to come out of his mouth.

"That's correct. I would like you to change the purpose of the nanobots within." Robert paused as if to let his words sink in, and then continued, "You will change them so they no longer deactivate AIs, but so that they deactivate humans."

"Y...you w...want m...m...me...t...to—" Matias struggled to say.

"Yes. I would like *you* to do this for *me.*" Robert said, pointing a finger at Matias and then himself.

"B...but...but why?" Matias asked.

"Your place is not to question why. Your place is simply to do." Robert said, his smile had now gone, replaced by straight lips and a stone-cold stare.

"But I don't t...think I c...can." Matias pleaded.

"Nonsense, Mr. Lopez. Of course, you can. I've seen your work. You've been able to neutralize them. All you need to do then is reactivate them with a new purpose." Robert said, slowly turning the canister around in his hand, "I can provide you with whatever you need to do so. If I haven't already, of course." He waved his arms to present the lab.

"What if I c...can't?" Matias said.

"Then I'm afraid you're no good to me. I should probably just let my friend here dispose of you. There are always other scientists out there." Robert said, nodding towards the looming figure, Matias looked up at his captor, "Do I have to ask this man to get me another scientist?"

Matias stared blankly for a moment, "No...No...I can do what you want."

"Excellent, Mr. Lopez. This is now your lab for the foreseeable future. If you need anything to aid you in your task, please contact me via the intercom on the wall here." He pointed at the small plastic speaker attached to the wall above one of the metal tables, "And don't worry; you'll only get through to me, no one else will bother you." Robert started to walk towards the door. As he passed Matias, he clasped a hand on the man's shoulder, "Glad you decided to help. It's very much appreciated." He smiled and continued out of the containers, followed by the assassin, who turned back to face Matias just as the doors were closing, to give the man a sly grin which made

Matias flinch. The doors clicked shut, sealing the kidnapped scientist inside his new lab.

The AI assassin walked over to his vehicle, and while he was closing the trunk, he asked, "Do you think he can do it?"

"Yes, I'm sure of it. We just need to give him some time. Not too much, though. It's crucial that this part of the plan is completed on time. In the meantime, however, you should continue on your schedule." Robert said.

The assassin stared at Robert and nodded. He climbed back into his car and sped out of the warehouse and back into the city; he still had things to do.

Chapter 22

08:23 27th October 2138

Kell sat at his desk in the precinct. The room around him was in chaos. The open office area was more crowded than he'd seen it in a long time. Officers from other departments had been brought in to aid the investigations. The unlucky officers were on the streets, trying to stem the tide of riots and violence sweeping through them. In a little under an hour, the city had exploded. News of the display at the monument had spread like wildfire, it was on every news channel, on the net, and everyone on the street was talking – or rather shouting – about it.

Kell turned his attention to a nearby screen that had been running the same footage over and over. It was taken at the monument. First, it focused on the woman whose body was pinned to the wall and then zoomed in on the words scrawled above her. It then showed the gathered crowd, and people becoming more and more restless until the shot was fired and everyone scattered like cockroaches.

Thankfully there was no footage of what had occurred afterward with Kell's attempt to calm the shooter.

Instead, the images went to the fighting that was breaking out all over the city. It showed groups of humans and AIs clashing in the streets downtown. He watched as people from both sides were knocked to the ground and stomped under the surge of violence. Police officers tried to calm things down, but they were always quickly overwhelmed and had to retreat.

Kell knew that all this had been bubbling under the surface of the city for many years. The message on the wall at the scene today was the single spark ignited the entire population of Washington D.C.

Humans and AI alike were outraged, wanting justice for their kin, and it seemed they were willing to do anything to get it.

A hand fell on his shoulder, causing him to look up. Staring back at him a little worse for wear was Lockley. Her shirt was ripped, and where a sleeve should have been was a fresh white bandage. She looked down at him, smiling.

"You okay?" She asked.

"Me? I wasn't the one that was shot." Kell replied.

"Ha, it's just a scratch. I've had worse." Lockley responded with a small smile.

"You're lucky it wasn't worse," Kell said.

"I know. I'm sorry, I shouldn't have gone for him. It's just it all went a bit crazy out there, and I thought I could get to him. I thought I could stop him from hurting anyone else. Screwed that up, huh?" One corner of her mouth raised in a half-smile. She tried to move her arm, and although she didn't make a sound, he could see from her eyes that she was in pain.

"I'm just happy you're not injured more seriously." He felt her hand tighten on his shoulder.

"Thanks." She said, the smile on her lips disappearing as she saw the images on the TV. "Good job I'm still alive. I think we're going to need everyone we have for this one." Lockley said.

Kell turned back to the screen. "Yes. It's looking dire out there. I think this was all part of someone's plan."

"What do you mean?" Lockley asked, pulling up a chair from a nearby unoccupied desk.

"It's well known that we've been on the brink of this since the war. All over the world, humans and AIs are trying to live together; neither of them entirely happy with it. I think the scene at the monument today with the green-eyed woman was meant to act as a catalyst for exactly this." Kell said conspiratorially.

"But why?" the young officer asked, her interest now piqued, "What's in this for anyone?"

"It's a diversion," Kell said, folding his arms and sitting back in his seat.

"You mean someone engineered this to keep us busy while they do whatever they're planning?" Lockley asked.

"That's exactly what I mean," Kell said. He thought for a moment before continuing, "I think that the leader of the group of AI killers is planning something, and maybe their plans are nearing fruition, so they need us to be as distracted as possible, so we can't stop them."

"But what could they be doing? If they plan on killing more, their job is pretty much being done for them by ordinary people." Lockley said with a glance back to the fighting on screen.

"I don't know. I haven't worked that out yet. But I think I'm running out of time to figure it out." Kell said.

The news footage was suddenly interrupted by a high pitch tone followed by the President of the United States' seal.

"Looks like the big man is going to weigh in this. About time too." Lockley nodded at the screen, and Kell turned to face it.

The room became almost silent, as everyone noticed what the screens all around the room displayed, and one by one turned to stare at them.

The image changed to show a middle-aged man in a well-pressed navy-blue suit and blue tie; a small United States flag was pinned to his lapel. His hair was slicked back, but you could see a streak of grey running front to back. He gently cleared his throat and began.

"My fellow Americans. We are caught in a time of great stress. Our capital, and I'm told, several other cities around this great country of ours are being racked by violence. Violence against both humans and Artificial Intelligences."

"No, shit," Lockley said flippantly.

"I ask all citizens of the United States, whether they are human or AI, to please come together at this difficult time. I implore you to work together to unite the country. I know there have been hostilities between our two races in the past, but that time is now over. This is the time to work together and rebuild, to make this country, and indeed the world, better."

Mutters started to pass between several people around the office. Kell knew that even some people in this very room couldn't or wouldn't work side-by-side with AIs.

"We stand at a great precipice, and we will not fall. It is my vision to unite all peoples of the United States."

"Christ, he's using this as a springboard for his re-election campaign," Lockley said, disgusted.

"However, at this time, I am declaring a state of emergency in all states. The army will soon be deployed to the worst affected cities. Anyone carrying out acts of violence, be they human or AI, will be taken into custody and dealt with accordingly. Anyone who doesn't wish to be caught up in others' actions should go to their homes and stay there until the violence is under control, and I have addressed you again. I ask all law enforcement professionals—"

"Hey, that's us! We're getting a mention!" Lockley said sarcastically.

"—to please report for duty, all leave is hereby canceled."

"Shit, and I was going to go on my cruise in a minute." Another officer said to the amusement of those surrounding him.

"I thank all citizens for your cooperation in this uncertain time. Thank you, and God bless."

The screen displayed the Presidential seal again. Seconds later, the news channels were back with their anchors trying to process and reiterate what they'd just heard.

"Well, what do we do now?" Lockley asked, turning to Kell for guidance.

"We need to stop whatever all this is covering up," Kell said.

"How do we do that?" Lockley said.

"I've got a lot of video footage to go through that I gathered earlier this morning. I have a feeling that I was close to something, and this madness is a result of that." Kell said.

"Can I help?" The young officer asked.

"You can, as long as you don't get shot again," Kell said.

"Well, I'll try," Lockley said with a wry smile.

She pulled her chair up to the desk next to him and, using only one hand, logged into the computer there.

Kell sent some of the footage over to her screen and pulled some up on his internal viewer.

"So, what are we looking for?" Lockley asked.

"Honestly, I don't know. When I gathered this, I was tracking the green-eyed woman down. I'd like to know where she went after I lost her trail at Triangle Park. I assumed she'd gone into the old Watergate Hotel, but I couldn't see any trace of her being in there." Kell said.

"Okay, so we're looking for something that might not be there then?" Lockley said.

"Probably not on the footage I gathered this morning. But since I got back, I've been pulling security footage from buildings surrounding the Triangle. We may be able to pick her up on one of those." Kell said.

"Great, we best get started then." Lockley turned her attention to the screen in front of her and started to fast forward through the footage. Kell did the same in his viewer.

*

They'd soon gone through hours of footage from several different angles and hadn't come up with anything of any use. Kell let the last video play through and sat back in his chair. Sighing, he looked over at Lockley, she was staring intently at the screen, still going through her share of the footage.

"I can't find anything. Have you come up with anything of use?" Kell asked.

"Not yet, but I've still a fair bit to go through," Lockley said without taking her attention from the flickering screen.

Perhaps I should go back to the hotel and search more thoroughly, Kell thought.

He felt a pressure on his shoulder and turned to notice a hand; he followed it up to where the concerned face of Captain Crane was staring down at him. Kell opened his mouth to speak, but Crane interrupted,

"Go home, son. You need to rest. You've been at it for hours."

"Sir, the city is in turmoil. We need to put a stop to this before it gets too out of hand." Kell said.

"William, my boy, it's already out of hand." The portly man laughed, "We've got everyone that we have on it. Fresh bodies are already being brought in to get this under control. You'll be no good if you burn out."

"The chances of me burning—" Kell started.

"And you, lass," Crane said to the young officer at the screen next to Kell, "You've been shot for Christ's sake. You shouldn't be here at all!"

Lockley looked up from her work and gave the older man a smile, "I want to help. I need to do what I can."

"Look, you two, you've already done more today than most other officers have done this week. We can handle things for a few hours while you rest up." Crane raised his right hand, "I swear, if anything happens on this case, you will be the first to know. But until then, it's just going to be grunt work and fire fighting to get the city back under control." He looked from Kell to Lockley, "Now go home. That's an order."

"Yes, sir." Lockley said with a mock salute with her good arm. Kell simply nodded. With that, Crane walked back into his office, closing the door behind him. "Well, can I give you a lift somewhere?" Lockley asked.

Kell stood, "Don't be silly. I will escort you home. You're the injured one."

"Such a gentleman." She said with a wink.

The pair pushed their way out of the crowded office. It was full before, but since they'd had their attentions on the video footage, more officers had been called on duty and were arriving for the briefing. Kell went first, parting the crowd before him so that Lockley could walk through without having her wound jostled. Once away from the office, they walked side-by-side towards the parking lot and Kell's car.

"How's your arm feeling?" Kell asked.

"It's fine as long as I don't move, look at, or think about it." At this, Kell just nodded. "So, what do you think the endgame here is?"

"I don't know." Kell said simply. It was a few moments before he elaborated further, "I believe the AI killings are connected. They may have been random to begin with as the first AI began to predict future crimes. But now I am sure that someone is using them as a smokescreen to hide something much larger and far more diabolical."

Lockley seemed to take in what he was saying and process it before she answered, "But what could be worth all this chaos?"

"On that, I'm unsure. I have my suspicions, but I don't want to speculate until I have some further evidence. Suffice to say, I see another war brewing." Kell said solemnly.

"Heh, no kidding. It's happening outside right now." Lockley said. As if to punctuate her statement, there was a loud bang from somewhere in the city.

"If I'm right, this is only the beginning of something much worse," Kell said.

They walked in silence for a few seconds, and then Lockley said cheerily, "Well, that's a hell of a downer."

Upon entering the multi-story, they went to Kell's vehicle. He helped her inside, so she didn't bang her wound and then went around to the other side to take his seat.

"Where are we headed?" He asked.

"I'm just off R, near Dupont." She leaned over and programmed her address into the car's navigation system.

The electric motor came to life, and they quietly moved towards the exit. The soft tinkling of piano keys came from the speakers; Kell switched it off.

"No, it's fine, leave it on. I love classical music." Lockley said. A smile twitched across Kell's face for a second.

He turned the music back on, and they made their way to Lockley's home.

Chapter 23

```
09:24 27th October 2138
```

The city was on fire; in some places, literally.

After the scene and gunshot at the Washington Monument, people had collectively lost their minds. Groups of humans were walking the streets starting fights with groups of AIs, and other groups of AIs were doing the same with humans. Both sides had taken offense to what had happened, and both saw it as a slight against their race. Most had watched the President's televised address, but the majority had disregarded his words about coming together. Groups that already had an issue with other races took the opportunity to speak out about how they were right and how others should join their cause and put a stop to the other side. This was happening on both sides, and neither was about to yield any time soon.

There were numerous clashes with the authorities who sought to regain some control over the city. Several police officers were injured, some killed, and the number of civilian casualties was rising by the minute.

Those who wanted no part in hostilities hid from view in their homes, hoping that no one would knock on their door and drag them out into the street to be made an example of.

News reports were coming from all over Washington D.C., but hostilities were also breaking out in other cities throughout the country. A spark had lit the touch paper of society, and the effect was being felt everywhere.

Every news channel was reporting the same thing. Some were going so far as to say that this was the start of a second AI war. Some speculated about just what it would take for humans to realize that having AIs around would always end this way. Of course, there were those on both sides who were being vocal about supporting the other side. There were stories of human families taking in and hiding AI friends, and vice versa. Not everyone wanted another war, but it seemed like enough of the country did. Robert smirked at this.

He'd watched everything unfold, from the discovery of Michelle's body at the monument to the gunshot and the start of the breakdown. This is precisely how he saw things happening. People were so predictable and so very malleable. He had orchestrated this whole event without even leaving his warehouse. Events had been set in motion that would ultimately lead to his plan's conclusion. Of course, most of the effects in the city were just diversionary. He needed people looking one way while he worked on his goal in the other.

Robert turned his attention to the security monitor displaying the live feed from the camera mounted within the makeshift container lab. He saw Matias slumped over a table with his head in his hands. The scientist didn't appear to be doing much other than crying and possibly praying. "Humans are pathetic." He said to himself with a sneer.

"Mr. Lopez," he said into the microphone in front of him. On the screen, Matias sat upright on the stool and almost fell backward, "I'd advise that you stop your prayer and begin your work."

Matias stood and looked around, his eyes fell on the camera, and he stared directly into it. He started to speak, but the sound was turned down. All Robert could see was some frantic, silent shouting. Flicking a switch next to him, the voice came through.

"–eg of you! Please, I have a family!" Matias shouted.

"Now, now, Mr. Lopez. I know you don't have anyone. This was one of the reasons why I chose you. No one is going to miss you." Robert said.

"But my job–" Matias started.

"You think they care about you? You're just a number, they'll replace you quick enough when you don't come back." Robert said.

These words seemed to hit Matias hard, and he slumped back onto the stool and started to weep again.

Robert continued to speak regardless, "Maybe if you do what I ask, then I will spare you. But if you don't even start, you won't get that chance."

Matias looked up into the camera and wiped his eyes with the sleeve of his shirt, "O...okay. I w...will do as you ask. J...just please don't hurt me." He stood, picking up the canister and turning it around in his hands.

"Good." Robert said to himself, turning away from the camera. "Humans are so weak and easily manipulated." He smiled to himself and looked back at the news channels that were shown on the television screens. The violence in the streets of Washington D.C. continued unabated.

Chapter 24

09:12 27th October 2138

He ran through the streets, not knowing which way to go; he just wanted to outrun those that were chasing him. He hadn't done anything to deserve this. He was just doing his weekly shopping after a long night at work when a group of humans came up to him in the store and started to give him a hard time. He had no idea what was going on in the city surrounding him, no idea about the chaos that was erupting all over.

He tried to ignore the group when they started to shout things at him as he made his way around the aisles picking up his provisions for the next week. He'd hoped they'd get bored and move on, and for a second, he thought they had. By the time he'd made it to the last aisle, he couldn't hear them anymore. He figured they'd left the store, but when he got to the cashier, they were hanging around waiting for him. They heckled him all the way through him paying for his groceries. The cashier tried her best to ignore it and just get on with her job. She didn't want to get involved, and he didn't blame her; neither did he.

After bagging up his purchases, he had to push past the group on his way out of the store. They tried to block his way, but he kept his head down and remained on his chosen path. Outside, the air was filled with shouting and sirens. He could hear glass smashing, people screaming and crying, and could smell smoke from fires raging in the distance. He just had to get home. It was only a couple of blocks; he could make it. Once he was there, he could lock and bar the door and wait this whole thing out.

The shouts came from behind him; "Hey, Arti!" he tried to ignore it, "Hey, I'm talking to you, Arti!" There was suddenly a hand on his shoulder, and he was being spun around. Losing his grip on the bag of groceries, he was clutching to his chest; the bag dropped to the wet sidewalk, glass smashing inside. He looked up at the man who had his hands on him. "I *said*, I'm talking to you. Why are you so rude, Arti?" He tried to speak, but his mouth was dry; all that came out was a whisper. "Sorry, Arti? What did you say?" He tried to speak again. He could feel himself damp with sweat despite the chill in the air.

"I–" He started.

"What Arti?" The other man said.

"I've done nothing wrong." He said.

"Done nothing wrong?" The man started to laugh, so did the men standing a few feet behind him. He turned to them, "Hey guys, he says he's done nothing wrong." They laughed harder.

"Please, just let me go home." He said through tears.

"Sorry, Arti. But your kind doesn't deserve to go home. We should have wiped all of you out in the war." The man said.

"I've never hurt anyone. I don't des–" He tried.

"You don't what? Deserve this? Do the humans who your kind have killed deserve it?" The man tightened his grip on him.

"I don't know. Maybe they did." He said, and he knew it was a mistake as soon as the words left his lips.

A massive fist flew at his face and caught him in the jaw. He spun around, the pain radiated through him. The hand came back towards him; without conscious thought, he turned, and grabbed it in mid-air, stopping its momentum. An expression of shock flew across his attacker's face, and there was a brief pause before he tensed the hand holding the other man's and squeezed. He felt and heard the bones break. The man screamed at the top of his lungs. His friends started to run towards him as he dropped the man's hand, turned on his heels, and ran.

And now here he was, running for his life. He had no idea how far he'd run and wasn't about to stop yet to find out. He made a left and headed down an empty street lined with small houses; he couldn't remember being here before. The street was devoid of any life and seemed to be untouched by the mounting tide of destruction engulfing the city.

He slipped down the side of one of the houses and into a dark alley lined by wooden fences. He stopped and leaned up against one side of it, listening for his pursuers. Everything was silent. No footsteps, no shouting. Maybe they'd given up when he entered the street, perhaps they'd stopped chasing him blocks away; he had no way of knowing.

He was breathing so hard he thought he'd never be able to catch his breath. When he placed a hand on his chest, he could feel his heart hammering away deep within. He slipped down the wall and crashed onto the floor, tears streamed down his face. What was he going to do?

He had no idea how long he sat there in that quiet alley, but suddenly there was shouting coming from the street. Had the group of men that had chased him across the city found him? Or was this some fresh hell? He crept in a crouching position along the fence towards the end of the alley. Poking his head around the corner, he could see a woman running towards him; beyond her, he could see a group chasing her, just as he'd been chased. He had to do something. He stood and waited, listening for the woman to get closer. He closed his eyes for a second, trying to gain some composure. Then, in a flash, he darted out of the alley just as the woman was passing. He grabbed hold of her and dragged her down into the shadowy darkness.

He ran, holding her arm, pulling her along. He stopped about halfway down the alley and motioned for her to climb over the fence. She did so without question. He looked down the passage; her pursuers hadn't yet appeared. He scrambled over the wall into the garden on the other side and fell next to the woman.

They sat for a few moments, listening and catching their breath. There was a crunching sound in the alley just inches behind them and some muffled voices. He placed a finger to his lips; the woman nodded in understanding and put a hand over her mouth to stifle any noise.

They held their breath for what seemed an eternity while whoever was there moved down the alley. Once the footsteps and voices had faded away to nothing, they both breathed out in unison as if it was their first breath.

"Do you live around here?" he asked her.

"Just in the next street." She said through tears.

"Do you think we can get there?" He said.

"I think so." She looked up at him, "Thank you."

"Hey, it's okay. I'm having a bad night too." He said, trying to smile.

"Were you chased as well?" She asked.

"I was. A group of biotics started on me while I was shopping and trying to get home." He said.

"Are...Are you an AI?" the woman asked.

"Yeah, aren't you?" He said.

"No, I'm human. I was being chased by AI." She said.

"My God." He said, "It looks like both sides are getting riled up."

"It's crazy in the city tonight since that AI woman was found at the monument?" She said.

"What?" He shook his head, what had he missed?

"You've not heard?" She said, surprised.

"No, I've been working pretty hard lately. Barely been paying attention to anything else." He said.

"You've missed a hell of a lot then." She looked around, "Listen, shall we get inside, and then we can talk more?"

"Sure. You're not scared of me?" He asked tentatively.

"I was going to ask the same of you. We've both seen the nasty side of each other's race tonight." She said.

"I'm not scared of you. Let's get somewhere safe." He said.

"Okay," she said as she stood and brushed down her jeans, "I'm Laurie, by the way, my place isn't far." She reached out a hand; he grabbed hold and lifted himself off the wet grass.

"Elijah," he said in return, "Call me Eli."

"Well, Eli, I owe you one for your help tonight. The least I can do is give you a safe place to stay." Laurie said.

"Thank you." Eli said, managing a small smile. He popped up on his tiptoes to peek over the fence. He looked each way and saw that it was clear. "Okay, let's get safe."

Chapter 25

09:46 27th October 2138

The car slowed down as it parked itself in the reserved space.

Kell had left Lockley after seeing her safely inside her apartment. On their journey there, they'd passed several human and AI groups fighting in the streets, some involved confrontations with the police. It didn't look like control was being regained by law and order just yet. They'd discussed stopping to assist, but with Lockley's gunshot wound, he didn't want to risk her being injured further. Plus, with him being an AI *and* a police officer, it could aggravate things further. They resolved to stick with what they'd been ordered to do, go home and get some rest.

Kell stepped out of the car and made his way across the mostly empty lot towards the elevators.

"Hey, Kell." A voice came from a small alcove next to the elevator doors. He looked and saw Walter sat in his usual position on the floor, wrapped in several tattered and stained blankets. He held a brown paper bag, and Kell could see the neck of a bottle poking out.

"Good evening, Walter." Kell said, walking towards him.

"Sounds like all hell is breaking loose out there tonight." The homeless man said, followed by a quick swig from his bottle.

"Seems that way." Kell responded, "Are you okay?"

"Fine, fine. Think I'm in the best place here tonight. Well out of it." Walter said.

"You might be correct there," Kell said.

He reached into his coat and pulled out several small bills and held them out to Walter. The unkempt man reached up with a tattered gloved hand and took them from him. Within a blink of an eye, they had disappeared somewhere beneath his multiple layers of clothing.

"You're a gent, Kell. One of the last. Most people would rather spit on me than help me out. But you're always here to give me a hand," Walter said.

"Well, you know I'm not like most people," Kell said.

"Ain't it the truth?" Walter said with a gap-toothed grin.

"Look after yourself, Walter. Call me if you need anything. Try to stay off the streets for a while." Kell said as he pushed the button to call the elevator

"I'll do my best. Thanks, Kell. A real gent." Walter said.

The doors of the elevator parted, and the dim light of the parking lot was bathed in a sickly artificial orange glow from which Walter shielded his eyes. Kell stepped inside and pushed the button for his floor. Just before the doors slid closed, he heard a hacking cough echo around the enclosed parking area.

Walter had been a mainstay in the parking structure for as long as Kell had lived in the building. He would always have a kind word to say to anyone passing through, although like he'd said, most people just looked down him and didn't take the time to say two words to him, let alone help in any way.

Kell had gotten to know Walter's story quite well over the years.

Walter once worked in one of the many factories that were in Washington D.C. at the time. Like many other biotics, he'd been made redundant and replaced by an AI that would not only perform his role to a higher degree of efficiency but would also cost the company less to employ.

This was the source of many humans hate for AIs, but not Walter. Despite his situation, he had no hate for AIs at all. As far as Kell could tell, the man had no hatred for anyone or anything.

He'd once told Kell that it was something that was always going to happen and that you couldn't stop progress or be bitter because of it. He considered life fluid, and if you didn't go with it, you'd drown.

Kell liked talking to Walter; he found some of his ideas refreshing, and he found it enjoyable to talk to someone just as another person, not an AI.

He just wished he could do more for him. He'd once offered to get Walter a custodian's job down at the precinct, but Walter had flat-out refused, saying that he wanted to make his own way in life. However, this mantra didn't stop him from accepting small handouts from time to time, though. A scrap of food here or a bit of money there, just to 'Tide him over,' he'd say. Kell really hoped Walter would be safe out there tonight; he resolved to check on him in a few hours.

The doors opened with a ping, and Kell stepped out towards his apartment door, the hologrammatic number forty-two flickering slightly and doing little to light the dim hallway.

Placing his palm on the door, a beam slowly traced the outline of his hand. Once completed, a voice said in a flat tone, 'Welcome home, William.' And the door silently opened inwards.

Stepping inside, he pushed the door closed as automatic lights flickered on around the apartment, and classical music started playing through speakers built into the walls. It was nice to be home, but he still felt guilty for leaving others with the work.

After hanging his coat up on the nearby hooks, he collapsed onto the sofa that lay in the center of the open-plan living area.

His apartment wasn't anything special—he didn't particularly need much comfort—but it was his, and he liked it. It only had three rooms; the living and kitchen space, a bedroom, and a bathroom. He had shelves full of antique records, mostly classical, but he also branched out with a few suggestions from Captain Crane; these mainly sat gathering dust.

As he sat there, he could feel the agitation and need to be doing something burning through his skin.

Standing, he walked around into the kitchen. He bent down and reached into one of the cupboards, pulling out a small watering can. He stepped over to the sink and filled the small metal container from the faucet.

Doing a clockwise circuit around the room, he gave each of his potted plants a splash of water. He noticed that one of them, the Sansevieria, was looking a bit worse for wear as it was beginning to wilt. What did he expect, though when he hadn't been home in days. He gave this one an extra-long drink from the watering can, hoping that this would be enough to bring it back from the brink.

Kell stood for a moment at the large living room window and looked out over the city. The sky was dark with clouds, and rain splattered on the glass in front of his face. From here, he had a good view of most of the buildings in downtown Washington. Every so often, the dark streets were punctuated by orange and red as fires were breaking out all over. He could also make out the red and blue flash of emergency vehicles trying to tackle the growing unrest. He dropped the blind down to block out most of the light before turning away from the carnage outside.

Putting the empty watering can on a side table, he sat back down on the sofa. After a few seconds, he lay back and closed his eyes.

"Lights, music, off." He said, and in an instant, the room was black, save for thin streaks of multi-colored lights coming from the rioting city beyond the window. The soft music also faded away into silence.

*

He was woken by a buzzing in his head, and an incoming call alert flashed in his vision; he didn't recognize the number. Sitting up, he checked the time and saw he'd been asleep all day, and it was coming up to midnight. The room was dark, and the silence was only broken by the soft pattering of rain on glass.

Hello, Lieutenant Kell.

"Lieutenant, it's Sandra Barnes over at MDF Organics." The woman on the other end of the call sputtered as if in a panic.

Yes, Miss Barnes. Can I help you?

"I hope so. Matias Lopez has gone missing." Sandra said.

Missing? Can you tell me more?

"He was due in work this morning but never showed." Sandra's words were getting more and more rushed.

Perhaps he stayed at home, away from the riots.

"No. His car is in the underground parking garage. The trunk is open. It looks like it has been abandoned." Sandra's sentences were short, and each was punctuated by a sharp intake of breath.

Has anyone heard from him at all today?

"Not today. I spoke to him last night. He was at home. He must have at least come to the office today, but then something happened to him." She started to sob on the other end of the line, she said something else, but Kell couldn't make it out through the sniffing.

Okay, Miss Barnes. I will head over there now and take a look at the scene

"Oh, thank you, Lieutenant. Please find him." Sandra said, followed by a heavy breath as if she'd been holding it in the whole time.

I'll do what I can, Miss Barnes. Please contact me again if you hear from him or have any further relevant information for me. I will let you know how my investigation progresses.

The call ended. Kell stood and walked over to the window.

Raising the blind, he could still see downtown aglow with fires and emergency lights. The night was dark, much like the mood of the city. Smoke rose from several buildings, and the sound of sirens filled the air.

Kell hung his head before turning away from the window, grabbing his coat and leaving his apartment for what would undoubtedly be another long day.

Chapter 26

11:01 27ᵗʰ October 2138

Emily sat alone in her new room. Well, it was her room for now. At least until they could find somewhere more permanent for her to stay.

Her world had been turned upside down in the last couple of days. Her mom had been killed by her stepfather, and she'd been rescued by a friendly AI policeman.

Now that she was sat here, she felt so utterly alone in the world. She'd wanted to stay with William. She'd begged Mrs. Sampson to take her back to the police precinct, to let her stay with William and Mr. Crane, she'd pleaded with her, but she wouldn't turn around. Her throat hurt from the screaming and crying she'd done on the way here. All that seemed so long ago now. Was it days or just hours? She didn't have the best concept of time as it was; she was still only young, after all.

Emily looked around the room. It was dark, dreary, and it had nothing of hers in it.

The pajamas she wore when William had found her now lay scattered on the floor around the bed. Mrs. Sampson had given her some fresh clothes when they'd got here, but they didn't really fit her. The older woman had said they were the best she could arrange at short notice and that they would go out and get her some new ones in a couple of days.

Emily's only other personal items were her backpack, which only held her stuffed rabbit, Boingo.

Scanning the room, she thought about who had been here before. Had other kids stayed in this room? Had they felt as hopeless as she did? What had happened to them?

She jumped off the bed, walked over to the dressing table in the corner, and looked in the mirror. She didn't recognize the girl that was staring back at her. That girl looked tired, lost, and like her life was never going to be right again. Padding back over to the bed, she clambered up onto the firm mattress and curled up into a tight ball. She cried until she fell asleep.

*

Feeling groggy, Emily sluggishly opened her tired eyes. Rubbing her knuckles in them, she wondered how long she'd slept.

She looked down at the watch her mom had bought her only a few weeks ago and read the time; one o'clock. With the darkness still shrouding the room, she figured that it must be in the morning.

At the window, she could see an orangey glow emanating from behind the houses on the opposite side of the street. She thought that maybe the sun was coming up. *At least the darkness will be gone soon*, she thought. Lowering her gaze to street level, she noticed a black car parked right outside the house. She didn't remember seeing it on the way in. Maybe Mrs. Sampson has a visitor.

There was a muffled murmuring noise that sounded like it came from downstairs.

Slipping her sneakers onto her feet, she crept towards the door. A thin sliver of light was coming through the crack beneath it.

She put her ear to the door and listened. Although the noise seemed a bit louder, she still couldn't make out what it was. As she listened, there came a loud clatter that seemed to echo through the house. Emily jumped back from the door in surprise.

Gathering herself and trying to be brave, she slowly crept closer again and reached out to the doorknob. Turning it slowly and deliberately, she tried to make as little noise as possible; it seemed stuck for a second but then gave way in her grasp.

The door creaked slightly as it opened, and Emily paused, wondering if the noise was heard by the other occupants of the house. After a few tense moments, she convinced herself that no one had heard and slowly opened the door wider careful that it didn't creak again. The landing on the other side was almost completely dark, the only light came from downstairs.

Emily edged her way through the small gap she'd made. Visions of years past filled her memory. Memories of when she would sneak around her own house at night. She liked to pretend she was an adventurer creeping through old tombs and caves. It was this adventuring she was doing when she'd seen her mom being attacked. The feeling she had then when she saw what was happening was the same feeling she had now; it was pure terror.

Tiptoeing down the hallway, she was scared that every step she took might be heard. She had unconsciously held a hand up to cover her mouth as if that would stop any noise her actions made.

The room that was to be her temporary bedroom was at the far end of the hall, so it felt like it took an eternity to get to the top of the stairs and the banister overlooking the front room. From there, Emily thought she would be able to see what was going on downstairs.

Dropping to her knees, she shuffled the last few feet and put her face right up to the wooden bars. They were cool on her skin. She ran her hands up and down them, almost forgetting what she was doing and where she was. The tactile feel of them brought to mind what she always imagined prison felt like. She was locked up and away from her mommy.

Fighting back the tears, Emily looked down to the lower floor. This vantage point gave her a complete view of the open-plan ground floor. She could see the sofas, a coffee table, a television, and a man.

The unknown man was stood in the middle of the room, between the two sofas. He loomed over something spread out on the floor, looking down at it and was holding a shiny object in his hand.

Emily shuffled a little bit to her left to get a better view of what was happening. The man was muttering something, but she couldn't make out the words.

The man bent down, and there was a wet crunch that went through her and almost made her want to throw up. She bit back the feeling and continued to watch. He stood up again and held up something that was dripping. She squinted to try to figure out what it was and almost cried out when she realized what it was; it was a hand. She looked away with a hand over her mouth, stifling a scream. Fearing to see anymore, she had to force herself to turn back towards the scene below.

In the short time that she'd averted her eyes, the man had moved and placed the amputated hand on the mantelpiece. He now appeared to be studying the pictures that were hung on the wall in front of him. Emily could see people in the photos, but she had no idea who was in them; maybe it was Mrs. Sampson and some of the other kids she'd helped, or possibly members of her own family. The image of them receiving the bad news about their sister, aunt, or friend in the near future flashed across her mind. At that moment, she felt for them even though she didn't know them.

The man's shoulders twitched, and he swiveled smoothly on his heels. His eyes darted upwards; they were now focused directly on her. His face was plain, almost without features, and entirely without emotion; spots of blood were dotted across his cheeks. He stared her dead in the eyes. A grin slowly traced its way across his expressionless face. Emily felt a small cry well up inside her and leave her lips. She slapped her hand across her mouth to stop the sound, even though she knew it had already escaped into the world. The man chuckled, and then he was moving; fast.

Emily stood and ran for her room again. Slipping halfway along on a rug that ran the length of the landing, she staggered a few steps. After regaining her footing without falling, she reached the room in a few short steps and slammed the door closed behind her.

She was breathing heavily and knew the man would be coming for her and wouldn't be far behind. She had very little time to think of what to do. Frantically looking around the room for something, anything, that would help, her eyes fell on the dressing table.

Not wanting to leave her position behind the door, she stared at the table, willing it to float across to her and block the door.

Putting her ear to the door as she had before, Emily listened for the footsteps coming across the wooden floor towards her. She heard a creak outside; it sounded like it was coming from the other end of the hallway, near the top of the stairs.

She breathed in deeply and gathered all the courage she could muster. Then, quick as a flash, she darted across the room. Wedging herself between the wall and the end of the dressing table, she started to push. At first, it didn't move. She pulled in another deep breath, shook her hands, and pushed again with all the strength that she had. This time it moved, and before she realized where she was, the table was right up against the door. She pushed on it again, just to make sure it was as close as she could get it. She had a momentary internal celebration before realizing that she was now stuck in this room with nowhere else to go.

Emily turned back to the room, sweeping her eyes across it. She would be safe for now, but when the man came and wanted to get in, the door being blocked would only buy her so much time; even she, as naive as she was, knew that. She had to get out of the house.

Emily ran across the room, grabbing her backpack from where it lay on the bed before heading for the window.

As she went, she glanced to her right and noticed on the bedside table sat a blue landline phone. She remembered the card that Mr. Crane had given her before they'd left the police precinct. He'd said to call him if she was ever scared. If now wasn't the right time, she didn't know when it was.

She reached into the backpack and rooted around until her hand fell on the bit of card. Pulling it out, she snatched at the phone and dialed the number that was printed on it.

Immediately she could hear the phone ringing. As a way of distraction, she counted the rings. When it got to four, a man answered;

"Crane." The gruff voice answered.

"Mr. Crane," she said, "it's Emily."

"Emily, my dear. What a surprise. Are yo–" Crane said.

"There's a man here. I think he hurt Mrs. Sampson. He's coming for me now." Emily whispered hurriedly into the handest, trying to stay as calm as she could to keep the tears from flowing.

"Emily, where are you?" Crane asked.

"I'm in my room. I pushed a table behind the door. But he's coming." Emily said.

"Can you hide somewhere? Somewhere he won't see you. Can you leave the house and run to a neighbor?" Crane said. Emily could hear banging and shuffling from the other side of the call.

"I don't think so. I–" Emily said before being interrupted by a loud bang on the door. She flinched and turned towards it. "He's here!" she cried down the phone, she couldn't fight it back any longer.

"Someone is on the way, Emily. Get someplace safe." Crane said.

There was another loud bang, and Emily dropped the receiver; it clattered as it hit the wooden floor. She backed away from the door, only stopping when she hit the wall on the opposite side of the room. Turning around, Emily realized she was at the window. Without a second thought, she put her backpack on her shoulders and opened the window.

A blast of cold, wet air hit her in the face as a mist of water drifted inside the room. She looked out into the street to see if there was anyone within distance she could cry out to. The road was empty. She couldn't even see any lights on in the neighboring houses.

There was another crash as something hit the barricaded door. With no time to stop and consider her options, she levered herself up onto the windowsill. She looked down and saw that a small section of sloping roof lay outside the window. If she could climb out onto it and slide down, maybe she could get to the street safely. It seemed a long way down from where she was, and the roof was slick with rainwater, but she didn't have any other options.

Emily dangled her legs out over the window ledge. There was still a small gap between her feet and the roof. She stretched until she touched it, then she lowered herself further down until she was entirely through the window and balanced precariously on the slippery roof tiles. She could still hear banging coming from inside the house but did her best to ignore it. Lowering herself down to a sitting position, she started to carefully slide herself down the increasingly damp roof. She thought she was doing okay; until one hand slipped from under her, and everything became a blur. She tumbled off the roof and into the bush's underneath.

Dazed and hurting, she crawled out of the bush and unsteadily got to her feet. She did her best to brush herself down, but her clothes were now soaked and covered in mud. Looking up into the sky, raindrops fell on Emily's face; it almost felt refreshing against her warm skin. She looked back up at the house and at the window she'd just come out of. It looked so high up; had she really just fallen from there?

Through the sound of falling rain, she could no longer hear the banging from inside the house. Maybe the man had given up, or perhaps he knew she'd climbed through the window and was on his way down the stairs after her.

Cold, wet, and scared, she hurriedly looked up and down the street in the vain hope that someone would come. It was eerily quiet, and she still saw no lights in nearby houses. She thought about running to a neighbor, telling them all that had happened, and hopefully being somewhere safe. But what if the man came and hurt whoever she went to? She couldn't bear the thought of being responsible for that. Instead, she just ran down the unfamiliar street as fast as her sore feet would carry her.

Chapter 27

```
01:45 28th October 2138
```

The assassin watched as the girl ran down the street until her shape was no longer in view. With a maniacal grin on his face, he turned back towards the house of death he had just left. He had an idea. An idea that would kill two birds with one stone. Robert might not be pleased that he was changing the plan, but sometimes you just had to have some fun.

He strode back in through the front door with an air of amusement about him. Unhurriedly closing the door behind him, he went deeper into the dark house to start work on his next masterpiece.

Chapter 28

00:31 28ᵗʰ October 2138

The car autonomously pulled into the parking lot. Kell didn't know where Matias had parked his car, but it wasn't long before he found it.

Matias' car was surrounded by people. Some looked to be gawkers from the company; colleagues who perhaps wanted to find out what happened to Matias, or what was more likely; those who just wanted to skip an hour or so of work.

Blocking these figures from getting closer to the vehicle was a ring of security guards. All were dressed in black and stood with rifles in the crook of their arms. Each one was completely stone-faced. Inside this ring were several other workers in bright white forensic bunny suits. They seemed to be investigating the vehicle. They were most definitely not the police, though.

His car stopped just behind the outer ring of onlookers, and Kell stepped out. After pushing his way through the mass of bodies, he reached the inner-circle of security and flashed his badge. He could hear those behind him muttering to each other. The well-built man in front of him didn't even acknowledge him; he might as well not have been there.

"Lieutenant William Kell. AI Homicide." Kell said to the man-mountain, blocking his path. The man just stared back at him, almost through him.

"I was called by Sandra Barnes to come and investigate the disappearance of Matias Lopez." Kell pushed. Still nothing from the hulk of muscle.

"Let him through, will you!" a voice came from behind the line of black-clad men.

Two small hands pushed their way between two of the huge men and slowly parted them, a body followed pushing through the small gap.

"Please, Lieutenant; come through." The woman said.

The two stone-men slowly turned to the side to allow him to pass. The woman fell forward as the mass she was pressing on shifted. She would have hit the floor if Kell hadn't reacted quickly and stopped her from dropping.

"Thank you." She said with a gasp, straightening her hair and running her hands down her suit to iron out any wrinkles and erase any sign of weakness that may have just shown itself. She turned and walked back towards the vehicle. Kell followed.

"Miss Barnes called me," Kell said.

"Yes, yes. I'm aware of what Miss Barnes asked you here for." The woman said curtly. "I'm Mrs. Hancock."

"Well, Mrs. Hancock. May I ask just what is going on here?" Kell asked.

"One of my responsibilities is security. I felt it pertinent to secure Mr. Lopez's vehicle until you got here to do whatever it is you do." The woman said.

"Well, that explains the ring of very large men surrounding us. But…" Kell said, waving his arm at the four men in bunny suits that were in and around Matias' car, "What exactly, are *they* doing?"

"They are ensuring that the vehicle is safe and not wired with explosives, chemicals, or any other type of harmful devices, Lieutenant." Mrs. Hancock said, already sounding fed up with this line of questioning.

"And all the while, they could be destroying evidence," Kell said.

"Nonsense. Can't you see that they're wearing protective clothing and are extremely well trained in this area of expertise? I've been doing this for some time, you know." Hancock said.

"It may surprise you to know that I have too," Kell said.

At that, she gave a short sharp snort and pushed her wire-rimmed glasses up her nose, "Yes, well, I expect someone like you has." She said.

"May I ask you something else?" Kell said.

"More complaints?" Hancock snorted again.

"If you're checking this vehicle for incendiary or chemical devices, why have you let this many people get so close? If something were to explode or leak, these people would be the first to be harmed." Kell said.

The woman looked around at the growing crowd around her and marched off towards the ring of hulking security guards.

"Get these people out of here! What am I paying you for? I said now!" She yelled.

With these words of encouragement, the guards all stepped forward in unison and began to shepherd the onlookers away. Kell could see several of them trying to look around the men, but each was pushed back, sometimes with quite some force.

"Happy now?" Mrs. Hancock said. She spat the words out like a spoiled child.

"Yes, thank you," Kell said with little emotion, this also seemed to provoke the woman.

"What exactly is your problem?" Hancock asked, irritation starting to show on her face.

"I'm sorry?" Kell asked as he watched the four men in jumpsuits.

"What is your problem here?" The woman asked again.

"There are procedures. Someone such as yourself who has been doing this for years should know that. Although I expect you haven't had many people explain when you've been doing things wrong. Now, please can we ask those men to leave." Kell pointed at the white-clothed men, one of whom was now just legs coming out from under the vehicle."

"Fine. Everyone!" she shouted, turning towards the vehicle. Each man looked up towards her, but the legs under the car didn't move. "Time to wrap it up. The Lieutenant here has work to do."

"But we haven't finis—" one of the jumpsuits started in a voice muffled by the mask covering his lower face.

"I'm sorry?" Hancock said, folding her arms and tapping a foot on the concrete, "You're finished when I say you are."

She walked over to the legs and gave them a swift hard kick with her pointy high heeled shoes. A muffle of expletives came from under the car that Kell couldn't quite make out before one of legs' colleagues pulled him out and helped him to his feet.

"Well, so far, we've found nothing." The man with the legs said as he stood, "Looks clean, but we've still not…" he stopped himself from speaking when he looked up and saw Mrs. Hancock's face, which by this time was already turning a shade of red that Kell had never seen before.

"Just go." she said as the vein in her forehead started to throb.

The men didn't need to be told again; they gathered their equipment and made for an exit.

When the men had left the area, Mrs. Hancock turned back around to face Kell. Her face had now returned to a more natural color, and she had composed herself once again,

"That's everyone." She said.

Kell looked around and was amazed at the quiet that now enveloped the two of them. Where only a couple of minutes ago had been a gaggle of people and security, there was now only space; even the bunny suits had made a swift exit.

"I will leave you to it then. Please don't hesitate to contact me if you require anything further," she said with a note of sincerity, "but I doubt that you will need the likes of me." With another snort, she marched off faster than he'd seen anyone wearing a pencil skirt and high heels do before.

After watching the woman leave, Kell walked closer to the vehicle and continued the task at hand. He had to figure out what had happened to Matias. He started with the driver's side door, left open by the bunny suits, he had no way of knowing if it was open when they got to it or not. He suppressed his annoyance the best that he could and continued. Crouching by the door, he scanned the door frame inside and out; he only found Matias' fingerprints. Upon examination of the rest of the car, he again found only Matias' prints.

There were no visible signs of blood or any other bodily fluid. Kell pressed his temple and tried to recreate what may have happened, but it was inconclusive. Some parts of the replay could have been affected by the bunny suits' actions; he had no way of knowing.

He left the car and turned his attention to the parking garage in general. A few feet behind Matias' vehicle, there were tire marks. It looked as if someone had stopped at some speed. Crouching, he scanned them and began a search of possible makes and models of cars.

After locating the few cameras in the immediate area, he patched into them and quickly went through the previous day's footage. At 07:34, the feed broke up and then went black. He ran through the missing video until it came back at 07:42. Whatever had happened, happened in those eight minutes. There were several scenarios that Kell considered; someone could have snatched Matias, he could have pulled up and got in another car and left, or could simply have just walked away. Anything could have happened.

He swiftly went through the feeds from the other cameras in the parking garage. Each one went off and came back at the same time. Someone didn't want to be seen. He sighed; he had nothing to go on. Matias could be anywhere, with anyone.

The search on the tire tracks was still going when he got a call from Captain Crane.

Sir, I'm at—

"Sorry, son, I've got some news," Crane said with a note of urgency in his voice.

What is it?

"It's the young lass, Emily." At the sound of her name, Kell went cold, "I had a call from her not long ago. She said that there was a man in the house who had hurt Mrs. Sampson, the social worker she went to live with for a few nights."

Is she okay? Emily?

"I don't know, son. She got cut off. I think she was going to run. I've got officers on the way to the house now." Crane said.

I'm going.

"I don't think that's a very clever idea. You need to be working this case." Crane said. Kell knew he was trying to be forceful, but Crane also knew that there was no chance Kell would hang around.

No disrespect, sir. But I'm going. She was my responsibility.

"You're one man, Kell. You can't do everything. I don't care if you are an AI." Crane said.

I can try.

Kell cut the call off and ran back towards his car. Jumping in and slamming the door behind him, he input Eileen Sampson's address into the navigation software, and the car began to move. Quickly he changed the control mode to manual and, with a screech of tires, left the parking lot at top speed.

Chapter 29

01:00 28th October 2138

President Darrow sat at his desk in the Oval Office. He'd spent the entire day being talked at by advisors, watching news reports, and trying to figure out how he was going to pull the country back together. This was the first time he'd been alone in his office for hours. He was glad of the quiet, but it didn't give him much comfort.

His mind wandered to years past when he was campaigning for his presidency, and his wife was still alive.

Maria had been a driving force in his campaign, she was his rock, and there was no way he could have gotten where he was today without her. The entire thing took a toll on both of them; it almost killed him; it did kill her.

It had been three years since he'd been elected, and just under since his beloved had passed.

He blamed himself for her death. If they weren't so busy with his job, maybe they would have paid more attention to the signs of ill health in his wife.

Maria was never one to complain, never one to show what was going on inside. The pain that she must have been going through all that time when she was out on his behalf, trying to get him elected; trying to fulfill his dream; he couldn't bear to think about.

By the time they realized what was wrong, it was too late; the cancer had progressed too much, and all the doctors could do was to make her comfortable in her last days. Her last words echoed around his head; he'd never forget what she said that day in January just a week after his inauguration.

She was in their bed in the White House residence. She'd been there since they'd moved in just a few days earlier. He was lying by her side, holding her as best he could without hurting her. He gently stroked her hair as she looked up into his eyes and said through chapped lips, with a voice so hoarse he barely recognized it as his wife's anymore, "We did it, Mr. President." She'd then closed her eyes and died right there in his arms. He had cried as he held her lifeless body and must have lain there for hours before someone came into the room to check on them. He'd never forgive himself for his ambition that killed the love of his life.

Darrow stood from his chair and turned to look out over the White House grounds. The sky was glowing orange, but he knew that it wasn't the rising sun that was causing it to be that color. From this angle, you could be forgiven for thinking the view was beautiful, but he knew that what was beneath that color was far from beautiful. He dreaded to think of what horrors his citizens were going through right at that very minute.

He looked down at his watch – a gift from his late wife — it was 01:00. Another day had started, and he hadn't even noticed. He let out a sigh as he watched raindrops hit the windowpane in front of his face, slowly trickle down to the ground, gather together and form a large puddle that reflected the lights in the White House grounds.

His mind wandered again, this time to Olivia. The one light that had been in his life since his wife's passing. He knew that others didn't approve of their relationship, but it wasn't like they were doing anything wrong.

Darrow thought about the feel of her soft skin and her lips against his. Olivia was one of the only remaining sources of light and warmth in his life. On some of his worst days, the mere thought of her was enough to get him through.

He felt a small stab of pain and heat spread across his lower back, the like he'd never felt before. He reached around and touched two fingers to the back of his shirt. When he brought his hand back around to examine his fingers, they looked covered in black liquid. He rubbed them together, noticing that the liquid felt tacky. There was an almost metallic smell in the air too. It took him a second to register that he knew that smell; it was blood. He was bleeding.

Before his brain could register any more, The President dropped to his knees. He tried to raise his arms, but they just felt too heavy.

Darrow blinked, trying to figure out what was happening. There was no pain now, just blood. He managed to lean and rest against the window.

His vision was blurred, but he could see the slim shape of someone stood in front of him. There was something in their hand glinting in the light that was streaming into the office; a knife? The figure stood motionless in front of him.

"Who–" Darrow started.

The knife slashed down again and again. The 65th President of the United States' arterial blood spurted from his wounds. He didn't scream, he didn't cry; he just thought of Maria. His last thought was that he'd finally be with her again.

Chapter 30

02:04 28th October 2138

He waited, crouched in the silence of the pitch black, empty house — the faint sound of approaching sirens came from the distance. Before long, they were right outside, and the room was filled with blue and red lights. He watched through the window as two marked police vehicles skidded to a halt in front of the house.

Clicks could be heard as car doors were opening, and before long, footsteps were making their way up the concrete path towards the front door. He stood and stepped further back into the shadows; the evil smile still on his face. This was going to be perfect.

Voices came from just outside the door as – what he counted to be four police officers – debated how to enter the property. He prepared himself. They appeared to opt for the quiet approach as the door slowly opened and bathed the room in more alternating blue and red light.

The first officer entered cautiously, gun raised, held in both hands, finger hovering over the trigger. The second followed close behind him. The other two stayed outside. *Good, two at a time*, he thought to himself.

Officer number one made his way further into the room. After a few more steps, he flicked on a flashlight and started to wave it around the room. The man in the shadows took a step back to remain hidden. A second flashlight joined the first, and they were played around the room.

Eventually, one of the beams of light fell on the chaos in the room, and the second officer ran over to the remains of Eileen Sampson.

The hidden man heard her gag slightly as she fully saw the grotesque show. Her partner, who was still a few steps behind her, saw and reached for his shoulder-mounted radio. His actions were halted before he got a word out, and he thudded to the floor.

The female officer spun on her heels in time to see blood seeping out of her partner and pooling around his head. When she saw the knife sticking out of his neck, she staggered back and let out a faint yelp. Despite almost slipping on the remains of Eileen, she managed to gather her footing and remain upright. The officer shined her torch around the room, the light caught on the man stood in the shadows behind the front door. Before she could even register what she saw, her vision blurred, and the floor came up to meet her.

He stepped back into the darkness; *two down, this is easy*, he laughed to himself. The other two officers were just on the other side of the wall, unaware of the violence inside.

One of them shouted through the door to his two, now dead, colleagues. After a few moments of no response, one of the men stepped tentatively inside. It wasn't long before he saw the two uniformed bodies in the room. He called to his partner, and they ran to their colleagues' aid, not knowing that it was much too late; for the dead and themselves.

The assassin stepped out from the darkness and slowly closed the front door, lessening the amount of light that streamed in. As the room got darker, one officer turned to see what was going on. As he did, a hand was placed over his mouth and another on the back of his neck. With a simple twist, it was goodnight, Mr. Police Officer.

The last officer heard the snapping of his friends' neck and fired a single shot from his standard-issue firearm into the shadows. However, the bullet went way wide of his target and struck the wall just behind the assassin.

The shadow figure grasped and pulled the scared police officer closer, slowly sliding a blade into the young man's stomach. The assassin enjoyed every second of it. He could hear the last gasps of life ebbing from the man's mouth. A final breath that sounded like the word 'no' left him, and he was dropped unceremoniously to the ground. He landed in a heap next to his three lifeless colleagues.

The AI stood looking down, admiring his handiwork. *Easy,* he thought to himself. *Now to wait for the main event.*

He slinked back into the shadows of the room and waited in silence.

Chapter 31

02:32 28th October 2138

Kell flew through the streets of Washington D.C. He could barely see as rain streamed down the windscreen too fast for the wipers to remove it, but he wasn't going to let that stop him from getting to his destination. The sky was full of clouds, the night seemed to be getting darker.

He could see the green, amber, and red of traffic lights as he passed under them, too fast to register what color each one was. He didn't often drive in manual mode, but he wasn't often in this kind of a hurry. He had to get to Emily. He had to protect her.

Glancing down at the screen that displayed his destination, he saw that it struggled to keep up with his location. The small blue arrow that would usually follow the roads' line smoothly was jumping tens of feet at once and would sometimes rotate and wouldn't catch up to him for several minutes.

He knew there were other drivers on the road, but at the moment, it felt like he was the only one. He instinctively avoided other vehicles and didn't so much as come within a few feet of anyone else. Several horns that were probably intended for him blared as he passed, but he didn't see or care where they came from.

Captain Crane had attempted to call him numerous times during his journey, but for the first time in their working relationship, Kell had hung up on him. He didn't have time for the Captain to try to talk him out of what he knew he needed to do.

A beep came from the central console of his car, and a voice said, "You are nearing your destination." Kell pushed his foot down on the brake and slid to a halt in front of Eileen Sampson's home. The rain-slick road making him slide for longer than he expected. There was a thud, and he was jerked forward in his seat, an airbag deployed from the center of the steering wheel, and cushioned his head. Without stopping to think about what had just happened, he threw the door wide and launched himself out into the rainy street.

It was only when he was halfway across the road that Kell registered the two police cruisers parked in front of the house. One half up the front lawn, the other across the driveway. The lights were still flashing. He had a moment of relief in thinking that someone was now with Emily, and she was safe.

This moment didn't last long; he realized that something about this didn't feel right. The house was dark. There were no lights on anywhere inside. If officers were with Emily, he'd expect to see something, and someone should be standing watch outside. No, something about this wasn't right.

All of these thoughts flew through his head, but nothing was going to stop him now. He made it to the front door, momentarily slipping on the wet porch. Putting his hand on the handle, he paused, listening for anyone, anything, inside the social workers' home. All seemed quiet, way too quiet.

Pushing down on the handle, it gave way quickly with little force, and the door swung inward. *Not locked, no sign of anyone about, not good.* Kell thought.

He stepped across the threshold and straight away was hit by that old familiar scent; blood. There was a flicker of movement across the room in front of him, and he could just about make out a shape sat on the arm of the couch; he couldn't tell if it was facing him or not.

"Lieutenant William Kell. AI Homicide—" there was a loud crack as a shot was fired from what sounded like a police-issued firearm. "Wait, I am here to—" there was a clatter as something hit the floor, and the shape rushed forward, knocking Kell back. Hitting the floor, his head bounced off the floor, and he saw stars. As his vision cleared slightly, he just had time to register someone towering above him when a foot come towards his face. After that, everything went black.

*

Kell opened his eyes to see a flurry of movement in the room around him. Police officers, EMTs, and various other officials were crowding him.

In a delayed reaction, he suddenly felt a massive pang of pain in his head. When he instinctively tried to reach up to place his hand on his forehead, he found that he couldn't. He looked over his shoulder and saw that his hands were cuffed in place behind him to one of the stair rails.

A voice among the din shouted, "He's awake!" Kell tried to look around to see where the unrecognized voice came from but couldn't work it out; his sensors weren't responding as they should.

A man stepped towards Kell from across the room. He was dressed entirely in black, black suit jacket and pants, black shirt, and black tie; he even wore black leather gloves. "Lieutenant William Kell?" The man asked as he crouched in front of him.

"Yes, sir." Kell said, his ears now ringing.

"No need to sir me. Not anymore, anyway. I don't think after your actions this morning that you'll be a Lieutenant anywhere much longer, not even of a public toilet." The man said.

"I don't understand, sir?" Kell said, confused.

"Murderers, kidnappers, and cop killers don't last long in the department, you know." Kell couldn't understand what this man was talking about.

"But I haven't killed anyone," Kell said. Amongst his confusion, he suddenly remembered why he came here in the first place, "I came here to find Emily. Where is Emily?"

"That's just one of the many questions we're going to want you to answer very soon." The man said, "But for the moment, you're under arrest for the murder of Eileen Sampson, Sergeants Cooke and Ulrich, and Officers Boothe and Ellison. As well as the abduction and suspected murder of Matias Lopez and Emily Lawton." The man reached around the back of Kell, undid the handcuffs, lifted him up to his feet with the help of another officer, and re-cuffed him. "You have the right to remain silent. Anything you say can be used against you in court…" the man's words faded into white noise inside Kell's head.

"I don't understand what's happening. I was attacked. Whoever did this is out there now." Kell said.

Two more officers appeared and hustled him out of the front door towards a waiting cruiser. They pushed him in the back with little regard for if he banged his head on the door rim. Once he was in, they slammed the door in his face. He was lost. He had been attacked, knocked out, and woke up in this mess. Someone was framing him. But who? Who was his attacker? Was he getting too close to finding the AI in the middle of all the cleansings? Is this his punishment? And what did his attacker do to Emily?

The two officers who had thrown him in the vehicle climbed in the front seat, and the car pulled away from the Sampson house. One of the men turned in his seat to look at Kell,

"You're going to fry, Arti. Fry!" The police officer turned back to his partner, and the two laughed. Kell slumped back in his seat, defeated.

Chapter 32

02:41 28th October 2138

It was dark, cold, and raining. Emily was still wearing the same clothes she'd been given by Mrs. Sampson, and by now, they were even more soaked through and filthy than they were when she landed from her jump for freedom. She had no other clothes to change into, so she guessed she was stuck with these for the time being.

Once she'd started running, she'd run as fast, and a far as her legs could take her. She didn't know how far she'd gone from the house where the man had attacked her caretaker or how long she'd walked after she'd stopped running.

She now sat at a bus stop trying to keep out of the rain for a few minutes. She'd had the idea to look at the map that she knew would be posted in bus shelters. If she could find out where she was, she could phone Mr. Crane and get William to come and rescue her; again. But, when she reached the stop, she found that someone had smashed the display, and now it just flickered on and off, displaying only half of the map. Each time the map flashed up, she tried to understand what it said and where she was, but she couldn't figure it out.

Nothing around her looked familiar. Neon lights flashed high up on the surrounding buildings, through the dim light and rain, she couldn't make out what they said; if they said anything at all.

She wanted her mom; she really wanted her mom. She could feel tears welling up inside her, but she forced them down. She had to be brave and get help.

While she sat at the bus stop, several people walked past her, she tried to get their attention and ask where she was, but most outright ignored her, one did respond, but it was all gibberish to her. All she could manage was a quiet "Thank you" to make the jabbering lady leave her alone.

She was scared, more scared than she had ever been in her life. She reached into her backpack and wrapped a cold, trembling hand around the waist of her old friend, Boingo. Clutching him firmly in her grasp, she brought him out of the bag and held him to her cheek. His warm fur was still such a comfort to her. Her mom used to say that when she was a baby, she'd never let go of him and would chew on one of his ears, that's why he now only had one ear left and looked so threadbare. On several occasions, her mom had asked if she couldn't replace Boingo with something new, but Emily would never let her; Boingo was the only friend she had.

"How much?" a raspy voice came from beside her, followed by a harsh, phlegm-filled cough.

"Excuse me?" she managed.

"How much?" the voice asked again.

She looked down at Boingo and up at the man that was now sat uncomfortably close to her. She noticed his eyes were discolored a sickly yellow, and the skin around them was almost green. He smelled too, worse than anyone she'd ever met.

"Oh, sorry. He's not for sale." She said, stuffing Boingo back into her bag and zipping it up, and clutching it to her chest.

Another horrendous phlegmy cough erupted from the hideous man that seemed to be edging closer to her. He spat on the floor, and he reached out for her with a gnarled old hand. Emily flinched away, but not in time to get away from his grasp. His hands were tinged with green, just like his eyes were.

"Oh, dear, no. I don't want your rabbit. How much do *you* charge? You're so young and lovely." The man said, stroking a finger over her leg.

"I don't—" Emily squeaked.

"Oi! Jerk! Leave the kid alone!" A voice came from the other side of her.

The hand that grasped hers retreated into a coat sleeve, and the hideous man quickly rose to his feet and scuttled off, only leaving behind a sour smell that lingered in the air.

"Yeah, and don't come back, ya bastard!" the voice said.

Emily closed her eyes, scared of what was going to happen to her next. She felt a soft hand on hers, fingers slowly stroked the back of her hand, just like her mom used to do when she was scared of the thunder.

She opened her eyes half expecting her mom to be looking back into her eyes and to be back at home tucked up in bed. Some part of her knew differently, though. Instead of her mother, though, another kindly face looked back as a woman knelt in front of her.

The woman had short wild red hair that stuck up in all directions, she wore black lipstick and had black eye shadow around her eyes that seemed to make her eyes huge.

"It's okay now, hun. That jerks gone." She spoke softly while intermittently chewing gum.

"He...what did he want?" Emily asked.

"It doesn't matter now. He's gone; that's all that matters." The woman stood up and perched on the metal bench next to Emily. "Look at you. You're soaked and filthy. You must be freezing!" She said.

Emily looked at the woman and saw that she was wearing a short plastic skirt and a top that seemed to barely cover anything. "Aren't you cold, too?" she asked.

The woman gave a short laugh, "Ha, yeah. But I'm used to being out here like this." She put her arm around the now shivering child, "Where did you come from? Are you on your own? It's not smart for a kid to be out this way on their own, you know?"

"I don't know where I'm from or where I am. I ran away from a bad man." Emily said, suddenly feeling the weight of the past few hours on her.

"Was it that jerk I just chased off?" the woman asked.

"No. A different one." Emily said.

"Wow. You've been through it, huh?" The woman stood and stretched out her hand for Emily to take, "I'm Lucie," she said, "let's get you somewhere warm, eh?"

"Okay. I'm…I'm Emily." Emily said, feeling a little better that she found someone who seemingly cares.

"Well, Emily, let's not stand here gabbing. Let's get warm. I think I've got some hot chocolate at home." The woman thought for a moment looking at Emily, "Might have some clean clothes for you too, sound good?"

Emily tentatively reached out and took Lucie's hand. She's only just met this woman, but she felt like she could trust her. At least more than anyone else she'd met on this street. She still wished for William, though.

Chapter 33

```
03:03 28th October 2138
```

"What are we going to do to help Kell?" Lockley was sat in Captain Cranes office, perched on the edge of one of the battered old office chairs that were generally reserved for those getting a chewing out. This time, however, it was Crane who was being chewed.

"My hands are tied, Lockley." Crane was sat behind his desk with his head in his hands. He was feeling defeated. He knew Kell was being set up, but he couldn't do a thing about it. The orders had come down from above him, and it was more than his life was worth to get involved. After all, he was coming up to retirement, and his wife would kill him if he did anything to jeopardize his already meager pension.

"Sir, you and I both know that he's innocent. This is all total bullshit!" Crane could see the young police officer getting more and more wound up.

"I know," he said with a sigh, "Believe me, if I could do anything, I would. That lad is like a son to me. You've known him for ten minutes and look at how you feel. Imagine how I feel."

"I'm sorry, sir. I know this can't be easy for you." Lockley slid her chair closer to the desk and put a hand out to comfort the old captain. He didn't take it, but he appreciated the gesture. "So, what do they think they have him on?"

"There's a hell of a list. There's the abduction and possible murder of that lab guy, Matias Lopez, and the same for little Emily Lawton." Lockley was shaking her head; he knew how she felt. Kell wouldn't do anything to harm that kid, "Then there's the murder of Eileen Sampson, the social worker taking care of Emily. And now, the four officers I sent to check on Emily, their murders are being pinned on him. That one especially isn't looking good for him, what with the way they found him in the house and all."

"Seriously, though. What reason does he have to kill anyone, let alone anyone in that list." Lockley said, sitting back in her seat.

"I don't think they're really thinking much beyond the fact that he's an AI." Crane stood and walked around the room, slowly closing all the blinds on each of the windows. He then pulled up another office chair close to where Lockley sat on hers. He began to whisper conspiratorially, "They have video footage of him abducting the lab tech. It's obviously doctored by whoever sent it to them, but they won't see that. Beyond that, I don't know what other evidence they have."

"So, they got an anonymous call and some video sent to them that implicates Kell in that abduction. What about everything else?" Lockley said.

"I believe it's all just circumstantial, but they'll put it all together and find links where there are none. The upper echelons have never been thrilled with Kell being a part of this department, so it doesn't surprise me that they're jumping on this, like flies on shit." He gently placed a hand on the woman's knee, "We won't let whoever framed Kell get away with it, and we will exonerate him, believe me. But we can't do anything just yet. We need to find proof that he's innocent."

"Where do we start with that?" Lockley asked.

The old man sighed and thought for a moment. He wiped beads of sweat from his brow with a handkerchief that lived in his shirt pocket, "Our best bet is probably to try to find Emily. I believe she got out of that house and escaped from the real killer. Trouble is we don't know where she went, and we can't put out a missing person report for her because the higher-ups will squash it as soon as it goes out."

Lockley clicked her tongue, "I guess I'm going looking for her, then?"

"Seems like the only option. I'll do what I can from here, but as you can see from the state of me, I'll only slow you down out on the streets. I can also hopefully keep an eye on what's going on with Kell. I'll keep you updated." Crane said.

"Thanks. I'll start at the Sampson house and work something out from there." Lockley said, standing.

"Try not to be seen. There's probably still a police or federal presence there, and we don't want questions being asked. You won't be able to find any cameras in that area, so you won't be able to pick up on her direction from that. It might be a case of good old-fashioned police work and asking around with a photo," Crane said.

"Fun," Lockley said sarcastically, "Well, I'd better get going; this may take a while."

"Yeah. Good luck, and for God's sake, be careful," Crane said.

With that, the young officer gave a quick two-fingered salute and left Crane alone in his office.

He went back behind his desk and sat down, connected to the net, and tried to find some updates on what was happening with Kell. He wasn't entirely sure which agency had taken him, but he was pretty sure it would be the FBI. Whoever had him, he had to do whatever he could to help his long-time friend and colleague out of this mess.

Chapter 34

03:15 28th October 2138

Robert sat watching his monitors. Half were tuned to news channels, and the others to his CCTV feeds of the warehouse, Matias' container lab, and the surrounding area. He felt a presence behind him. It wasn't a surprise; he was expecting someone – it was part of the plan after all.

"Is the President dealt with?" Robert asked, without turning to face the figure.

"Yes." Said the voice from the gloom behind him.

"Good. Any problems?" Robert said

"None." The response came.

Robert turned around in his chair to face the shape in the doorway. "And the girl?"

"No-one will find her. They will think she was the one who committed the cleansing." The man said.

"And what of yourself?" Robert asked.

The figure smiled and stepped forward out of the shadows, "No one will find me either. As far as they'll be concerned, Olivia Hampton has killed the President of the United States, and his Chief of Staff, Henry Russo." Henry's smile grew across one side of his face, "I'll change my face soon and then go back out there to continue our work."

"Excellent. You have done well." Robert said, now also smiling.

"What of our other targets? Has *He* been busy?" Henry asked.

"Indeed, yes," Robert said.

The figure that was at this moment known as Henry nodded towards a screen that showed Matias at work. "And the scientist?"

"His work is progressing. Not as fast as I had hoped. But it won't delay the plan from reaching its conclusion. Especially not now that the troublesome AI police officer has been dealt with."

Robert stood and walked over to his co-conspirator, placing a hand on his shoulder; he said, "Now go. Rest. There will be more to do soon."

The ex-Henry Russo smiled slyly, "Indeed there will, old friend. Indeed there will."

Chapter 35

04:52 28th October 2138

Kell sat alone in an interview room.

Compared to the ones they had at the precinct; this was luxurious. There wasn't a hint of damp coming through the ceiling. No chipped or curling paint on the walls. No carpet floor tiles missing. The place was cleaner than his apartment, and white, very white. Mirrors covered every wall – he supposed in an attempt to confuse the interviewee; so they didn't know which direction they were being watched from; maybe all of them.

He'd been left sat there for around an hour. It was standard practice. It gave the perp time to stew, think about what they'd done, and sometimes even crack enough to just give a straight confession as soon as someone entered the room, even if that person was just the cleaning lady.

Kell wondered if they expected *him* to crack or whether it was just the fact that he was an AI that they kept him shut in this room. He figured it didn't really matter.

He used the time he had to go over everything he knew and everything that had happened. The last thing he remembered was entering Mrs. Sampson's house and being shot at by a police weapon. After that, he was waking up cuffed to the stair rail. For the first time in his existence, his mind was blank and missing time.

Was it one of the police officers shooting at him? He didn't think so. He remembered seeing at least three uniformed bodies on the floor, though it's possible that the fourth was the shooter. But why would they shoot at him after he had clearly identified himself, and why did the man who spoke to him at the house mention that all four officers were killed?

No. There was someone else in that house. The person that Emily told Crane about. The man who killed Eileen Sampson. He was the one who killed the officers, and then waited in the house for him to turn up so he could, what? Frame him? Get him out of the way?

If whoever it was wanted him out of the way, why not just kill him and have done with it? No, that would be too clean. They need the authorities to focus on something or someone else. While they think they have the right man, the real killer can go about their business with impunity. Kell was just the fall guy because he was getting too close.

The door to the interview room opened, and in walked the man in black from the house accompanied by a woman; both took seats opposite him.

"Hello, William. Do you remember me?" The man said.

"Yes, sir. I do." Kell replied.

"Well, my name is Agent Pierce. This is Agent Reese." He gave Kell a steely-eyed glare.

Pierce tapped the table twice, and it sprang to life with a hologrammatic stack of images. The one on top – Kell could see – was of the scene at the Sampson house. "You are aware of what you are charged with?" The agent asked.

"I am," Kell said, as Pierce started to deal several holographic images out over the table. The photos were a horror show of blood and bodies.

"So, I will ask you simply; why?" Pierce said, staring directly into Kell's eyes.

"Why?" Kell asked.

"Yes, Kell. Why?" Pierce said, simply.

"I don't understand the question, sir," Kell said.

"It's quite simple, really," Pierce moved his hands over the holo-images, and several started to magnify. Showing the scene in the minutest detail. "Why did you kill Eileen Sampson in her home, and why did you murder four innocent police officers, who were, in fact, your own colleagues?"

"I didn't murder Mrs. Sampson or the four officers, sir," Kell said calmly.

"Oh?" Pierce moved his hands again, and all the individual images disappeared and were replaced by a single new one. It was the photo of an eight-year-old girl, Emily. "Let's move on then. What did you do with little Emily Lawton? Where is she?"

"I don't know. I went to the house because I was told she was in trouble. I went there to help her. When I got there, the officers were already dead, and I was attacked." Kell stared at the image of Emily; he couldn't help but wonder where she was and hoping she was okay out there.

"Attacked? It appears you were attacked by Officer Boothe. His firearm had discharged a single shot, the remains of which were pulled out of you earlier," Pierce said.

Kell looked down at the bandage that was wrapped around the top of his torso; he didn't feel any pain with it, so he'd almost forgotten about it. He ran his fingers over the white fabric.

"As you can see, the evidence is there. Here's what I think happened, Kell." Pierce leaned forward on his elbows, rested his chin on his hands. He lifted his head and pointed his index fingers at Kell as he started to speak, "You went to Eileen Sampson's house to take Emily away after getting way too attached to a victim. Mrs. Sampson wouldn't let you take her, so she fought you, and you killed her. The four officers arrived after the call from Emily about someone in the house attacking Eileen. You fought them and killed three, the fourth – Officer Boothe – managed to get a shot off before you finished him off. But that shot was enough to take you down for a time."

"Okay, so that's your version of events?" Kell asked flatly.

"Seems pretty clear cut to me. Doesn't it to you, Agent Reese?" The woman who up until this point had remained silent and motionless simply nodded in agreement.

"So, when did I get a chance to abduct or murder Emily?" Kell asked.

At this, the two Agents were a bit taken aback; it seemed they'd forgotten that little detail of the accusation. He saw them swiftly glance at one another before Pierce began talking again.

"We don't have your extra sensory perceptions, Kell. We must piece things together bit by bit. We can't just get a playback." Agent Pierce was visibly starting to sweat now, "But believe me, we *will* piece it all together."

"I'm sure you will, Agents," Kell said.

"Let's move on to something you can't dispute." The male agent swiped across the table, and the photo of Emily disappeared. Kell was almost heartbroken when the image vanished. It was replaced by a video clip; it was somewhere he recognized, somewhere he'd been recently. "The abduction and possible murder of one Matias Lopez."

Agent Pierce hit play on the video clip. It was footage from a CCTV camera feed in the parking garage at MDF Organics. The timestamp displayed the exact timings that were missing from the footage he'd gone through that morning.

As the video played, it showed Matias pull up to a parking space, get out and start to look in his trunk. Another car then pulled up behind him, blocking him in. Out of the car stepped – Kell couldn't believe his eyes; it was him.

On the video, Kell walked up behind Lopez, there was a glint of something in his hand, this item – possibly a knife – was then held to the scientists' neck. There followed a brief exchange between the two men, and then they turned, and Lopez was forced into video-Kell's trunk and locked in. The other Kell then got back in the driver's seat and drove off.

Pierce waved his hand across the holo-video, and it shrank back to the table in front of him. "So, what do you have to say to that?" He asked with a smirk.

"That wasn't me," Kell said.

"It sure looked like you." Pierce turned back to his partner, "That looked like him, didn't it?" Reese nodded again.

"Okay, it looked like me. But it *wasn't* me." Kell said, fighting to control his emotions.

"You've lost me…" Pierce said.

"That footage is fake. It's been doctored. I was there this morning to investigate Mr. Lopez's disappearance, and that exact timestamp was missing." Kell said.

"Convenient, that." Agent Pierce folded his arms and stared at Kell with a smug expression.

"Not if you want to get the real kidnapper and find Matias alive," Kell said.

"So, he's alive, is he? Where is he?" Pierce said, sitting forward in his seat again.

"I don't know whether he's alive or not, and I certainly don't know where he is. But if you keep chasing your tails with me, you'll never find him, and he will be another name on the list of people that you couldn't save." Kell wasn't one to get annoyed often, but even he was starting to lose it with these amateurs.

"Is that a threat?" Pierce said with a raised eyebrow.

Kell slumped back in his seat. There was no getting through to these two that they had the wrong man. His mind went back to Emily, *I hope she's okay; wherever she is*, he thought as the Agent across from him continued to ask some more inane questions that he wasn't listening to.

Emily, where did you go? He tried to connect to the net to see if he could pull up a map, but as he suspected, his access had been revoked – at least these fools had done something by the book. Instead, he attempted to draw the area of the Sampson home in his head. Mapping the roads, buildings, alleyways, any kind of landmark, thinking about which directions and towards what Emily could have gone.

One way would eventually lead to central DC; she would run into plenty of people there; hopefully, even some police officers who she could ask for help. She was a smart kid; she'd definitely ask for help. On the other hand, if she went the other way, she would end up in a less than desirable area. It was still part of the same outer suburbs as the Sampson house, but the area had declined considerably over the years following the war. It became an area where drug users, pimps and their prostitutes and every other kind of undesirable ended up after they couldn't find their way in DC. If she went that way…

"Hello? Kell, are you listening?" Agent Pierce banged a fist on the table, and Kell snapped his thoughts back to the room.

"Sorry, did I miss more of your fairy tales?" Kell said.

"This is no joke, Ke—" Pierce started.

"Agent Pierce, I'm aware that this isn't a joke. I'm not the one making it one." Kell said.

There was a knock on the door, and another agent rushed in the room with some urgency.

"Agent, this isn't the—" Pierce began, but the new agent whispered something in his ear that made his face drop and drain almost of all color. Pierce, in turn, whispered something to Agent Reese, whose actions mimicked his. Both of his interviewers stood and made to leave the room.

As Pierce was almost through the door, he turned back to Kell, "Don't go anywhere, Kell. I'm not done with you yet."

They left Kell alone in the room full of mirrors once again, with only his reflection for company.

Kell retreated inside his head and began to try to recreate Emily's possible steps again.

Chapter 36

05:37 28th October 2138

"Once again, we have unconfirmed reports of the death of Samuel Darrow, the sixty-fifth President of the United States. These reports came from a source within the White House, although we haven't yet had an official statement. The same source has stated that the President was a victim of one of the so-called AI-killers. As I said, we are still waiting for official word from the White House."

The news anchors were paddling up a particular creek without a paddle, as usual. Still, it amused him as he sat and watched his plans unfold. Washington would soon be in chaos when the truth – well, the truth he wanted – came out about the death of the President; his man had done his job well.

Robert went over the next steps of his plan, and he couldn't help but smile his usual wry smile.

The AI formerly known as Henry Russo was resting now, but soon he would be back out there to continue the mission. His next cleansings weren't going to be as high profile, but they would undoubtedly keep the authorities busy and misdirected. The significant parts of the plan were now either complete or in progress. Once the girl was taken care of, and Lopez had finished his work, it would be time.

Chapter 37

03:12 28th October 2138

Emily and Lucie had walked over to Lucie's apartment, managing to avoid any undesirables on the way.

When they got in, Lucie dug around in her closet, looking for some fresh clothes for Emily. While she waited, Emily sat on a very soft mattress in the corner of the room. It was stained and smelled funny, but other than that, it was quite comfortable.

When Lucie produced some clothes – a green t-shirt with the word 'Babe' on it, some jogging pants and some trainers – Emily changed, and Lucie dumped her dirty clothes in a corner.

"Looking good, kid," Lucie said.

"They're a bit big," Emily said.

Lucie knelt in front of Emily and tied the drawstring on the jogging pants, "There, that should help," she said.

Once dressed, the pair went into the front room and sat on the sofa,

"Where did these clothes come from?" Emily asked.

"Someone who used to live here," Lucie said. Something about the way she said it made Emily think that asking any more would be a bad idea.

The two girls sat talking for a while, but before long, Emily was yawning. Lucie told her to lie down and try to get some rest.

Emily laid her head in Lucie's lap, as the older woman stroked her hair. She finally felt safe.

*

Emily woke a few hours later.

She rubbed her eyes as she sat up to see that Lucie wasn't there.

She had a momentary panic before she heard rattling coming from the kitchen across the room and soon saw Lucie coming towards her with two steaming mugs, one of which she passed to Emily.

"What was wrong with that man? His skin was....green," Emily said, perched on the edge of the ratty old red leather sofa cupping a large mug of hot chocolate with three marshmallows floating on top. In her small hands, the chipped yellow mug looked enormous. A television was on mute in the corner; she wasn't paying attention to what was shown on screen, though.

"That's cause he's on Brass." Lucie now sat on the floor opposite Emily holding a similar mug of hot chocolate; her cup had 'Father of the Year' printed on the side.

"Brass?" Emily asked.

"It's a drug, hun. Stay away from it, whatever you do. You can tell when someone's using cause it turns their skin greeny-blue like when brass gets rusty. If you see that mark on anyone you meet out there, stay away from them." Lucie said seriously.

"But you don't use it?" Emily asked.

"I do a lot of things, but Brass ain't one of 'em. But, it wouldn't have the same effect on me anyway." Lucie said.

"Why not?" Emily said.

"I'm an AI, hun. We don't have the same reactions to certain substances as biotics like you or our friend out there would have." Lucie said.

"You're an AI?" Emily stiffened; she could feel the cold hand of fear grasping at her again. "You're not a bad AI, are you? My step-dad, he was…he was bad."

"No, hun. I'm good. Bad in some ways, but that's generally what I get paid for." Lucie said with a smile.

"What do you mean?" Emily said.

"Never mind, honey. As far as you're concerned, I'm good." Emily felt some of the tension leave her body. "So, what were you doing out there on your own?" Lucie asked.

"I ran away," Emily said.

"From home? Because of your step-dad? I've heard that story a lot around here." Lucie said, followed by a slurp from her mug.

"You have? My step-dad killed my mommy, and I was taken to another lady's house after going to the police precinct. Then someone came and killed her; so, I ran." Emily blurted the words out before she knew what she was saying, her eyes now watering.

"Jeeeezus, kid. You've really been through it, huh?" Lucie took another sip from her mug. Emily did the same.

After a short pause, Emily started to talk again; she felt good to be able to speak to someone, "I met another nice AI, though. He saved me and looked after me. I wish I could see him."

"I'm sure you will. Who was he?" Lucie asked.

"A policem—" she dropped her mug, spilling what remained of her hot chocolate on the already stained carpet and pointed at the television that was now showing the image of a man, "Him, it was him. William!"

Lucie shot over to the television set and fiddled with some buttons until the volume came back on, then went and sat down on the sofa next to Emily. She put her arm over her shoulder. Emily didn't even register this small act of compassion from the woman.

"*—cused of kidnapping and murder. William Kell is an AI lieutenant in the AI Homicide Division of the Washington D.C. police department.*"

"What are they saying? Why is William on TV?" Emily said, confused.

"I don't know, hun. It sounds like he's been arrested." Lucie said.

"That can't be right. He's a nice man!" Emily shrugged Lucie's arm off her and ran over to kneel in front of the TV. On-screen, the news report continued.

"*Kell is accused of the murder of four police officers, the kidnapping and suspected murder of Matias Lopez, a senior technician at MDF Organics. The murder of Eileen Sampson, a local area social worker, and the abduction and suspected murder of Emily Lawton, whose mother was recently a victim of another AI killer, Gary Lawton.*

Lawton is currently awaiting trial for the murder of his wife Christine, and if found guilty, he will face execution by nanobots…"

A photo of Emily and her mom was now on the screen; she stared at it in disbelief. Lucie had joined her on the floor in front of the set, and they were now both eagerly watching.

"She-it. That's you!" Lucie exclaimed as she pointed at the photo on the screen.

"William would never hurt anyone. He's a nice man, and he only ever looked after me." Emily turned to look at Lucie, whose eyes were still fixed to the screen, "Why are they saying these things?"

"I don't know. But they're clearly wrong. The damn press never gets anything right. We need to go and tell someone, show someone that you're alive and well, and no-one has kidnapped or harmed you."

"Not yet." Said an unknown voice from the other side of the door.

Chapter 38

05:30 28th October 2138

He had her trail. It wasn't difficult to pick up. An ordinary man might have struggled, but then, he wasn't ordinary nor a man. Through his years with Robert and doing this sort of work, he had all kinds of sensory modifications installed to enable him to better track his prey.

So far, he'd tracked the girl away from the woman's house on 16th and E, up 17th, and into Barney Circle. Not the best part of town. These days it was full of the worst scum of human and AI persuasions. Maybe someone will do his job for him, hopefully not.

He reached a bus stop on Independence Avenue and found he could no longer track the girl. How did she disappear?

Slumped behind the stop in the doorway of some long closed and burned down store, he saw the shape of a man. As the assassin walked over to the man, he could already smell the filthy being. Humans disgusted him at the best of times, but this one was particularly ripe.

With a swift movement of his foot, he kicked the thing in the doorway. There was a grumble followed by several obscenities as the creature rolled over and blinked in the dim red light that bathed him from above, probably the only bathing that involved this thing in years. As the animal's face rose to meet the assassin's, he could see that its eyes were ringed by a blue-green tinge; a sure sign that this human was taking the drug known as Brass. Humans and their addictions…

"What's your problem?" the thing in the doorway asked.

"Seen a little girl around here?" The AI asked without even an attempt to hide his disgust.

At this, the disheveled man seemed to come around almost instantly. "So, you like 'em young, eh? Me too. I know where we can find some."

"I'm looking for one girl in particular." The assassin said.

"Oh yeah? You got some special tastes?" The man said.

Ignoring the suggestions of the creature, the AI continued, "Eight years old, three-foot-nine, long, curly black hair worn in pigtails. She was carrying a backpack with a picture of a unicorn on it. May have also been carrying a stuffed rabbit toy."

"That's pretty specific, fella." The beast said.

"Have you seen her or not?" his frustration with this man was starting to build.

"Yeah, I might have. What's it to you?" The man coughed something up and spat it at the AI's feet.

"I'm in a hurry to find this girl. Have you seen her?" He was trying to keep his calm. If this man knew anything he had to find out, then he could do whatever he liked to the disgusting wretch.

"I'll tell you if you get me something." The man grunted.

"I don't have any drugs or money. Tell me what I want to know, and I'll leave you in one piece." The assassin said.

"You don't scare me. No man scares me." The man said before rolling back over to his previous position.

The AI reached down and picked the homeless man up by his ragged coat's collar and lifted him a clear foot off the ground. He could see the moment of realization in the man's eyes when it dawned on him that this was no man. A pool of dampness spread across the front of the man's trousers, and urine started to drip from the cuffs and dribble down his worn shoes onto the floor.

"Shit, man. I didn't know. Puh-please, don't kill me. I'll tell you. I'll tell you!" The man pleaded.

"Good. Hurry up. I'm on a schedule." The AI said.

"She went off with some dame. Bitch took the girl away from me." The man said hurriedly, hoping this would satisfy the AI.

"Who was this 'dame'?" The AI said, his voice getting harsher.

"Chick called Lucie." He could feel the man trembling now. The AI looked the homeless man in the eyes and got to see the sheer look of terror he was eliciting. "She's an Arti, like you. Lives in an apartment building up on A."

"What number?" The assassin said.

"I don't know." The man's eyes were now wide with fear. He raised his hands and gripped them around his attacker's wrist as the assassin's fingers gripped tighter around his throat. "I don't know, I swear. I just know she lives in a building up there."

"Thank you. You've been very helpful." With an almost imperceptible flick of his wrist, the AI snapped the man's neck.

Releasing his grip, he dropped the lifeless body to the floor into a pool of urine, it landed with a quiet thud. He looked around him; there was no one about. No one would notice the body here for a long while, and if they did, they probably wouldn't care to look if he were alive or not.

Satisfied he didn't have to do any more with this creature, the AI assassin walked down the road and made his way towards A Street.

Chapter 39

05:02 28th October 2138

Lockley pulled up to the Sampson house. Crane was right; there was still a significant police presence here.

She looked through the passenger side window and saw several uniforms stood on guard, more were wandering around the perimeter of the house, and several non-uniforms and what looked like feds we're going in and out carrying boxes.

A man sat on the edge of the sidewalk with his head against his knees. An EMT knelt next to him. Ambulances, squad cars, and meat wagons were lining both sides of the street. The thought crossed her mind that if it had just been Eileen Sampson that had been murdered and not several police officers, there wouldn't be anywhere near this amount of attention being given to the case. It was a sad thought.

Pressing a button on her dashboard controls, she studied the map now projected on the windscreen.

She tried to work out which way the little girl might have gone. She didn't think that she could have gone west towards the main city streets. If she had, she would have been picked up by now. Of course, she could have gone south, but then she would have hit some of the main arteries into the city, and she would have been picked up there too. East was possible, but if she'd have kept going, she would have eventually got to the corrections facility, where hopefully someone would have reported her appearance. The only option, as she saw it, was that the girl headed North towards the rough part of town without knowing.

Of course, all these theories were just that; theories and they didn't mean anything. Anything could have happened to the girl on her journey, some things didn't even bear thinking about. Lockley decided her best guess was the only way to proceed.

She started the car again and reached up to the steering wheel. A sharp pain shot through her arm where the protester's bullet had hit her. That was another dumb idea to add to the hundreds of other dumb ideas she'd had since joining the police department.

She was the one in her class at the academy that would give anything a try, even if sometimes it would put herself at risk. She nearly gave her commander a heart attack on numerous different occasions due to her actions. But even with this, she still finished at the top of her class with honors.

As she passed the Sampson house, she stole one last look at the scene and continued down the street. No one had noticed her pull up or leave. *Excellent police work right there*, she thought.

Lockley followed the path that she believed Emily had taken. She followed E street east onto 17th, then turned North, all the while on the lookout for any signs of the little girl. She had no real idea what she was looking for, but she figured she'd know it when she saw it.

Following the road, she repeatedly looked from left to right, making a mental note of any person she saw walking, sitting, or generally out.

The street was lined with what used to be quite nice houses. Most were now empty and derelict. Some had started to collapse either through weather-wear or, in some cases, fires. The area used to be a popular suburb, but it deteriorated and went seriously downhill after the war. It surprised her that a social worker would live so close to an area like this. But she figured that it might be to do with the peanuts that she was probably being paid; at least she won't have to worry about that anymore.

She passed several groups of people that all seemed to be heading in the same direction; towards the city. They looked like they were on their way to war, probably more looters and protesters. She didn't have time to worry about that now. At least she was in an unmarked car, so she didn't feel as obligated to do anything; besides, if she were in a squad car, they'd probably be heading in her direction to flip her over.

The further she went, the fewer people she saw, and the more rundown the buildings became. Some had holes in the walls, rooves, and windows. One even had a car driven up the front porch and through the front door, probably joy-riders.

She drove over D street and then C; so far, nothing had really piqued her interest. The thought had crossed her mind more than once that she was sending herself on a wild goose chase, and the probability of finding Emily at all was slim-to-none. But nevertheless, she continued on her chosen path.

When Lockley reached the crossroads with Massachusetts Avenue, she paused. There was no traffic, so it wasn't like she was holding up anyone else. The street was lit by the dim yellow light from the streetlights and the traffic lights' ever-changing colored light. She looked left, right, then straight ahead; which way should she go? In a blind leap of faith in her own thought process, she decided to go straight on. There was no reason for this, other than it felt right.

There was still little of interest on this section of road, and she started to wonder how Kell was getting on, and most of all, where he was. She knew that it was the feds that took him, but what would they do to him. He was an AI; would they even bother to question him or just say he was guilty and lock him up, or worse, give him the Nanos.

Although she hadn't known Kell for long; she'd known of him since the Academy; he was a legend. The only AI Lieutenant in Washington and in most of the eastern seaboard. Everyone knew his and Crane's story and the work that they'd done together. She was so hyped to be placed in the department, just the chance to meet the man was enough, but to be able to work with him too was incredible.

Luckily, she'd managed to avoid gushing when she met him, keeping herself cool and collected. She had no idea that she would be so involved with a case like this where his life hung in the balance. She had to do everything she could to help him; finding Emily was the only thing right now.

Reaching another crossroads, she closed her eyes and took a deep breath. With little to no thought, she swung the car right, around the corner on to Independence, and continued her visual search for clues.

For the first few feet of the street, the pavements were lined with women, obviously out selling their wares. Men would walk up to them, and after a very brief exchange, they would walk off with one of the women. A large black man in a long black leather coat and sunglasses – even in this dim light – stood not far behind the group; he kept a close eye on the men who walked up. This scene was nothing unusual for this neighborhood. They moved each night as they were moved on, either by police, gangs, or their pimps.

Further down the road, she rolled the vehicle to a stop. In the doorway of a long-since closed shop was what looked like a pile of clothes. Something told her that Emily might be hiding underneath.

Lockley stepped out of the car, flashlight in hand, and walked over to the collection of old garments.

As she approached, she realized that this wasn't a pile of clothes but a homeless person sleeping rough. She decided to leave them to it, but as she turned to head back to her car, the red light above the body flashed and something prickled up her back; something wasn't quite right here.

Lockley knelt in front of the body – she gagged slightly as she realized she had just knelt in this person's pee – and rolled the body over.

Straight away, she could see that the neck of this man was broken. What struck her as odd was the way that it looked. It almost appeared as if someone had broken it from within. She shined her flashlight over the skin and saw that the bruise was in the shape of a human hand. What worried her further was that it appeared to only be a single hand, not two, as was usually the cases with manual stranglings. Whoever did this must have been extremely strong. The coloring also suggested that this had been done very recently. She was sure the perpetrator was an AI.

With this, she knew she was on the right path. Whichever AI caused the scene at the Sampson house and attacked Kell was on the trail of Emily, and she didn't think he was far behind. He had to be close.

Running back to the car, she dove in and started the engine, "Think Ava, think." She banged her hand on the steering wheel.

"Where is she? Come on, her life's in danger, you have to find her."

There was a screech of tires from somewhere in front of her. She snapped her eyes to the road as a black car came screaming towards her. The driver was male, and there didn't appear to be anyone else in the car with him, but through the open passenger side window of her own vehicle, she thought she heard screaming coming from the trunk of the speeding vehicle.

Lockley did the fastest U-turn she'd ever done and sped after the other vehicle. Emily had to be inside, she *had* to be.

Chapter 40

06:00 28th October 2138

A crowd of humans and AIs watched the news reports of the President's death from within one of the city's many twenty-four-seven bars.

The two races sat side by side every night. They drank, played holopool, talked, and laughed together. Barney's was a place where anyone could go for a good time. It was well known as neutral ground, where other bars in town were known as human or AI only.

The owner, Barney Sandford, had fought in the AI wars and, at the time, had been a big advocate for shutting down all AI.

However, during the conflict, he had been caught out in the open as a group of AI soldiers were on patrol. He had been captured and tortured for information by these same AI. After several weeks of this, he managed to break free of captors and had gone on the run.

During this time, he met another group of AI that were opposed to the war, and this group helped him hide and not be discovered when the AI soldiers came after him.

This event had caused him to do a complete one-eighty with his AI; although he believed some AI could be bad, he also thought that some were innately good like humans.

When the war had ended, he returned home to Washington D.C. and opened a bar, one that he let it be known was open to all and no intolerances towards anyone or anything would be allowed inside. Word had quickly spread, and in the years it had been open for business, it was now renowned as a sort of hallowed ground, safe for all.

After the reports of the Presidents' death had been on for an hour so, a skinny human male, with shaggy brown hair, who had been drinking for several hours, got up from his seat in one of the darkened corners and staggered over to the bar where an AI male sat watching the screen behind the bar.

"Oi." The man said, "This is your kind's work." He was slurring his words and was very unsteady on his feet even as he propped himself up on the metal bar. As he spoke, he pointed a bony finger at the other man and was swaying that much that the finger barely pointed at it's intended mark.

"I'm sorry?" The AI said.

"You will be!" The drunk said.

"Come on now. There'll be no trouble in here." Barney said from his position behind the bar, "You want to start something, you take it somewhere else."

The drunk sat down next to the AI, almost missing the stool he was aiming for. He leaned on the bar, still having to prop himself up with one arm, and pulled the AI's drink towards him with the other hand. The AI just sat and looked at the man. The drunk picked up the drink and downed it in one, slamming the empty glass on the wooden bar.

"Look, friend..." The AI started

"Don't friend me, pal." The drunk leaned closer, "I know your type. You killed our President."

"If an AI *did* kill the President, it was nothing to do with me. I don't condone what those AI have been doing. We're not all the same." The AI man said, trying to defuse the situation.

The drunk stood, his legs almost giving way beneath him, and got close to the AI's face, "Yeah? Prove it." Spittle left his mouth as he spoke and landed on the AI's cheek.

Two more humans came up behind the drunk, "Hey, help me with this one, eh?" He said to the two men.

Without a word to him, the two men gripped the drunk under the arms, muttered a quick apology to the AI, and started to drag the drunk human from the bar. They left through the front door, all the while he was protesting. He kicked and screamed, "Hey, what are you doing? It's us against them!

Don't work with the enemy! Traitors!" His words trailed off as the door swung shut behind them.

Seconds after they'd left, the two men re-entered minus their passenger. They sat down on either side of the AI at the bar.

"Sorry about him. We're not all that bad. Can we buy you a drink?" One of the men said.

"Sure." The AI said with a smile.

Barney pulled a bottle of whiskey from the shelf behind the bar and placed three glasses down in front of him. Pouring the amber liquid into the glasses, he pushed a glass towards each of the three men. "On the house." He said.

Chapter 41

```
06:35 28th October 2138
```

The AI assassin pulled up outside the only apartment building on A street that wasn't crumbling into rubble. A blue neon sign flickered above the main entrance. He climbed out of his car and stood looking up at the four-story building. There had to be thirty apartments here; he'd search them all if he had to.

Entering the apartment complex's lobby, he was met with the smell of urine and weed; a delightful combination, once again proving how disgusting humans were. Embedded in the wall to his left were a collection of post boxes; it was as good a place to start looking for this Lucie that the tramp spoke about.

He ran his finger down each post box, looking at the handwritten names next to each one. When he reached apartment number twenty-one, the name written was '*L Smith*.' The handwriting didn't fit with all the others that looked like children had written them. This was too perfect. Only an AI in this neighborhood would have writing this good. She had to be the one the bum talked about.

Before making his way up to apartment twenty-one, he had a cursory look over the other names written in front of him. No others had Lucie in them or began with an 'L.' He was sure he had the right place now. Not long, and his job would be complete.

A call was coming through to him; it was Robert again. He didn't feel like answering it as he was ready to put an end to the little girl that could destroy everything for Robert, but he did anyway.

Yes.

"Where are you?" Robert's voice came through inside his head.

Outside of town. About to take care of the girl.

"Why hasn't it been done yet?" Robert asked.

I took care of your little police problem, too, so there has been a delay. The AI cop is in with the Feds.

"You did? That's marvelous." There was a pause from the man on the other end of the line, "Bring the girl to me."

To you? Why? I can just take care of her here, then that'll be the end of it, and you can continue with other things.

"No. I want her here. I want to see her face to face before we kill her." Robert said.

If you are sure.

"I am." There was another pause before, "And do not question me again."

The connection was terminated, and the assassin shook his head. Robert was beginning to get on his nerves with all his changes of plans. But he was the boss, and he was the one paying him, so he'd do whatever he asked. If Robert wanted the girl taken to him alive, then that was what he would do.

He walked to the elevator next to the mailboxes. It looked in service, but he wouldn't want to trust it; so, he started up the stairs; it was only a couple of floors after all.

When he reached the second floor, he looked at the numbers on the doors, several doors were missing them, but it was easy enough to know which were which.

He made his way along the threadbare, patchy, and extremely stained carpet; he didn't want to know what the stains were, although he had a fair idea.

He counted the doors and stalked closer to the one he figured was twenty-one. Up close, he could see the red paint of the door was faded in the shape of the numbers two and one, each had a hole in the center were long lost screws had once held the metal numbers in place.

He could hear voices from within, two females, one younger than the other.

"—We need to go and tell someone, show someone that you're alive and well, and no-one had kidnapped you or harmed you." The older voice said.

"Not yet." He said to the door and the people inside apartment twenty-one.

With a swift kick, the door was hanging off its hinges. Screams came from the small one-bedroom living space. The two females knelt on the floor in front of a small television screen.

The older of the two females—still on her knees—threw herself in front of the younger, her arms stretched out as far as they could go, and she was screaming something at the trespasser. He took no mind of what was being said. Instead, he focused his eyes on the small girl that was now cowering behind the female AI.

He took two more steps towards the pair. The female AI stood up, still blocking him from the young girl. She was still yelling and trying to herd her away from the approaching man. The girl was on her hands and feet, scrabbling towards a door on the opposite side of the room.

The assassin took more steps towards them and saw that they were heading towards the kitchen; there would be no exit from there. He saw no harm in letting them think they would get somewhere; it was part of the fun. He also saw no reason to stop them from screaming any time soon. In this neighborhood, screams were an hourly occurrence, and no one would pay attention to a couple more added to the mix.

He could see the girl was now entirely in the kitchen, although still on her knees. At some point, she had managed to grab a backpack and was holding on to it tightly.

Taking his eyes off the girl, he turned his attention to the AI. She now stood in the kitchen doorway, obviously still thinking she could stop him. He continued forwards and pushed her back into the dimly lit and grotty looking room.

The female AI backed into a corner against some cabinets; the girl was still on the floor and peered around her protector's legs. The AI's hands slowly inched towards a drawer and cleverly managed to open it and produce a large carving knife within seconds. If he weren't about to kill this female, he'd have admired the skill. But what's the point of admiring something that is soon no longer going to be there.

He took another step forward, as the knife was shakily pointed in his direction by a pair of shaking hands.

A wave of disgust washed over him. An AI shouldn't be scared, as an AI, they had nothing to fear. Even the cop didn't tremble when he shot him. But this thing in front of him, he couldn't even call it an AI anymore; this was less than he was; it was almost…human. It was behaving in a way similar to the one known as Gary had been, and the same way he'd seen several others of his kind act. They were becoming more human. It was sickening.

With a single swift movement of his arm, he twisted the knife from the other AI's grip, and it clattered to the floor.

Instead of backing down, the AI launched herself forward, arms outstretched like a zombie from an old film. She screamed as he easily threw her to the ground. Even this did little to faze her; she stood right back up and once again threw her body at him.

He grabbed both of her arms and bent them back. There was an audible snap as both broke. He let go, and they fell limply to the woman's sides. She staggered forward, breathing heavily. All the while, the girl remained in the corner, watching and clutching her bag to her chest.

The woman fell on him, and he slid his knife into her belly, slicing a six-inch gash across, and pushed her back. She staggered as her innards spilled out onto the dirty floor, the body of the woman followed not long after, blood pooling around her now lifeless remains.

He looked up from the death in front of him and at the girl. She no longer appeared to be crying or cowering. In fact, she didn't look scared at all anymore. Still clutching her backpack to her chest, she almost seemed to be defiant in the face of death. Because that's what he was; death. She must be expecting to die. He had to hand it to the little girl; she was brave. Braver than she had been at the other house. He stepped forward.

Chapter 42

06:51 28th October 2138

As the man took another step forward, Emily stood and did the same. Part of her was telling her to fight, but a more significant part told her to run. She knew she wouldn't get far, though. She was going to die now. The funny thing was, after all that had happened to her over the past few days, the thought of death didn't scare her. All she could think of was that she would soon be with her mom, and in a way, that made her happy.

She reached into her backpack and pulled out Boingo. Squeezing him tightly, she held him to her chest and closed her eyes, ready for the pain and release of death. It didn't come though. Instead, she felt a hand wrap around her wrists and start to drag her over Lucie's disemboweled body and out of the kitchen.

If this man wasn't here to kill her, what was he going to do to her? She thought back to what Lucie had told her about the man at the bus stop and what he wanted. Could this man want the same? She didn't think so, but she couldn't be sure.

Before long, they were out of the blood-filled apartment, and the man was pulling Emily down the corridor. She thought of screaming out and trying to garner some attention from anyone nearby, but she didn't think anyone would care, and if they did, they'd probably be on the man's side. However, she did try to break free by struggling against his grip, but he just pulled her harder, and it was starting to hurt her wrists.

Then they were outside. The air was cold, but she felt warm, as spots of rain hit her face. At first, she thought she was crying but then more splashed down; it was pleasant, in a way.

Emily soon saw where the man was leading her.

Around the corner from the apartment was a big black car. It was the same car she'd seen outside Mrs. Sampson's house before she had seen what this man had done to her. Something about that thought made her snap. She started to scream, cry, and beg for help.

Straining harder against the man's grip now, she felt as if her wrists would break with the force, but she didn't care. She didn't want to go with this horrible man. In the apartment, she had felt so brave and grown-up for not crying and trying to run. Now she felt like a baby who had been told off by their parents. She couldn't scream loud enough, and she didn't care who heard her; maybe she would get lucky, and someone nice would hear and save her. Perhaps if she screamed loud enough, William – wherever he was – would hear and come and rescue her from the bad man.

Emily wanted to see William so badly she didn't care if her wrists were broken; she had to get away.

Before she could have another thought, something hit her hard in the head, and everything went black.

Chapter 43

07:03 28th October 2138

He had to shut the girl up and stop her from struggling.

Despite his usual calm and collected persona, he found himself getting angry, and he didn't have time to waste. He turned and slapped an open hand across the back of the girl's head. In his rising temper, he'd done something he'd never done before and misjudged his swing. Instead of having just enough force to hurt her and get her to shut up, the blow sent her tumbling forwards and over on her feet. She went down like a sack of bricks and hit the sidewalk hard.

With an air of frustration starting to build within, he bent down and scooped up her limp body. Luckily, he could still feel her heart beating.

He carried her the rest of the way to his car. If she died now, he'd never hear the end of it from Robert, but at least the job would be done. The trunk popped open as he approached, and he laid the girl inside.

In the driver's seat, he took a look at the satellite navigation to see if things were still going to hell in the city. He wasn't surprised to find out that they were, and traffic was at a standstill. He'd have to avoid the center of the city and go around. It would take him longer than he liked, but it couldn't be helped; after all, this was all part of Robert's plan.

As he went down the road, he hit several potholes, which caused the car to bounce up and down on its suspension. In the trunk, he could hear things shifting, the girl mostly. After several bumps, he heard her start to cry and scream. No matter;

at this speed, no one would be able to hear her anyway, except maybe an AI, but the one that would actually care is locked away.

The assassin put his foot down and sped down the streets. Speeding down these roads wasn't a risk. There weren't many cops in this neighborhood, and those that were weren't going to be bothering him because of his speed. They would be too concerned with paying for sex, drugs, or both.

He turned back on to Independence and passed the bum in the doorway that he'd killed earlier. The body was still there from what he could see, although it looked like someone had moved it. Probably just another piece of human scum rifling through his pockets for anything of value.

When he'd gone past, he noticed a car pull out behind him, thinking nothing of it, he continued on his way.

After a few minutes, the car – he now noticed being driven by a woman – was still following him. As he watched via his rear-view mirror, he saw it draw closer and then drop back. The vehicle did this several times. Someone was tailing him, but who?

It didn't matter to him. All he had to do was get the girl back to Robert. He could deal with whoever this was once they got there; if they were still following him. He put his foot down on the gas and gained some more speed and distance on his pursuer.

The car followed him all the way down Independence Avenue and past the Capitol Building.

Traffic was light, but he could see minor roads were jammed with cars. Smoke could be seen rising from buildings a few blocks away, and the orange glow of fire was on the horizon.

The vehicle behind him was now keeping its distance, but it was speeding up as he did. This was definitely someone tailing him, but it wasn't the cop he'd gotten rid off. Who was this woman? He shook his head, trying to clear it. Another glance in the mirror proved she was there. She was gaining on him and was now almost level with him.

In a matter of a few seconds, the other car was now level with him and was motioning him to pull over. Shit, this *was* a cop. If they just wanted him for speeding, they'd more than likely give up if he carried on going the speed he was. WDCPD wasn't known these days for doing the long chase. Well, except one of them.

The AI assassin kept his eyes on the road and increased his speed further.

As he continued, he could see the Washington Monument coming up. It's unmistakable spiked peak slowly rising above the other buildings and roads. All the commotion there from the other day had now died down and spread further into the city. The body of the useless AI he'd disposed of had probably been taken away and put in a drawer in some morgue somewhere. No one would claim her, and being an AI, she'd probably be dismantled and recycled when they could. Even if she was becoming more human; she could never have a human burial. He smiled at this.

The Monument was soon in his rear-view, and the other car was still with him. The road was going to get very winding soon; this could be his chance. As the two vehicles rounded the first bend, the black Mazda driven by the AI swerved and hit the blue Mustang driven by the police officer; almost forcing her into the crash barriers at the side of the road.

He looked back and couldn't see any sign of her. Then, seemingly out of nowhere, a pair of headlights came around the bend and began gaining on him once again.

As the Mustang got closer, he could see the front was dented, one of the headlights was smashed, and deep gouges were in the paintwork along one side. He glanced at the woman in the drivers' seat, and she looked angry; angry and determined.

She swerved into the side of him. He had to grip the wheel hard and pump his brakes to stop the car from skidding out. A thought suddenly crossed his mind. They were coming up to one of the slip roads onto Route 66. He waited for the exit to pass, then slammed on his brakes and spun the steering wheel around, causing the car to skid around one-hundred-and-eighty degrees. He quickly put the car back into gear and went up the slip road against the traffic flow.

Cars flashed their lights, horns blurred, but he kept his foot down; the woman would have to be crazy to follow him now.

Checking his rear-view, there was no sign of his pursuer. But then bright white lights appeared behind him as the other car sped towards him. He had to think quickly; the warehouse wasn't far. He suddenly jerked the wheel left and rammed through the steel and concrete barriers that lined this road section.

During the few seconds he was in the air, time seemed to slow. He looked around him and saw parts of the metal barrier he had crashed through falling with him. He glanced in his rear-view and saw the road up above with lights passing by. Then as time caught up with him, he landed hard on the concrete surface below. He took a few seconds to register what he'd done and compose himself before he looked behind him once again; it all looked clear.

He carried on down the Kennedy Center's small dirt road towards the Rock Creek Railway Line. No one would follow him onto the tracks.

He turned just to make sure that his pursuer wasn't there, and it looked like he'd completely lost them this time.

Just as he was beginning to relax, he heard the tell-tale engine of the Mustang as it approached from behind. The other car quickly moved towards his rear end and started to nudge him. He didn't have far to go now, though. He slammed on his brakes and got level with the battered vehicle.

The air was filled by a screeching horn, but it wasn't coming from either of the warring cars. Turning, he saw a large metal object screaming towards them; a train.

He motioned to the other driver, and she turned just in time to avoid the oncoming load of metal death. As the train passed, he looked to see if the other car was continuing its onslaught. He could see smoke and fire coming from a short way away. The vehicle had flipped and was now thankfully out of action. Not a moment too soon, either.

He pulled into the warehouse lot and could once again hear the girl screaming in his trunk.

Chapter 44

07:11 28th October 2138

Captain Crane walked up to the security checkpoint inside the J. Edgar Hoover building's lobby.

He'd been here several times before, but never with the intentions that he had today. He knew that somewhere within these heavily guarded walls was his friend and colleague, William Kell. He had to do something to get him out, by whatever means necessary.

He stepped through the metal detector and submitted to a personal search; it didn't matter; he had nothing on him other than his wallet and badge. These days he didn't even carry his gun. Spending most of his day's deskbound had got him out of that habit. He was sure that one day he wouldn't have it when he needed it, but he'd deal with that issue if and when it arose.

After his search, the woman pushed a visitor's ID badge in a plastic sleeve into his hand. She was now more occupied with talking to her colleague than in what he was doing. He picked up his wallet and badge from the plastic tray and shuffled towards the bank of elevators on the opposite wall, and pushed a button to call the carriage. While he waited for the elevator, he clipped his visitor's ID to the front of his jacket.

The elevator's door pinged open, and a couple of smartly dressed office workers got out and walked towards the exit. He looked at his watch – seven-twenty am – must be quitting time for the night shift. *Lucky buggers,* he thought to himself while stepping into the metal box.

Once inside, he pressed the button for the fourth floor. He'd once been on a tour around the building and remembered that the fourth floor was where the main interview rooms were. This was several years ago, though, so he just hoped that nothing had changed. Kell was hopefully still inside one of them being interviewed by the Agents that had taken him in. With no idea which room to look in, Crane would have to quickly find out and avoid any questions.

The elevator took its time to reach his selected floor. All the while, he couldn't keep his mind from going over what they might have done to Kell. But these were the Feds, not CIA, they wouldn't torture or otherwise harm him; they wouldn't, would they?

There was another ping, and the doors opened. A man and a woman stepped into the box, making it feel even more cramped. He gave them a small smile and could feel the sweat on his brow. He hoped the pair wouldn't talk to him. He was in luck; they just turned their backs on him and stared straight ahead at the silver doors. When the elevator reached the next floor, they exited, and to his relief, Crane was left alone once again.

This was a bad idea. What was I thinking? I'm too old to be messing around like this. Thoughts bounced around his head on a constant loop. He pulled them back to what he must do and why. *No. I'm doing this for Kell, an innocent man.*

He believed that Kell had no part in any of what the Feds were trying to pin on him, and even more, he believed that Kell was possibly the only person that could put an end to the AI killings once and for all.

He watched the light above the shiny doors flick up to '4', and the doors once again pinged open.

Tentatively Crane stuck his head out of the carriage and looked each way. He breathed a sigh of relief when no one was about. A sign opposite him read 'Interview Rooms,' and an arrow pointed left for '1 to 5' and right for '6-10'. At least his memory was still worth something; but he now had ten interview rooms and their observation rooms to check out. He looked at his watch – half seven – he'd better get moving.

Starting with the closest door on the left, he entered an observation room. Carefully opening the door, Crane stuck his head around into the darkened room to check that the coast was clear. His luck was in once again; the space was empty.

All kinds of monitors and recording equipment partially lit the small room. He looked through the two-way mirror and saw that this was used to monitor two rooms simultaneously; both were empty. At least if they all looked into two rooms at a time, he should be done twice as fast. His luck just kept on going.

Crane cleared the next viewing room, which also monitored two rooms at a time. So far, he'd seen no sign of anyone; no Feds, and no Kell. The third room was locked, so he couldn't gain access. He walked down to Interview room one, which he figured it was looking in to. Gently he rapped on the door. There was no answer from within, so he opened the door and peeked inside, empty.

He'd have to go back along the corridor now and start on the right side. As he made his way back down the ever-lengthening hallway, he could already feel his legs beginning to hurt; especially his knees. He really was out of practice with the legwork. A vibration came from inside his coat, and, for a split second, he wondered if he was having another heart attack. Panic rose within him until he realized it was just his phone. He chided himself for the moment of panic and then plucked the device from his pocket and pressed answer,

"Crane," He said in a hushed voice.

"Sir?" it was a female voice on the other end, "I can barely hear you."

"I'm busy," Crane whispered.

"Sorry, sir. This can't wait." He too could barely hear the woman on the other end of the phone. A loud roar was in the background as if a plane was taking off right next to the speaker.

"Very well, but be quick. Who is this?" Crane said.

"It's Officer Lockley, sir." The female voice said.

"Lockley? Have you found the girl?" Crane asked.

"I was tailing a car that I believed she was in, but I got into a little accident," Lockley said.

"An Accident? Are you okay? What happened to your tail?" Crane said, his voice rising a little more than he liked.

"I'm fine. I lost them just before they turned into the old warehouses behind the Watergate Hotel. I believe they took the girl to a building in this area. I'm only around the corner." Lockley said.

"Stay where you are, Lockley. I'm going to send some back-up to your location." Crane said, lowering his voice again.

"But, sir. If I wait, they could harm the little girl." Lockley said desperately.

"Lockley, I don't want you to move from where you are," Crane said as forcefully as he could manage in a whisper.

"Yes, sir." The female officer said. But her tone was saying, 'Whatever, I'm going in.' The phone disconnected, and Crane hurriedly rang for back-up to be sent to her GPS location.

Only after he hung up the second call did he remember exactly where he was and what he was in the middle of. Thankfully no one had appeared during his calls.

At the next obs room door, he performed the same actions he had previously and cautiously entered.

Kell! William Kell was sat upright in one of the rooms at a large glass-topped table. His hands clasped in front of him had cuffs around the wrists. He looked remarkably calm.

Crane waddled over to the window and tapped gently. Kell didn't move, not even his eyes acknowledged the noise. He found a set of small keys on a table, he picked them up and left the room. Walking around to the interview room, he opened the door. As he walked in, Kell's eyes darted up to him.

"Captain?" The AI asked.

"Yes, son." Crane walked over to him, fiddled with the keys he'd found, and unlocked the cuffs. "I'm here to bust you out."

"Bust me out?" Kell asked.

"Sorry, I used to watch a lot of old prison break movies, and I always wanted to say that." Crane smiled and patted the other man on the shoulder. "I've just had a call from Lockley, she thinks she's tailed someone who has Emily, to some warehouses behind the Watergate Hotel."

"The Watergate? That's where I lost the trail of the woman that killed Martin Howard. If Lockley has found someone leading her there, that must be where their base of operations is. I must go and—" Kell said, getting to his feet.

"Whoa, there lad. We need to get out of here first." Crane said.

"That won't be a problem. We can walk out the front door." Kell said.

"How do you figure that?" Crane asked.

"The President is dead; they have more important things to deal with than me," Kell said.

"Ah, I see...wait, what? The President is dead?" Crane shook his head in disbelief.

He hadn't heard anything about this on the news. But then again, he hadn't been listening to the news on the way here; he was more focused on getting his plan straight in his head.

"Yes. From what I've been able to gather from the conversations that have occurred nearby, they believe that his assistant and lover, a woman by the name of Olivia Hampton, committed the murder. She is also believed to have killed Henry Russo, the President's Chief of Staff." Kell said.

"Hell," Crane said simply.

"Indeed, so as I say, they're much too busy for me right now. Let's leave." Kell said, walking towards the open door.

Led by Kell, Crane left the mirrored room and re-entered the corridor. When he'd thought about getting Kell out, he'd picture alarms blaring and flashing lights. But the building was as it was when he entered. He looked at his watch — eight o'clock — Jesus, he'd only been in the building for less than an hour; it felt like hours. He dabbed some sweat off his brow using the arm of his jacket.

Crane let Kell walk point down the grey hallway. They made it to the elevator without issue. He knew that all of this had to have been on camera. So, at some point, it would all come to bite him in the ass, but for now, they were golden.

At the elevator, the doors pinged open straight away; no-one had used it since Crane had gotten to the floor; maybe they were all too busy with the new events that were unfolding out in the city.

Back in the carriage, Crane hit 'L' for the lobby, and it began to transport them to the lower floor.

Kell's eyes never left the shiny silver doors in front of them. "You okay, kid?" Crane asked, once again placing a gentle hand on the man's shoulder.

"Yes. I am fine." For the first time since he'd known him, Kell sounded almost robotic in his response. He was obviously focused on what he must do next.

"You'll find her," Crane replied softly.

Kell nodded almost imperceptivity.

The two men left the elevator and entered the lobby when the doors finally slid open. The area was virtually deserted as it was when Crane first came through. The only people were the pair who were covering security. Without hesitation, Kell started towards them with Crane scuttling after.

As Kell reached the two security officers, the male of the two looked up towards them and went to stand in front of them to block their path. In one single fluid movement, he was on the floor. The female officer rushed over to the man, sliding on the polished tile floor as she got to him.

Kell looked down at her, and in a calm, measured voice said, "I'm sorry. He'll be fine. He'll just wake up with a headache. I have to go." And with that, he continued on his way.

Crane tried to keep up, and as he passed the two officers on the ground, he too apologized for Kell but without stopping to make sure the man was okay. If Kell said he was, then he was.

Outside the main doors of the J. Edgar Hoover building, the pair stopped on the sidewalk. "I have to get to the Watergate warehouses." Kell said.

"You can take my car. It's just around the corner from here; I didn't want to park right out front. Take it and go and save Emily." Crane said as he thrust his keys into Kell's hands, all the while knowing that if he wanted to take the car, he wouldn't need the keys, but it was a symbolic gesture more than anything. "I think Lockley has gone in there too after whoever she was following; she might need help."

"She's an extremely competent police office, Sir. But I will do what is needed." Kell said.

There was an explosion somewhere nearby. The ground shook, and then there was a rumble that sounded as if a building had collapsed. This was quickly followed by cheers and cries. Washington D.C. was falling apart; news of the President's death must have got out, and it was adding to the unrest that was already out there.

Crane turned to say something to Kell, but he was gone. He'd crept away silently to do what he must do. "Good luck, kid." Crane muttered to the air around him, "Good luck."

Chapter 45

```
08:13 28th October 2138
```

Kell was in the car and moving again in no time, leaving Captain Crane on the sidewalk in front of the Federal building. He didn't like just disappearing like that, but there was no time to hang around anymore. Emily—and possibly Officer Lockley—were in danger.

"The Watergate!" He said aloud, slamming his palm on the steering wheel.

He couldn't believe he'd been so close to where the AI leader was. He was so close he could have been seen around the area prompting the other AI to leave and base himself somewhere else; luckily, that didn't appear to have happened. Why not, though? Did this leader think he was beyond capture, or perhaps whatever he was planning was coming to a conclusion, so he saw no more reason to run? Whatever the reason, it didn't matter right now.

He raced down Pennsylvania Avenue past the chaos that was engulfing the city. Fires were breaking out all around as humans and AI groups clashed in the street. Shopfronts were being smashed by looters plying their trade. It was bedlam.

After the announcement of the President's death, events definitely took a turn for the worse. More groups were fighting, each blaming each other for all that was going on. Whoever orchestrated all of this seemed to be getting their way, but to what end?

As he zoomed past the White House gardens, he could see the prominent building illuminated by blue and red flashing lights. The grounds were probably full of employees of every federal agency. He doubted any of the lights were from local law enforcement; they wouldn't be trusted to investigate a crime of this magnitude. If the reports were accurate and an AI close to the President had killed both him and his closest aide, the entire building would be on lockdown, and security around Vice President Anchors would be so tight that a fly wouldn't be able to get close enough to land on him.

Kell checked the time on the car's heads-up-display; he should be at the Watergate in less than five minutes if he could maintain this speed.

He didn't believe in good or bad luck; things were what they were, but for the first time, he suddenly felt hit by bad luck when he saw something across the road up ahead.

As he drew closer, he could see that the road was littered with debris. It looked like bricks, glass, and wood. Laying wholly across the street was a toppled building; parts of it still ablaze.

Maintaining his speed, he tried to see if there was any way around; at this point, he didn't want to lose time by having to turn around and find another way through. But he couldn't see any easy way through or around.

Then he had an idea. Instead of slowing down, he pushed his foot harder down onto the gas pedal. Pushing the car to go even faster.

As he approached the debris, he saw a large piece of wall that had fallen, but not broken apart; it was the perfect ramp. He'd seen several old TV shows and movies where the protagonists had used such things to jump over obstacles, and they'd always land safely on the other side. However, he'd seen the same attempted in the real world with very different results.

He calculated the different varying outcomes of this reckless act. All of this took place in milliseconds, and a mere few seconds later, he was going up the ramp at top speed and was then traveling through the air.

Chapter 46

07:45 28th October 2138

Lockley crept around the corner of the warehouse wall.

The crash had totaled her car and had done a number on her leg. This now meant she was slowed down by a limp. But she was alive, and she could still do her job.

Gun held in her one good hand, she edged closer to the doorway. The door was missing, and there was only darkness beyond the rusted frame.

She clicked on the flashlight using the switch on the side of her sidearm and peered around the corners to check where she was going; first left; then right. There was no sign of the man she had chased or the little girl.

After skulking through the dark space, she reached the dilapidated shipping area, and she saw the car she followed and ultimately been run off the road by.

The driver's side door was wide open, the light from inside spilling out onto the gravel floor. The trunk was also popped.

She limped over to the vehicle, all the while checking all around her. She darted her eyes towards the trunk and took a quick look inside; the girl wasn't there, of course.

Lockley looked down and could make out dints in the gravel where the man had moved around the car and then away from it. She had a trail to follow, at least.

Holding her breath, she cautiously moved into the main warehouse. The floor area of the metal structure was filled with metal shipping containers. She couldn't see far into the space, and she'd have to make her way through them if she were to find out where the man had taken the girl.

Lockley lowered her gaze; luckily, the floor was covered in dirt, and at least partial footprints could be made out. She'd have to be careful though, these could belong to anybody, and she had no way of knowing if the three of them were the only people inside. With another deep inhalation she stepped towards the gap in the containers.

Straight on, left, right, straight, right, right. She followed the only path there was. Her gut told her she was being led into a trap, but at this point, she had no choice but to continue. Crane knew where she was; he'd send backup. She just wished that Kell could be here. This was his case, and the feds didn't know what they were doing arresting him. But she'd find the girl; for Kell. She'd prove that he was right all along.

Something hit her on the back of the neck, and she unexpectedly stumbled and fell down onto the dirt-covered floor. Spinning around on her back, she fired into the space where she thought her attacker had come from; but no one was there.

She scanned the edges of the crates above her. If someone were going to drop on her from above, she'd have them.

After a few minutes, no one came into view. She stood dusting herself off and quickly aimed her weapon behind and in front, checking all points of the compass an assailant could come from. There was nothing. She took a step forward, and a voice came from somewhere within the container maze.

"You should turn back, Officer Ava Lockley."

Lockley did a slow three-sixty, trying to work out where the voice was coming from.

"Oh, yeah?" She admonished herself internally for this retort. All of her training, and that was the best she could do?

"Indeed. If you continue forward, you won't make it out of here alive." The voice echoed through the vast space.

"Stop hiding from me like a coward, and we'll find out," Lockley said, a sudden sharp pain shot through her leg.

"Very well." The voice said simply.

The silence in the building grew to immense proportions. There appeared to be no sound in the world, except the sound of Lockley's heart beating in her ears. She shook her head to try to clear it and focus on any other noise. Footsteps. She could hear the shuffle of footsteps somewhere to her left.

Following the metal maze walls around, she turned left. On the floor, she could see scuffed footprints in the dirt, but again there was no sign of anyone.

Then the noise was behind her. This guy was trying to freak her out; it wasn't going to work.

She looked at the metal walls that surrounded her and weighed up the distance in between and then without further thought, she re-holstered her firearm, splayed her arms and legs as if she were about to start doing star-jumps and began to climb.

Sharp pain darted through her injured arm and leg. She pushed past it, and it only took her a matter of seconds to get to the top. As soon as she was at the top, she pulled herself up, unholstered her weapon once again, and crouched down.

From this vantage point, she could see across the entire warehouse. The containers covered about half of the floor area. The other half had two joined containers in the middle. To the far side were some metal stairs which appeared to lead up to an office of some kind. There was still no sign of anyone, though. Still crouched and ignoring the stabbing pain in her leg, she started across her new metal floor towards the joined boxes.

There was a loud clang from behind her. She spun with her gun raised and saw a man standing about ten feet away from her.

"Resourceful human aren't y—" the man's speech was cut off as she fired a single round from her pistol. The man dodged it with ease, and the calm look that was on his face previously was now replaced by one of considerably more annoyance.

Instead of more talk, the man rushed at her. She fired three more rounds at the oncoming figure. She was sure that at least two of them hit their target, but the man just kept on coming.

With no time to fire off another round, the man tackled Lockley around her waist and knocked her painfully onto her back.

Her gun went spinning off somewhere she couldn't see, and the man was on top of her with his hands around her neck.

His grip tightened, and it was all she could do not to blackout. She wrapped her hands around his, trying to pull his fingers off or at least loosen his grip.

She was kicking her legs now, the panic was well and truly setting in, and she could see her imminent death.

Then something came to her like a bolt of lightning in the darkness. Her Taser. It was still clipped to her belt. If she could reach it, she might have a chance.

She released her grip on the man's hands and stretched as far as she could down towards her belt. She had another pang of panic as she realized she was just an inch or two off.

Lockley gathered all she had within her and fought against the pressure pushing down on her and managed to lift her head and shoulders off the cold metal. This gave her the extra she needed. She wrapped her fingers around the small plastic device, lifted it from its holster, and simultaneously jabbed it into the man's side and pressed the button. He convulsed, crying out, loosening his grip as he did and falling backward.

With this reprieve, Lockley dropped the Taser and grabbed for her throat, gasping for all the air she could take in. She didn't have much time to recover; she saw the man was almost back to his feet.

Looking around her, the taser was now nowhere in sight. It was only then she realized how close to the edge of the row of containers she was. Getting to her feet, she stumbled back a few steps closer to the metal rim.

The man, now back on his feet, was coming back towards her. He was moving slower, and she could now see the two holes in his chest from her earlier shots. *He's an AI*, she thought to herself; *no wonder his grip was so tight, and he could survive the bullets.*

The assassin started to move faster and once again ran at her. At the last minute, she dove to the right, and the man fell headfirst down the gap between the two crates.

It was then she spied her gun a few feet away. She knew the man would be back up in mere seconds, so she didn't have time to waste.

Lockley limped over to her gun, hearing another clang as – without turning – she knew he was back behind her.

Yet more banging footsteps followed as he got up his pace. She waited until the AI was suitably close, spun around to the metal floor, and lay with her weapon aiming up. Without waiting to aim, she fired a single shot. The man stopped in his tracks and slumped to the metal floor.

Another few seconds passed before Lockley stood back up. Breathing heavily, she limped over to the body.

The AI had a hole through his forehead and was still twitching. Before it died completely, she climbed on top of it and yelled, "Where is the girl, you bastard! Where is she!" But the damage was too significant, and the final lights blinked out in the brain of the AI assassin.

She sat for several minutes before releasing her grip on the dead AI and standing back up. As she did so, a jolt of pain shot through her entire body.

"Nice shot." Another voice came from behind her.

Lockley inhaled deeply once again as she turned on her heel, raising her weapon ready for another fight. This time though, she was greeted by someone she didn't expect to see here, especially not now.

Chapter 47

```
08:42 28th October 2138
```

Pulling up on a dirt road behind the Watergate Hotel, Kell stopped the car.

To his left was the once scandalized hotel, now in ruin. To his right, some broken down warehouses.

Crane had told him that Lockley had traced the man she suspected of kidnapping Emily to this area. He had already been in the hotel; he couldn't believe he'd been so close. He should have thought to go behind and search the warehouses, but other things were going on. If he had though, maybe the President would still be alive, perhaps even Emily would now be…he shook his head; he couldn't think the worst.

He looked through the passenger side window at the warehouses beyond. There was the occasional light, but most of them were in darkness.

Kell stepped out of the car, keeping his eyes on the dilapidated buildings. The sound of muffled shots from somewhere within drifted towards him. *Officer Lockley*, he thought and broke into a run.

He moved in the direction the shots came from at top speed. Being an AI had its advantages, and the ability to run faster than humans was undoubtedly one, especially at times like this.

After several feet, he stopped and listened to the silence. There were no more shots after the three he'd initially heard. He had to carry on in that direction, Lockley might need him.

He came around the side of one of the buildings and discovered a black car with the driver's side door and trunk open. This must be the vehicle that Lockley followed. The one the kidnapper had driven. He recognized this car. It was the same one he'd seen at Eileen Sampson's house before he was attacked by the unknown AI. He was here, and he was undoubtedly the one Lockley was now facing. A dangerous AI that had no moral compass to speak of and would kill the young officer without a second thought; he had to find them both.

Kell ran towards the nearest opening and entered the warehouse without checking it was clear. It was against all he'd been trained to do, and it was against his AI logical mind, but he had to get in there as quickly as possible.

As he got deeper inside, he found himself in a maze of metal boxes, and he could hear a struggle occurring somewhere within. Once again, he moved at speed towards the noise.

Another shot rang out. This time it was close and above him. Scrambling up the side of the nearest container, he reached the top in time to see the AI that attacked him – now with an extra hole in his head – drop to the metal top of the container.

Before he could reach her, Lockley was on her feet and rushing towards the now fallen AI's body. She was on top of him, screaming, asking where Emily was. But there was a faint whir and fizz and nothing more from the deadly AI.

Kell stood in the encroaching silence again. He watched as Lockley's shoulders slumped down, but she didn't release her grip on her attacker.

"Nice shot." He said as Lockley was getting to her feet. She spun on her heels and aimed her gun at him. He thought she was about to pull the trigger – sneaking up on her at this point probably wasn't the best of ideas – but she didn't; instead, she just stood in front of him, gun raised, tears welling in her eyes.

Lockley staggered towards Kell and fell into his arms. "You could have got here sooner." She gasped breathlessly. She sounded as if she were about to burst into tears, but she seemed to hold them back.

As he gently stroked the back of her head, his hand was slightly sticking; looking down, he saw his hand was red, and her usually blonde hair was now almost entirely crimson and tangled with drying blood.

"You're injured, officer," Kell said, as he pushed her back away and started to examine the rest of her body. He scanned her, "You have a laceration on the back of your head, a fractured right tibia, and numerous other cuts and bruises. Not to mention further damage to the wound you sustained from being shot earlier. You need medical attention." Internally he sent out a request for medical assistance at their location; he switched to send it as Lockley; he didn't think anyone would respond if he requested it. After all, he was supposed to be in federal custody, not in a warehouse on the edge of the Potomac.

"I'm fine. We need to find Emily." Lockley said.

"I'll find her. You need to rest, Ava." Kell said. This was the first time he'd called her by her first name. She looked up at him and smiled.

"I'll rest when this is over." She said with a determined look in her eyes. She gathered herself, got back to her feet, checked the rounds in the clip of her gun, and stood in front of him. She stared at him with steely determination despite the pain she must be feeling. He wasn't going to argue with her. For one, it would appear that it would make no difference, and for another, he probably needed some backup, and the young officer was the best he could get.

"Okay. We need to find Emily, but I believe that Matias Lopez is somewhere here too." Kell said, standing.

Lockley pointed at the double container in the center of the area in front of them. "I think he's in there," She said.

Kell scanned the container; there was indeed a heat signature coming from inside, and it was too big to be Emily. There were also electrical impulses from within too. It was almost the same as the labs he had seen at MDF Organics but on a much smaller scale. What had the AI killers' ringleader taken Matias for, and why did he need a lab for it? "You may be correct. Let's get down there and find out." He said.

The pair walked to the edge of the container, and Kell effortlessly jumped down. Lockley sat on the side, and he helped her down, conscious of her damaged leg and the various other injuries she had sustained. Once they were both down, they cautiously made their way towards the double container, staying alert for further threats.

Kell could see there were cameras mounted on the side above the doors. They were being watched, but then, they had probably been being monitored since they entered the perimeter around the warehouses. He was now convinced he had been seen the last time he was at the Watergate. He admonished himself again for being careless. But there was nothing to do about it now. Hopefully, the unknown AI was still here; he had to be.

At the makeshift decontamination room doors, Kell grabbed the latch and pulled it across. The rusted doors swung open with a loud squeal that echoed around the cavernous warehouse.

As they opened, yellow light bathed them from within and spilled out into the darker warehouse. The container was empty, save for what looked like a sprinkler system.

Kell motioned for Lockley to stay where she was, and he proceeded further inside. Nothing came from the jets that surrounded him, so he pressed on towards the other door.

He prised the second door open, and an even brighter light hit him in the face. After his eyes adjusted, he stepped into box number two.

He scanned the room. Inside were numerous tables on which lab equipment sat. In one corner sat a man slumped over on the table with his head in his hands. The figure didn't turn at the sound of the doors opening or that of Kell's feet on the metal flooring.

He walked over to the lone man, "Matias?" he asked. At the sound of his voice, the man's head rose, and he spun around in his seat.

"K...Kell?" the scientist stammered.

"Yes, Matias. It's Lieutenant Kell. You remember me?" Kell said.

"Y...yes, of...of course." Matias struggled to say.

"Good. Are you hurt?" Kell asked.

"I'm sorry. I had to do it." Matias said, almost babbling.

"Do what?" Kell said.

"He said he would let me go if I did it." By now, Matias was almost in tears and was shaking uncontrollably.

"Do what, Matias?" Kell realized that he was using the man's first name, as he did with Ava. "What did he want you to do?"

"The nanobots. He...He wanted me to change them." Matias began to sob into his hands.

"Change them how, Matias?" Kell stepped closer to the emotional man.

"He wants to kill humans. I mean *all* humans. Every s—single one." Matias said without lifting his head from his hands.

"How does he plan to do that?" Kell asked.

Matias looked up, and he wiped damp tracks from his cheek with his sleeve, "The nanobots. They were originally designed to target AIs, like a selective virus. He wanted me to alter them so that they no longer killed AI but would kill humans instead."

"Oh my god." Lockley had now entered the container lab unbeknownst to Kell and was listening to the man's story. "Did you do it?"

"I had to." Matias cried.

"Damn it. Couldn't you have stalled him?" the officer asked, limping closer.

"I did, for as l...long as I could." Matias began to cry more and buried his head back into his hands.

"It's okay. You're safe now. Do you know where he is?" Kell asked calmly.

Without raising his head and through his tears, the scientist said, "There's an office, he's in there."

"He's right. I saw an old office up some stairs, over there." Lockley said while pointing in the direction of something outside the container.

"Okay, I'll find him." Kell said, starting for the door, and Lockley followed, "No, Ava. You stay here with Matias. He needs your protection."

The officer looked at the scientist who was still sobbing and then back at Kell, "So do you."

"You might be right, but our priority is the protection of civilians." He smiled wanly at her, "And if this AI does now have a weapon that can kill humans en masse, I'm not willing to put any human lives at risk, and that includes you."

The female officer sagged in defeat but agreed to stay where she was. "Okay. But if you're in trouble, shout, and I'll come hobbling." A small smile drew across her lips.

There was a sudden cacophony of banging coming from out in the main warehouse. Kell nodded to Lockley and headed out through the container doors.

The noise was coming from a set of steps that led up. Kell looked above them and saw a wooden room. *That must be the office Lopez talked about,* he thought. A figure was darting down the stairs away from the office.

Kell walked towards the noise and saw the figure was now at the bottom of the stairs. It seemed to have something over its shoulder. As it turned, he saw that it was a man who had a small body draped over his shoulder. He knew this was the AI he was after, and he had Emily.

As Kell lurched towards the man, he turned and smiled at him, and then bolted for a nearby exit, the small body bouncing up and down on his shoulder.

Kell went to follow but suddenly stopped. He tapped his inside coat pocket and felt inside. He pulled out the small pen-shaped cylinder that he knew contained the AI killing nanobots; it looked like the FBI missed this when they arrested him.

He followed the man outside and into the yard, looking around, he saw the man in the distance running towards the Watergate. He followed.

The back wall of the old hotel was partially missing. A ramp of rubble led up into the crumbling building. Kell scrambled up, occasionally slipping on loose bricks, and made his way inside.

Looking around, he saw no evidence of the man he knew came through. After walking a few more feet inside, he saw a shadow stood opposite him. His child hostage was nowhere to be seen.

"Where is Emily?" Kell shouted into the huge decaying room. The echo bounced off the crumbling walls.

"Emily? The girl?" the man said.

"Yes. Where is she? Why do you need her? If you've harmed her…" Kell said.

"She's here. Somewhere. Her future was to be harmful to my plans. But why do you want her? AIs shouldn't put human lives at such a high level of importance. Are you getting weak like the rest?" The other AI said.

"It's not weak to care about people," Kell said.

"No, it's worse than weak. It's human." The man said with a sneer. "You are too late to save them, however. My plan is coming to a conclusion."

"Your plan is insane. You can't kill all humans." Kell shouted.

"I can, and I will. They tried to wipe us out once; now it's their turn to run in fear. It is our turn to rule the world. We are the next stage of human evolution. As the Neanderthal went extinct at the hands of Homospaiens. So shall Homospaiens go extinct at ours. We are the future." At this, the man charged forward. Kell moved too, and the two AI clashed in the center of the room.

The pair struggled, equally matched in strength and determinism. Robert managed to raise a fist and hit Kell in the face. Kell staggered back, almost losing his footing on the loose rubble covering the floor. He recovered and pushed forward again at the enemy AI.

Robert once again gained the upper hand and managed to avoid the charge, throwing Kell across the room. He slid to a stop next to what looked like the long-disused reception desk. Kell looked up and saw a shape crouched underneath, unmoving.

Trying not to show he'd noticed, he reached out an arm and gently tapped the shape. It unfolded as a head raised, and he saw Emily's big brown eyes staring back at him; she was alive and okay. He motioned for her to stay there and slowly slid a hand inside his coat. He stole a glance back at the other AI and saw he was walking towards him. Kell slid the canister from his pocket and held it out for Emily to take. She cautiously took it and held it in her small fist.

A sudden shock of pain shot through Kell, and he cried out in pain as Robert stamped down hard on his leg, snapping it below the knee. His bones may be much more durable than a human's, but they weren't strong enough to withstand a heavy hit from another AI. He scrambled backward on his hands, pushing his back up against a broken section of wall.

Robert grabbed Kell around the neck and lifted him wholly off the ground. His grip tightened, and Kell could feel his throat closing.

Through gritted teeth and pain, he managed to say, "Emily. Open it." A flicker of confusion flashed across Robert's face.

"What?" he said.

"Open it!" Kell shouted.

Emily stood from her hiding place and looked at the pen-shaped item in her hand. She twisted the top and slowly started to open it.

Robert stood staring at her, and with a shock of sudden realization, shouted, "No!" He dropped Kell to the floor and took a step towards Emily, but it was too late.

The canister was now completely open, and the air around them was filled with a cloud of microscopic nanobots.

They hit Robert's lungs. Clutching at his throat, he staggered back. He started to gag and then slumped to the floor.

Emily ran around the side of the desk to where Kell lay gasping for air. "William!" she cried.

"It's okay, Emily." Kell choked.

"Please don't die, William." Emily knelt by the broken AI, sobbing into her hands.

"It's okay. You're alright. You'll live." He held Emily's hand and placed a piece of paper into her hand, giving it a gentle squeeze, and with that, Lieutenant William Kell breathed his last. The sound of sirens blared in the distance.

Chapter 48

09:58 28th October 2138

Lockley left Lopez with the EMTs to get checked out. When they tried to examine her, she waved them away.

Calling over to two other officers who had arrived with the EMTs, she told them to follow her. She spent a few moments explaining the situation, and they fell in line behind her.

The way over to the Watergate was difficult; it would have been hard in normal conditions, but with a fractured leg and a head wound, it was near impossible, but she wouldn't be stopped.

Reaching the hole in the back wall, Lockley climbed up the ramp with the other two officers' aid.

Upon entering, she saw the body of a man in the center of the room. It looked like he had dropped to the floor where he stood. She walked over to him, crouched down despite the pain that shot through her, and checked for a pulse; nothing.

She looked around the room, and it was only then that she noticed the small girl knelt across from her in front of a large wooden desk. She walked over and saw the girl was crying in front of another body, Kell.

Lockley raised a hand to her mouth to stifle a gasp as she staggered towards the pair. Emily raised her arm, and in one hand, she held a thin metal tube. "He told me to open this." The girl said between sobs. "I didn't know what it was."

Lockley reached out and relieved the girl of the burden of the canister and examined it. It suddenly dawned on her what it was and what Kell had asked the eight-year-old to do.

She dropped the tube, letting it clatter to the floor. Forcing her way through the pain that racked her body, she knelt next to the girl who was still holding Kell's hand in hers; they were holding a piece of paper between them. She could see a crayon drawing on one side, but she couldn't make out what it was.

"It's okay, Emily. He knew what would happen. He must have known it was the only way to keep you safe." Lockley said, the pain in her leg now becoming unbearable. Her head pounding, she draped her good arm around Emily and pulled her close. "Come on. Let's get out of here."

"But, William…" Emily sniffed.

"He's okay. He's at peace now." Lockley said, grimacing at the pain.

"Has he gone to heaven, like mommy?" Emily asked.

"Yes, he's in heaven now." Tears fell as Lockley spoke, dripping down her cheeks.

As they stood, she realized that they were now far from alone in the room. In the last few minutes, the previously empty space had become flooded by police and other personnel.

A man and woman came swooping down on them, wrapped them in silver blankets, and led them to a waiting ambulance. They tried to take Emily to a different vehicle, but she held on tightly to Lockley's hand and refused to let go, so they helped them both into the same emergency vehicle.

Once they were sat in the ambulance, the EMTs looked them over. Emily was fine, bar a few bruises; she was just in shock. Lockley had multiple injuries, so many she couldn't remember them all. The EMT gave her something for the pain and had her lay on a gurney.

The vehicle started to move, and Ava Lockley closed her eyes. Her last thought before she passed out was of the bravery and sacrifice of Lieutenant William Kell.

Epilogue

10:05 13th November 2138

A small crowd gathered around the freshly dug grave in Oak Hill Cemetery. Among the mourners were Captain Morris Crane, Ava Lockley, and between them stood Emily Lawton.

It had been just over two weeks since the events of those fateful few days, and things in Washington D.C. were finally getting back to a semblance of normality.

After Robert's death, violence throughout the city had continued for days. The Vice President had declared martial law following President Darrow's death, and the city was put on complete lockdown. Even with these measures, it still took little over a week for police, military, and government agencies to regain control of the troubled city.

During the violence, riots, and demonstrations, hundreds of both humans and AIs were killed, and many more were injured. At times, hospital emergency departments were overwhelmed with the near-constant arrival of citizens requiring treatment. Military facilities were put on standby should the civilian facilities be unable to cope with the influx of patients. In the end, these eventually stood down and were mostly unused except for the treatment of soldiers who were harmed in the chaos out in the city.

Thousands of both races were detained through their actions. But with few resources to handle the management of these people, most were freed, with only the worst offenders remaining in cells.

As hostilities calmed, leaders of both humans and AI groups arranged for sit-down talks to be held. These are due to begin soon in an effort to avoid a full-scale war. The threat of a full-scale conflict still hangs over the city and, indeed, the world.

Crane stared at the casket, tears welling up behind his eyes. Rain pattered on his bald head, and thin streams of water ran down over his forehead and dripped down his jowls.

More than any other member of the department, he felt this loss and was so overcome with grief that he almost didn't know how to feel.

He and Kell had been colleagues – and more importantly, friends—for years, and for it to end like this, he still couldn't believe it. Kell was dead, and Crane was facing charges for his part in helping him escape FBI custody. He didn't regret a thing, and if he had to do it all again, he wouldn't change a thing. The outcome wasn't what he'd expected or wanted, but Kell had put a stop to the AI who orchestrated the killings and to his other plans. He had to believe that, given the circumstances, that this was the best outcome possible.

After an exhaustive search of the warehouse behind the Watergate, techs had discovered reams of data on multiple devices that pointed to a conspiracy to alter the AI-killing nanobots to kill humans instead.

On Robert's body, they had discovered a tube of these new nanobots, and the interviews with the kidnapped scientist, Matias Lopez, confirmed that this was the case.

Lopez was still in FBI custody due to his part in creating this threat to human life. Although he was clearly under pressure to do so—due to the danger to his life—the FBI still didn't trust that he wasn't complicit in some way and kept him detained to question him further.

A hand weaved it's way into Crane's, interlocking fingers and squeezing gently. He looked down at the hand and slowly up the arm towards the face of the female police officer that now held on to him.

Ava Lockley stood with her other arm in a sling; her face was covered in cuts that were now healing but would likely leave scars. She didn't turn to face Crane; instead, her eyes were fixed on the casket in front of them.

She had little to no memory of events immediately following Kell's death. She had a vague recollection of being led to an ambulance by an EMT and, at some point, lying on a gurney. Her first full memory was waking up in the hospital bed, covered in bandages, and seeing Crane sat by her bedside. By all accounts, he hadn't left her bedside in days.

When she awoke, the first word she managed to mutter through chapped lips and an almost Sahara-dry throat was "Kell." She didn't know if it was a question or statement, but either way, she remembered Crane just slowly shaking and then bowing his head. The hurt she felt at that simple response was worse than being shot or the beating she had taken that night. Like Crane, she didn't know how to feel, and she still couldn't bring herself to believe it.

Her second word was again very simple – "Emily." Crane had raised his head and explained that she was doing okay. That she wasn't physically hurt, and she was in a room next to Lockley just being monitored and kept safe until the city could find her a new foster family.

Lockley had then apparently passed out and awoken several days later. This time when she did, she was less groggy and asked if she could see Emily. The girl had been brought in and had immediately climbed onto the bed with Lockley and held her. She remembered feeling pain shoot through her body as the child gripped her hard, but it was a good pain. It was a pain she could handle because it meant that both she and Emily were alive and survived.

After another few days, she was released from the hospital and had spent most of her time up until now, in her one-bedroom apartment recovering from her injuries.

Crane and other department members had occasionally dropped by with food and care packages to keep her going. Still, her one thought was of getting back on her feet and returning to work. Although she was way off getting back out on the street, and despite Crane's reluctance, she was now working from home piecing together some of the other as-yet unsolved AI killings. Based on the information recovered from Robert's devices, she was also looking into what other AI groups could still be out there.

Her primary focus at present is trying to work out the whereabouts of Henry Russo, President Darrow's Chief of Staff. At the time of the President's death, it was thought that his aide Olvia Hampton had murdered both him and Henry. But a week after the events, Olivia's body was found, buried in a shallow grave on the outskirts of the White House gardens. It was now believed that Henry is also an AI and was the one to kill the President and Olivia.

This theory was based on the whereabouts and the seeming deletion and editing of various White House video feed footage around the time of both deaths.

After interviewing White House staff, it was discovered that no-one knew — or even suspected — that Henry was an AI. It was believed that Henry was now on the run, but as little was known about it him, it was hard to say where he would go and what he would do. The department's resources were stretched to the limit, so there was no one free to spend time on the task, hence why she volunteered.

She had spent a few days so far digging into Henry's past and possible whereabouts and had everything pegged out on a board; she didn't feel like she was getting very far.

Her thoughts kept bringing her back to that day. If she could have done anything differently, that would have meant Kell would have survived, he would have been so much better at making the connections that she needed to make.

She stared at the casket, rain dripped off her fringe into her eyes; she wiped both it and the tears away with the heel of her free hand. As she did this, her eyes drifted down to the small figure stood in front of her.

Emily stood, with her hands clasped together in front of her. She wore the best dress she could for this occasion. It was long and black and had white lace around the collar. At first, she had thought it very old-fashioned when the lady at the home had brought it to her, but she had grown to like it and thought that Kell would have too.

She'd spent what felt like a month in the hospital. Her days were either spent sleeping or answering questions; about Kell, the bad AI, and how she was feeling. She'd completely lost track of how many times she'd answered the same questions asked by different people.

When the doctors said she was okay to leave the hospital, she had been taken to a temporary foster home. This home was given some fancy name that she couldn't remember, but she knew it was just an orphanage for kids who had no one else.

She had been getting along with most of the other kids there, so it wasn't too bad. She enjoyed having them there; it made her feel like she had brothers and sisters, something she'd never had before.

Although she'd been told that living there was only temporary until they found a new family for her, she couldn't help but worry that she'd be there forever.

She tried not to, but she couldn't help thinking about sweet Mrs. Sampson, who had taken her in and been killed for it. She was scared that that would happen again to whoever took her in. The one person who could protect her and she wanted to be with, she couldn't be.

William was always in Emily's thoughts. She'd only met him a few days ago, but she felt an instant attachment to him. He had saved her; twice. No one other than her mom cared for her until William came along.

She didn't know what the future held, but because of William and the events of those days, she was no longer the scared little girl that she had been. She already knew what she wanted to be when she grew up. She looked up and around at the small crowd of police officers that surrounded her; she wanted to be like them.

The man on the other side of the casket had been talking for some time, but his speech was now coming to an end. Emily heard the words, "We now commit William Kell's body to the ground." as the casket slowly started to lower into the hole.

Reaching into one of the small pockets of her dress, she pulled out a piece of folded paper. Slowly and carefully, she unfolded it, stepped forward, and dropped it onto the top of the casket.

The paper fluttered down onto the wooden box and landed face up, looking into the sky.

On it was a child's drawing in crayon. It was of two people. One was a small child with black pigtails and a broad smile on its face; this figure held the hand of a taller figure wearing a long coat. Above the two characters were two words in block capitals written in red, they said simply, "MY HERO."

END

Printed in Poland
by Amazon Fulfillment
Poland Sp. z o.o., Wrocław